D0835118

Poisoned
Honey

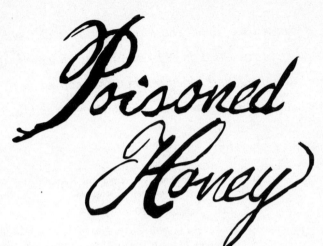

A STORY OF
MARY MAGDALENE

Beatrice Gormley

ALFRED A. KNOPF
NEW YORK

I would like to thank Daniel Ullucci, the scholar who read and commented on Poisoned Honey *in manuscript. I also thank Sasha Helper, M.D., for pointing me to valuable information about hallucinations in childhood.*

THIS IS A BORZOI BOOK PUBLISHED BY ALFRED A. KNOPF

Visit us on the Web! www.randomhouse.com/teens ·

Educators and librarians, for a variety of teaching tools, visit us at
www.randomhouse.com/teachers

The Library of Congress has cataloged the hardcover edition of this work as follows:
Gormley, Beatrice.
Poisoned honey : a story of Mary Magdalene / Beatrice Gormley.
p. cm.
Summary: Relates events from the life of a girl who would grow up to be a close follower of Jesus Christ, interspersed with stories of the Apostle Matthew. Includes author's note distinguishing what Scripture says of Mary Magdalene from later traditions.
ISBN 978-0-375-85207-7 (trade) — ISBN 978-0-375-95207-4 (lib. bdg.) —
ISBN 978-0-375-89361-2 (ebook)
1. Mary Magdalene, Saint—Juvenile fiction. [1. Mary Magdalene, Saint—Fiction. 2. Saints—Fiction. 3. Jews—History—168 B.C.–135 A.D.—Fiction. 4. Marriage—Fiction. 5. Matthew, the Apostle, Saint—Fiction. 6. Demoniac possession—Fiction. 7. Jesus Christ—Fiction. 8. Bible. N.T.—History of Biblical events—Fiction. 9. Jerusalem—History—1st century—Fiction.]
I. Title.
PZ7.G6696Poi 2010
[Fic]—dc22
2009005095

ISBN 978-0-375-84404-1 (tr. pbk.)

Printed in the United States of America

10 9 8 7 6 5 4 3 2 1

First Trade Paperback Edition

To Jeanie

CONTENTS

WHAT IS MY MISSION?

I was possessed. Possessed "with seven demons," as they say. That means as possessed as you can possibly be. Possessed, body and soul.

Now I am healed. Instead of being chained in some lonely place like a wild beast, I'm back in my family's house, fully clothed and in my right mind. I'm grateful for each simple blessing. Thanks be for the taste of bread dipped in olive oil at suppertime! Thanks be for the sound of voices—*human* voices—in the house at daybreak!

But what now? What about the mission that was revealed to me?

In the moment of my healing, when the rabbi drove the demons from my body, I caught a glimpse of the kingdom of heaven on earth. Rabbi Yeshua looked at me with eyes of love, and I understood that the Lord loves each person that way. I thought the whole world was transformed.

But the world was not transformed. My brother had not glimpsed the heavenly kingdom. He wasn't even interested in hearing about it. Neither was my mother or, of course, my uncle. They're relieved that I'm healed, but now they expect me to take up my part in their household without further fuss. And they expect me to leave quietly, before long, for the household of whatever husband they find for me.

Am I to follow the path trod by my mother, my grand-mother, my cousins, my sister—by every woman I know? Could it be that this ordinary path of women is itself the "high purpose" hinted at in my visions and dreams? Was it for this that my soul soared on eagle's wings, and that the prophet Miryam appeared to me?

No. No!

I am bewildered. And I am afraid. The demons aren't really gone. I don't hear their voices . . . yet. But I sense them lurking silently. If I abandon my mission, will that be the sig-nal for them to move back in?

I don't know what to do. If Rabbi Yeshua were here, I would plead again, "Help me."

ONE

A SPARROW FALLS

The first "voice" I heard was a sparrow's. So I'll begin my story with a sparrow falling—with the murder of a friend.

I was nine years old, growing up in the town of Magdala, where Mount Arbel casts its shadow onto Lake Gennesaret. When I was a young girl, Herod Antipas had been ruler of Galilee for many years. My family, though, had been in the sardine-packing business for generations. We were known for high-quality salted fish long before Antipas's father, Herod the Great, became king of Greater Judea, and even long before the Roman armies tramped into our land.

My name was Mariamne, which is the Greek version of the Hebrew name Miryam, and my family called me Mari. I lived with my father, Tobias; my mother, Tabitha; my widowed grandmother, Abigail; my older brother, Alexandros; and my younger sister, Chloe. We had our own house, but we shared the walled courtyard with my uncle and his family. As my grandmother's elder son, my father was head of the family group.

One morning, as the sun was coming up across the lake and my father was saying morning prayers on the roof terrace, I took grain to the courtyard to feed the chickens. It was important to give them just the right amount of grain. If we didn't give them enough, they'd try to escape to find food somewhere else. If we gave them too much, they wouldn't search for the bugs we wanted them to eat.

I tried to give each chicken its fair share, although that wasn't easy. There was one hen that the others pushed aside, for no reason that I could see. There was a sore on her neck where the others had pecked her. After I gave the flock their grain, I dropped a handful right in front of the pecked hen.

As the chickens gathered clucking around my feet, a sparrow flew into the courtyard. He stayed just out of reach of the chickens, several times his size. He was a neat, pert little bird, and his bold stare made me smile. *Give me some, too,* he seemed to say. *I'm hungry.* I threw a few seeds his way, and he gobbled them up before the chickens could run over to them. *Many thanks!* he seemed to say.

"You're welcome, sparrow," I said. I was so charmed by the little fellow that I didn't notice my brother, Alexandros, on the stairs behind me with his slingshot. I heard a whirr, then a sickening thump as a pebble struck the sparrow. The pebble clattered on the courtyard flagstones, and my sparrow fell lifeless.

"Got him, the little thief!" exclaimed my brother.

I screamed at him; I ran to Imma, our mother, with the sparrow's broken body. "Look what Alexandros did! On purpose! He's a *murderer*."

Alexandros ran after me to tell his side of the story. "But Mari was feeding the chickens' grain to the sparrows!"

Of course, our mother took Alexandros's side. She scolded me for giving good food to a wild bird, and she told me it was ridiculous to call the death of a sparrow murder. "If we grieved every time a sparrow falls," she said sternly, "we'd be in sackcloth all the time."

I saw that it was no use, and I hated Alexandros so much, I couldn't stand to look at him. So I went back to the courtyard.

Later that day, I talked Yael, our serving woman, into taking me down to the shore. On the rocky beach, I made a sort of tomb out of stones and laid the sparrow in it. "That's quite a fine sepulcher for a bird," Yael remarked. "In fact, it's finer than the one they'll lay me in."

"Really?" I asked. Forgetting my own sorrow for the moment, I gazed up at her glum face. I was shocked at the idea that no one cared as much for Yael as I cared about my sparrow, but maybe it was true.

"You're too young to know what a miserable world this is," said Yael. "But you'll find out soon enough."

How could Yael think that about the world? It was glorious. The world was full of wonders, from the artful design of a sparrow's feathers, to the snug feeling of my sister's back against mine in our cot at night, to the plump sweetness of an apricot from our orchard. In the synagogue, the Scripture readings often mentioned all the things the Lord created. Sometimes I imagined the One sitting at his heavenly workbench, smiling with pleasure as he turned out sparrows and warm bodies and apricots for us to enjoy. It made me sad that Yael didn't see this.

The very next morning, while I was feeding the chickens as usual, a sparrow perched on the courtyard wall. "Go away! Shoo!" I told him. I was terrified that my brother would kill this one, too.

Don't worry. I'll stay out of range of the slingshot, said the bird.

I don't mean that he *seemed* to say it; he spoke just like a person, only in a chirping kind of voice.

Here's what to do, the sparrow went on. *Save some of your bread from breakfast. When no one's looking, put the crumbs on top of the wall, right here.* He hopped sideways in one direction, then the other, to mark his words.

I knew that sparrows couldn't talk, so I must have been making this up myself. Still, I did as the sparrow told me. Later, when no one else was watching, I saw him come back to eat the crumbs.

The next time I had a chance to talk to Abba, my father, alone, I told him the whole story of the sparrows. He listened with his arm around me, his eyes serious above his gray-streaked brown beard. When I finished, he kissed the top of my head and said, "That second sparrow is wise beyond its years! It's true that you shouldn't give the chickens' food to wild birds. But if you want to share your own bread with them, that's your right." He added, as if to himself, "Alexandros shouldn't be slinging stones inside the courtyard; someone might get hurt. I'll talk to him."

After that, my father began taking Alexandros to work with him every day. I was glad to have him out of the house, although I think my mother missed him. I kept on leaving bread for Tsippor, or Birdie, as I called the sparrow. Whenever I was upset about something, I would sit on the stairs and talk it over with Tsippor while he pecked the crumbs.

One Sabbath, sitting in synagogue, I listened to a psalm that made me think of Tsippor: "For your name's sake lead and guide me, take me out of the net which is hidden for me. . . ." Those lines brought such a vivid picture to my mind: of the One tenderly untangling a terrified bird from the hunter's net. Later, I overheard Alexandros stumbling as he tried to recite the same psalm for Abba. How could he have trouble memorizing such unforgettable words?

I didn't tell my younger sister, Chloe, about my sparrow friend, but one day she overheard me talking to him. I asked her if she heard the sparrow answer me, but the idea seemed to frighten her, so I said it was just a game. During the next year or so, I talked to Tsippor less and less, although I still fed him.

I suppose I always knew, as girls do, that I'd get married someday. But I didn't realize it clearly until the year I was eleven and my cousin Susannah was thirteen. Susannah, my uncle Reuben's daughter and my father's niece, was my favorite cousin. She had a round, shiny face and merry dark eyes, and although she was older, she was always willing to play a game or sing a song with me.

Then suddenly—it seemed—Susannah was thirteen, and no longer just a girl but a maiden. Soon after she came of age, she was betrothed to a young man named Silas, a cloth dyer. A year later, their wedding took place, and Susannah left our compound for Silas's house. She came to visit now and then, but there seemed to be a screen between us: she was a married woman, and I was still a girl.

One day in Tishri, the month of the autumn harvest, Susannah came to help us make date syrup. All the women and girls in the family gathered in our courtyard, taking turns stirring the great pot. The sweet, heavy scent filled the air.

The work wasn't hard, and since it would take hours for the syrup to boil down, the gathering was like a party. We chatted and sang and played with Susannah's baby, Kanarit, a girl with a funny toothless smile.

I thought the baby looked like Susannah. Susannah said she looked like me. Our grandmother (we called her Safta) said that I looked like Susannah, only more serious, and the baby looked like both of us.

Next year, I thought, it will be my turn to be betrothed, then married, and then (the Lord willing) have children. I hoped to follow Susannah's example, rather than my mother's. Susannah seemed to enjoy everything: her baby, her husband, her house, her neighbors. Imma, on the other hand, treated everything in life as a duty to be borne or a temptation to be avoided.

As I was thinking about my cousin and my mother, Yael entered the courtyard carrying another basket of dates on her shoulder. "Oh, evil day! Evil, evil day," she muttered as if to herself, except so loudly that we couldn't help hearing.

My mother looked up from checking the date syrup. "Say what you're going to say, Yael."

Yael looked pleased to have everyone's attention. "Herod Antipas has done a dreadful thing, Mistress Tabitha. I heard some men telling it in the market, and it's true, because they'd just come back from Tiberias." (Tiberias is the capital city of Galilee.)

"Well?" Imma gave the stirring paddle to me and put the other hand on her hip.

Yael gave in and spat out her news. "They say that Herod Antipas has *slain* John the Baptizer. Cut his head right off." Then she clapped her hand over her mouth, as if saying so made the dreadful thing true.

"The Baptizer?" gasped Susannah. "The holy man from the desert?"

None of us had seen John the Baptizer, because he preached in Judea, several days' travel down the Jordan River. But everyone had heard about his fiery sermons, and I'd imagined myself among the crowds on the riverbank, listening. Now Yael's words forced me to see the preacher kneeling as Herod's soldier swung his sword. Evil! The sense of it smothered me, and I gasped, too.

"The Lord save us!" exclaimed my grandmother. "I wish we were on the other side of the lake from Tiberias. When the Lord's punishment strikes that wicked city, what will happen to us?"

"Nonsense," said my mother. "I'm sure the Lord knows it's not our fault. The heathen Romans rule the world, even our holy city of Jerusalem, and they let Herod Antipas, a so-called Jew worse than the Romans, rule us in Galilee. What can we do? Anyway, this is men's business, not women's. Mari, you aren't letting the syrup scorch, are you?"

With an effort, I pulled my mind back to the courtyard. "No, Imma." I gave the paddle a good stir.

Chloe, my sister, looked anxious. Maybe she was imagining fire from heaven falling on Tiberias, spilling over onto nearby Magdala. Or no—she was probably thinking about the beheading, because she looked a little green. "Safta," she begged our grandmother, "tell us a story about something nice."

"Not something *nice*!" I protested. "Please, Safta, something exciting."

"Please," my mother snapped, "a story with an uplifting moral."

My grandmother seemed relieved to turn from the shocking news. Looking around the courtyard at us women and children, she smiled. "Nice, exciting, and uplifting? I know just the story." She closed her eyes and took a deep breath, as she always did before telling a story.

"Long ago—after the Jewish people escaped from slavery in Egypt, but before they reached the Promised Land—they wandered in the desert. Hot wind blew grit into their throats and their eyes. But at the end of each day, when they made camp in the desert, their prophet Miryam found a well for them. No one else could see the well, but Miryam found it with the eyes of her soul."

I'd heard this story more than once, but each time Safta came to those words, "the eyes of her soul," a deep thrill went through me. If I could see with such eyes, and be such a blessing to my people!

"Then they drank the pure water, they splashed it over their hot, dusty faces, and they blessed the Lord and his prophet Miryam. And to this day," my grandmother finished, "Miryam's Well refreshes our people from its secret source."

"Where is it, Safta?" asked Chloe.

Susannah laughed. "If we knew, it wouldn't be a secret, would it?"

"Oh, we know it's somewhere in the lake," said my grandmother firmly. "When I was a girl, there was a man of great faith tormented by demons. He prayed for healing, and he was told in a dream to go out on the lake in a boat. He did so, and Miryam's Well appeared to him. As he bathed and drank from the well, the demons fled. He was healed."

"I like that story, Safta," said Susannah, "but . . . how could there be a *well* in the lake?" She made a frustrated, squinting face. "I can imagine the wide blue lake, and I can imagine a stone-rimmed well like the one in this neighborhood, where Yael draws water. But when I try to put the well in the lake . . ." She made a gesture to show the well sinking right to the bottom, and everyone but Chloe laughed.

Before our grandmother could answer Susannah, Chloe asked, "Where did the demons go, after they left the man? Did they go to possess someone else?" She looked anxious.

"These are idle questions," said Imma. "Chloe, you aren't skimming off the foam as it rises. You begged to help with the date syrup this year, do you remember?"

Although I'd laughed with Susannah, I had no trouble imagining Miryam's Well in the lake, and it seemed important to explain to the others. "But Miryam's Well *isn't* an ordinary stone well," I said. "The blessing water would bubble up through the lake, and it would look different from ordinary water. As if it were a different color, like wine."

Susannah rolled her eyes at me in a teasing way. "Mari can see anything. Why, she saw the whole spirit world in the lake."

"That's not what I said," I protested. Susannah was

reminding me of a remark I made once, when she and Chloe and I were down by the lake. The surface was calm, and the sunlight struck the water just right, so that the town and the mountain behind it were reflected. Only, the reflected town was upside down and wavering.

I'd said that the spirit world, if I could see it, would look like that. The very idea made Chloe squirm, and Susannah hastened to reassure her. "Mari's talking her usual nonsense."

Chloe hated to see things in a different way. When we were younger, I'd shown her how to lie on the floor and put her head way, way back until it seemed as if she could walk on the ceiling. I thought she'd be fascinated by the upside-down view, as I was, but Chloe burst into tears and ran to Safta.

Now our grandmother skipped over both Chloe's question about demons and Susannah's question about the well. Gazing into the sky above the courtyard wall, she murmured to herself, "It is a special gift, to see what is hidden from others."

I didn't think much about Miryam the prophet again until the next spring, at Passover time. In the synagogue, a lector read us the story of how Moses, Aaron, and their sister Miryam led the Jewish people out of Egypt. When they escaped from the Egyptian army, Miryam and the women danced to celebrate the victory. "Sing to the Lord, for he has triumphed gloriously," she sang. "The horse and his rider he has thrown into the sea."

Right there in the synagogue, I heard her sing. How did I know that the clear, strong voice was Miryam's? I *knew* it, as well as I knew my grandmother's voice. I could still hear the lector murmuring underneath, and I knew he was reading to the congregation, but I also knew that Miryam's words were meant for me. I had seen Miryam's Well with the eyes of my soul, and now I heard her voice with the ears of my soul.

I was so excited, I could hardly wait until after the meeting to tell someone. But whom should I tell? Not Chloe; it was just the kind of thing that would frighten her. Not Imma; she pooh-poohed anything that wasn't down to earth. Not Alexandros; I never told *him* anything. I could have told my grandmother, but this was so important, it seemed fitting to tell the most important person in the family.

On the way home, as we turned the corner into our alley, I took my father's hand. "Abba," I said quietly. "In the synagogue, I heard Miryam singing her song. She sang it for me."

My father looked startled, but then he squeezed my hand. "The Scriptures do speak to us, don't they, my dear? Even to women."

TWO

THE EAGLE'S VIEW

One day, after a large shipment of sardines had gone out, my father decided to take a holiday. "We'll ride to Arbel and visit my sister's family," he said. "I've hired donkeys."

Abba took along Alexandros, Chloe, and me, as well as Uncle Reuben and his young boys. My grandmother stayed home because the long ride would be painful for her sore joints, and Imma stayed home because she had more important things to do. The rest of us rode across town along the main street, my sister behind me on our donkey.

As we crossed the avenue leading down to the docks, the waterfront came into view. I recognized our family's packing-house among the buildings on the wharf. There the sardines were salted down and sealed in huge jars, ready to be shipped northeast to Damascus or west to Ptolemais. Offshore, at the entrance to the harbor, the stone lighthouse tower rose from a pile of boulders.

Past the wharf, the Jewish neighborhoods bordered smaller settlements of Syrians, Phoenicians, and Greeks—all Gentiles, or non-Jews. At the edge of the Gentile district, my father and uncle halted their donkeys in front of a house, leaned over, and spit on the doorstep. The house, as far as I could see from its plastered walls and tiled roof, was respectable—in fact, it was larger and finer than ours. My brother, riding ahead of me, also paused and spit. I called to him, "Why are you spitting?"

"Harbor-tax collector's house," said Alexandros. He wiped his mouth and twisted around to explain further. "Filthy Roman-lovers. His sons went to the same rabbi where I learned my letters. None of the rest of us would talk to them. Uncle Reuben complained and got the rabbi to teach them separately."

A tax collector! How dare he live in this well-built house, just as if he'd earned it with honest work? Tax collectors were the scum of the earth, parasites, bloodsuckers. Some of them, like the household-tax collectors, worked for Herod Antipas, ruler of Galilee. Some of them, like the harbor-tax collector, worked directly for the Roman overlords. But all of them made their living by cheating us.

I, too, leaned over to spit on the tax collector's doorstep, but just then the door opened. A young man, perhaps a little older than Alexandros, paused in the doorway. His thick eyebrows, tilting down and out from the bridge of his nose, gave him a mild look. For an instant, his face was unguarded, showing nothing but shock that a young girl, a stranger, was going to spit at him. Then his face turned hard, and he ducked inside and slammed the door.

"Oh, Mari!" Chloe tightened her arms around my waist. "I thought he was going to hit us."

I didn't think that, but I was shocked. The young man from the tax collector's household had looked so hurt. Surely such a despicable person had no right to be hurt! And yet, I felt uneasy, as if I might have done something wrong.

We rode on out of town by the south gate, then left the paved highway and followed a dirt road up the long, gradual south slope of Mount Arbel. We passed pomegranate orchards and olive groves, then rocky pastures where flocks of sheep were feeding. The higher we climbed, the clearer the air became, and I breathed deeply to draw in more of it.

The direct way to the town of Arbel and my aunt's house wound around the side of the mountain, but my father led us first to the top to see the view. Herod Antipas's army had a garrison with a watchtower up there, and there was also a Roman army post. The boys were curious to see the Romans, and so was I, since they were supposed to be some kind of demons. But Uncle Reuben told us sharply to stay away from the soldiers, and Abba herded us on to the lookout point.

"The lake is so little," said Chloe behind me on the donkey. "Is that our lighthouse, that dot?" She spoke in a small voice, as if she'd dwindled with the lake.

I felt just the opposite, as if I'd grown enormously tall. I'd never seen the lake from end to end, only the part of it visible from Magdala. I was so excited, I almost thought I could fly.

My father quoted a line of Scripture: "As it is written: 'They who wait for the Lord shall renew their strength, they shall mount up with wings like eagles.'"

I'd heard those words in the synagogue, and they always lifted my heart in a mysterious way. Now I felt I understood: the soul had wings, as well as eyes and ears. As my father glanced away from the view, I caught his eye. We exchanged a look, and I felt as if we were soaring together.

My uncle didn't seem moved by the eagle's wings; he was busy pointing out sights to the boys. In the valley to the west was the town of Arbel, our destination. Southwest was the peak of Mount Tabor, where the Temple priests lit a beacon to let the villages know when the holidays began.

Alexandros had been up here before, and he eagerly joined in to show off his knowledge. Magdala was right below us, with its stone breakwaters reaching two sheltering arms out into the lake. As we watched, a tiny ship slid past the lighthouse and into the harbor. That must be a merchant ship, Alexandros said. It wouldn't be a fishing boat; they fished at night and were pulled up on the shore by dawn.

My brother went on to point out the city of Tiberias, gleaming white on the lakeshore south of Magdala. From Tiberias, Herod Antipas ruled Galilee, the territory on this side of the lake, as far west as we could see and farther. Across the lake were independent Gentile cities, as well as Gaulanitis, where Herod Philip ruled.

As Alexandros talked, the landscape seemed to divide into sections, like embroidery markings on cloth. I wished I hadn't listened to him, because my sensation of floating above the world faded away.

Uncle Reuben interrupted Alexandros with a harsh laugh. "You know many little facts about this ruler and that, nephew. But there's only one big fact: all lands belong to the Roman Empire."

"Brother!" exclaimed my father. "It's not right to talk that way in front of . . ." He motioned toward Alexandros and Chloe and me and our cousins.

Uncle Reuben looked as if he'd like to argue, but he was the younger brother. He took my father's rebuke with a shrug.

"The Romans in their pride may think they own the

world," Abba added, "but we Jews know better. As it is written, 'The earth is the Lord's.'"

Again I felt the lift of eagle's wings, the wings of my soul.

One evening soon after the trip to Mount Arbel, Uncle
Reuben ate supper with us to discuss some business with my
father. We ate on the rooftop, as we usually did except during
the rainy season. Chloe and I served the bread and stew, the
olives and cheese and watered wine, while Abba and Uncle
Reuben talked. They'd been giving money to the family of an
injured fisherman, and Uncle Reuben thought it was time to
stop. My father thought they should support the family for
another year or so, until the oldest son in the family was big
enough to go out with the fleet.

My grandmother whispered to me to fetch a special basket from downstairs. As I took the basket from its peg, I
could guess from its sweet, spicy smell what was in it. Safta
had baked my father's favorite fig cakes again. Back on the
rooftop, she took the basket from me and set it in front of
him. "For you, Tobias," she said in a soft voice.

I saw a loving glance pass between them—and a flash of
resentment from Uncle Reuben. Abba offered the cakes to
my uncle, and he took one, but he chewed it sullenly. If I
were Safta, I thought, I, too, would favor my elder son.

When dinner was over, I carried the leftover stew down

to the kitchen. I started back to fetch the wine jug, but near the bottom of the stairs I met my brother, Alexandros. It annoyed me, the knowing way he looked at me. Had he come all the way down from the rooftop just to stare at me? "What is it?" I snapped.

"I can't tell you," he said solemnly. "It's men's business."

"Then why are you looking at me like that? What is it?"

Alexandros hesitated, but he couldn't resist showing off his information. "Abba had an offer for you."

An offer. An offer of marriage, that meant. My stomach dropped. "Who? Who is it?" In my mind, I pictured the young men of Magdala in our synagogue and sorted through the unmarried ones.

Shaking his head regretfully, Alexandros started to turn away. "I shouldn't have told you. But it's a good offer, and he'll probably accept it. Uncle Reuben thinks he should."

Ordinarily, I tried not to let Alexandros see that he bothered me, but now I was too upset to worry about my pride. I pestered my brother, hanging on his sleeve.

Finally, he gave in. "All right, if you have to know . . . it's Eleazar the merchant."

"Eleazar?" I couldn't take in whom he meant at first because I didn't know of any young men with that name. There was a certain merchant, Eleazar bar Yohannes, who sat in one of the best seats in the synagogue. But he was as old as our father.

"I shouldn't have told you," said Alexandros uneasily. "Don't say anything to Abba."

I felt sick. Scarcely hearing his words, I pushed past my brother and ran up the stairs to the rooftop. My heart pounded, choking me.

My father and Uncle Reuben were now leaning on the wall, gazing out to the waterfront and talking quietly. Uncle Reuben frowned at me as if I were a sheep struggling against being sheared, but Abba took my hand. "Mari, what's the matter?"

Gasping for air, I couldn't speak at first. I kissed his hand. "Abba, please, please . . ." When I finally managed to choke out the words, my father frowned, too. "Alexandros shouldn't have said anything to you. Nothing has been done so far. It was only a suggestion from Elder Thomas, Eleazar's cousin."

"But please, Abba, please don't . . ." I kissed his hand again. "Dear Abba!" Raising my eyes, I saw that I was embarrassing him, and I stopped talking.

"Surely," said my uncle, "Mariamne should speak to her mother about such matters. Then her mother could speak to you." He spoke in a pompous tone, as if he were the older brother. "To put it plainly, brother, this outburst is unseemly."

My father looked annoyed, but he put an arm around my shoulders and guided me away from Uncle Reuben. "Mari, my dear," he said in a low voice, "please calm down. You shouldn't get yourself so worked up. It would be rude of me to reject an offer right away, especially since Elder Thomas was the go-between. I must consider, then answer politely."

I nodded, already ashamed of my panic. It was Alexandros's fault, for talking as if my betrothal to Eleazar was bound to happen. "I'm sorry, Abba." I wished I hadn't made such a scene in front of my uncle. Squeezing my father's hand, I ran back down the stairs.

But at the bottom of the stairs, doubt nibbled at me. My father hadn't promised me anything. He hadn't actually said he would never betroth me to a man who was distasteful to me.

That night, I lay down on my cot beside Chloe as usual, but I didn't go to sleep. I listened to the sounds of the others settling in with sighs and clearing of throats. Someone coughed and rolled over; someone else (Safta, I guessed) made whistling noises in her sleep. When the whole family except me seemed to be asleep, I got up and stepped softly to the low wall at the edge of the rooftop.

The town was quiet and dark except for lamplight here and there in a window. As I watched, one window went dark, then another. From the shore came faint sounds of boat keels scraping on pebbles as fishermen set out for a night's work. The lake glimmered, lit by the half-moon at the top of the sky.

I yearned to soar above the broad expanse of water, into the broader sky. This house was such a small place, dear as the people in it were to me. How is it that my father and uncle can choose my destiny? I cried silently.

Your destiny is not theirs to choose, Namesake, said a voice close by.

I whirled around. A woman stood beside me, dressed in a wool tunic that left one shoulder bare. Her dark, wavy hair was loose except for an embroidered headband, and she carried a timbrel, a hand drum, under one arm. Lines fanned out from the corners of her eyes, as if she'd spent years out in the sun, searching the far horizon.

With my brothers, I led our people out of bondage in Egypt, she said. *No man chose my path for me, and none may choose yours.*

"What is my path?" I whispered. "Tell me what to do!" Trembling with fear and excitement, I reached out to take her hand.

She was gone.

Slowly I seemed to sink back into my small place in my family, in the Jewish community in the town of Magdala. I returned to my cot and lay down. But I felt certain that my life could never be the same. Miryam, the heroine of long-ago times, had spoken to me.

In the light of day, however, I wasn't so sure. My vision of Miryam had called me Namesake, yet many girls were named Mariamne or some other form of Miryam. They couldn't all become great heroines, could they?

Besides, how was I, a maiden of thirteen years, supposed to seek out my own path? I wasn't even allowed to go out the courtyard gate by myself, or to talk to anyone except relatives or family friends. It was baffling.

Still, I was sure that the vision was about something urgently important. It seemed connected with the breathtaking sight of the world from the mountaintop.

THREE

THE TAX COLLECTOR'S SON

The Jews of Magdala considered Alphaeus, the harbor-tax collector, a traitor to his people and a bad man. However, he was a good father to his sons, Matthew and James. Alphaeus sent them to a private teacher to learn to read, write, and do arithmetic. He taught the boys common Greek so that they could bargain and negotiate with foreigners. He tried to teach them his business.

Matthew and James's mother had died when James was still a baby, and Matthew didn't remember her well. Since then, Alphaeus had married three more wives, but each of them had died in childbirth. "You don't want to get too attached to a woman," he told Matthew the night after the third wife's death. "They're like pet doves. Very pretty, but you can't count on them lasting more than a few years."

James was slighter than Matthew, as well as younger, and Matthew looked after him when they were away from the house. At the private school, the other boys taunted them for being the tax collector's sons. Sometimes they even threw shards of pottery at them, and Matthew would step in front of James to shield him.

The rabbi who taught the school at his house was a mild man, patient with the younger boys. The only time Matthew saw him get really angry was when he'd caught the other boys bullying James. The rabbi ordered the ringleader, Alexandros bar Tobias, to copy a proverb over and over: "A fool's lips bring strife, and his mouth invites a flogging." But finally, because of the other parents' objections, the rabbi asked Matthew and James to come for their lessons at a separate time.

Alphaeus had an office near the docks, where he could keep a sharp eye on all the goods that came into the market, as well as the goods (salted sardines and dyed cloth) that were loaded onto boats leaving Magdala. Whether the goods came in or went out, the shippers and receivers had to pay Alphaeus the harbor tax. Exactly how much they had to pay was up to the tax collector, Alphaeus explained to Matthew. The Roman overseers let the tax collectors decide how much extra to charge to cover their own salaries. So a tax collector had to make quick judgments in each case:

—How much could the trader afford to pay?

—How much of a fuss would he make if you overcharged him?

—Did he have connections with powerful people?

"You might think I'd make the most money on the wealthiest merchants," said Alphaeus, "but actually, I have to go easy on them or they'll complain to the council. The smaller traders have to pay whatever I ask."

One day, Matthew was out on the black stone wharf with his father when the owner of a sardine-packing business received a shipment of salt. Matthew recognized the man as Tobias, the father of Alexandros bar Tobias, the bully.

However, Tobias seemed different from his son. Respectfully and sincerely, he asked Alphaeus for a deferment of the customs tax. "It's been a hard month," he said. "We lost a boat in the last storm. Three fishermen drowned, and I've been helping out their wives and children."

Matthew was impressed with Tobias's matter-of-fact manner. He was giving the widows and their families more than he could afford, but he didn't seem to think his generosity was anything out of the ordinary. Matthew looked to see his father's reaction.

"A sad story," said Alphaeus with a straight face. "My Roman supervisor would be moved to tears, if I were foolish enough to tell him."

Tobias flushed, but he kept his tone even. "I see your point. I'll pay the Romans' portion, but if you could see your way to letting me defer your cut . . . I can pay you just as soon as my buyer in Sepphoris pays me for the last shipment."

Alphaeus shook his head and folded his arms. Tobias hesitated, then drew out his money pouch and counted the full amount of coins into the tax collector's hand.

As the sardine packer left, followed by dockworkers carrying his salt, Alphaeus turned to Matthew. "What did you learn just now, son?"

Matthew said slowly, "I learned not to pay attention when they try to make you feel sorry for them."

"Good boy!" His father beamed and rumpled his hair. "They'll tell you anything to try to get out of paying." Matthew said nothing, but he wondered: Was the sardine packer just trying to get out of paying the harbor tax? Or was he really short on money because he was helping his fishermen's families?

"Another thing you should understand," continued Alphaeus, "is that the Romans rule the world. All the lands around the Great Sea, from the Pillars of Hercules to Damascus. That's the one big fact you have to know in this life: keep on the good side of the Romans."

"What about Herod Antipas?" asked Matthew.

His father nodded. "Herod Antipas . . . oh, we have to give him all due respect. The Romans let him rule over Galilee like a rooster on a dung heap and peck the maggots out of it. But he'll go too far one of these days, and then . . ." Alphaeus made a gesture of wringing a rooster's neck.

Matthew didn't like to think of Galilee—their homeland—as a dung heap, but he didn't protest.

While Matthew worked hard to learn Alphaeus's business, his younger brother, James, was a disappointment to their father. James would rather hang around the rabbi's house, reading and talking to the teacher, than learn how to collect taxes. In fact, James began to quote Scripture that criticized Alphaeus's teachings. One day he recited to his father, "It is you who have devoured the vineyard, the spoil of the poor is in your houses. 'What do you mean by crushing my people, by grinding the face of the poor?' says the Lord God of hosts."

Matthew, amazed and horrified, thought their father might throttle his brother. But Alphaeus only cuffed James on the side of the head. "Don't you quote Scripture at me! Who do you think paid for you to take lessons, you insolent brat?"

James sullenly learned to do the accounts for Alphaeus, but he never learned to stomach the tax collector's business.

Alphaeus hoped James would come around sooner or later, but Matthew knew he wouldn't. James was stubborn as a donkey. He told Matthew, "I'd rather be a common laborer than a tax collector. Haven't you noticed the way people shun us?"

"You mean the holier-than-thou folk in the synagogue?" said Matthew.

"I mean righteous Jews, like Elder Thomas and the rest of the council," said James. "They'd rather welcome lepers into the congregation than someone who helps the Romans to oppress us."

"Abba says the Romans have the right to collect a harbor tax because they're the ones who built the lighthouse," argued Matthew.

"Yes—they built it by forcing our people to do the construction work," said James. "And where do you think the fuel for the beacon comes from? They make the peasants on Mount Arbel take time out from tending their vineyards to deliver wood. Better for all the harbors in Galilee to be dark than to be lit by Roman fires!"

Matthew could see, without James's pointing it out, how the Jews of Magdala felt about Alphaeus and his sons. At the Sabbath meetings, Elder Thomas was more gracious to the Gentiles who came to listen, standing respectfully in the back of the hall, than he was to the tax collector. Other members of the congregation would glance at Alphaeus, then pointedly turn away. Once, as Matthew, James, and their father walked into the meeting hall, Matthew heard someone mutter a line from Scripture at their backs: " 'If one turns his ear away from hearing the law, even his prayer is an abomination.' "

One day, when Matthew was eighteen and James was sixteen, news came from Tiberias that Herod Antipas had executed a popular traveling preacher, John the Baptizer. At dinner, James was trembling with outrage. "John only spoke the truth: Antipas should not have divorced his wife to marry his brother's wife. It's against the Law."

"It's not our concern, is it?" asked Matthew in surprise. "We don't live in Tiberias."

"But we're all Jews," exclaimed James. His eyes were blazing. "Either we're a faithful nation or we aren't."

Alphaeus waved his hand, dismissing the question. "A wandering preacher has no right telling our ruler what to do. He should have left that up to the Jewish council of Tiberias. Insulting the ruler and his wife is . . . why, it's close to treason." He dipped bread into the dish of stew and chewed.

"How can you eat, Father?" James burst out. "It's a day

for fasting and mourning. Our ruler has murdered a holy man. As it is written, 'How the faithful city is become a harlot, she that was full of justice! Righteousness lodged in her, but now murderers.' "

Matthew laughed, almost choking on a mouthful of food. "Are you calling Tiberias, Herod Antipas's capital, a faithful city?"

"The 'faithful city' is a poetic symbol for the Jewish people, as you'd know if you paid any attention to the rabbi," said his brother. Matthew had never seen James so grim; it was frightening.

Alphaeus scowled. "James, eat. There's no reason to mourn the death of a fool. What did this John expect? Herod Antipas is always on edge about rebels. John talked like a rebel, and he got crowds of people to follow him. Antipas had to have him killed. Even if the tetrarch wasn't personally offended by John's insults, he had to show the Romans that he was in control."

That made sense to Matthew, but he could see that James wasn't listening. Under his father's eye, James pretended to eat a little, but he sat through dinner staring at the carpet. In the morning, he had disappeared.

James left a note on his bed, scribbled on a piece of broken clay pot. Matthew had never learned to read as well as

James, but he could make out that his brother was quoting the prophet Ezekiel. And the message was simple enough: " 'The son shall not suffer for the iniquity of the father.' "

Alphaeus stormed into the synagogue and complained to the elders, accusing the rabbi of turning James against him. He demanded to know where James had gone. The elders questioned the rabbi, a quiet, scholarly man; he was distressed but claimed to know nothing. When Alphaeus began to shout, Elder Thomas called the guards and ordered him to leave.

Later, they heard that James had made his way south to the Dead Sea and joined a religious sect. Alphaeus ordered that his name never be mentioned again. Matthew could see that his father was more hurt than angry, but that made Matthew all the angrier at James. He wanted to shout at his absent brother, "If you're so fond of Scripture, why didn't you remember 'Honor your father'?"

Alphaeus stopped attending Sabbath prayer meeting at the synagogue, and so of course, Matthew didn't attend, either. He was relieved not to have to walk into that hall full of unfriendly faces anymore, but he missed hearing the Sabbath readings. Sometimes on a weekday, he'd stop by the synagogue and listen to the scholars who gathered on the porch to debate points of Scripture. He'd wonder, What would

James say about that prophecy? or How would James inter-pret that law?

One morning several months after James disappeared, Matthew started to leave the house for his father's tax office. Opening the courtyard door, he noticed several wet globs on the doorstep. He just had time to recognize them as spit when he saw the two girls on a donkey paused in front of the house. The girl in front, about thirteen, was leaning over, but she raised her head and looked straight at him for an instant.

Before the girl could also spit on his doorstep, Matthew slammed the door shut. Somehow, the scorn of this maiden, with her fresh, passionate face, upset him more than censure from Elder Thomas. Matthew admitted to himself a shameful secret: he wished he were not the son of Alphaeus the tax collector.

FOUR

LIKE RACHEL AND JACOB

At first, I thought often about the night Miryam appeared to me. It seemed urgent to honor the vision, but what *was* the path that no one could choose for me? How should I follow it?

It must have to do with the way I saw and heard things differently from others. Miryam had found a well in the desert for her people, water that they needed but couldn't find for themselves. So maybe I, too, could find something precious for others—with the eyes and ears of my soul.

Meanwhile, to my relief, my father did refuse old Eleazar's offer for me. I heard my uncle reproach Abba for losing the profitable sardine business with the palace in Tiberias. Evidently, that would have been part of Eleazar's offer, or at least Uncle Reuben thought so.

My mother had no doubt about the path I should follow, or that it was her duty to push me along it. Now that I was old enough to marry, she watched me all the time. I'd always been a fairly well-behaved girl, except for flights of imagination, and I wasn't used to being scolded.

But these days, it seemed, my mother's eyebrows drew together every time she caught sight of me. "Don't run up the steps, Mariamne. *Walk.*" Or "When you speak to your father, don't meet his gaze but cast your eyes down. Likewise with Alexandros."

"Alexandros?" I said in disbelief. "He's my brother, and he's only three years older than I am." With growing indignation, I added, "Why should I respect him, when he never even learned his lessons properly?"

"But Alexandros is a man," said my mother sharply. "And you are a maiden. You need to get in the habit of being more modest with *any* man."

One afternoon, after my mother had corrected me six times in a row, I ran to my grandmother to complain. "Imma hates me! Nothing I do is right!" I paced in front of her with clenched hands. "Why should I treat my brother like a prince? He doesn't deserve it."

"Soften your voice, Mari dear!" My grandmother caught one hand and straightened my fingers, stroking them.

"Tabitha is only worried for your sake. You know your father is looking for a suitable match for you, don't you? When he finds one—before long—there will be a meeting of the families. The groom's family will watch your every movement, and if your behavior isn't perfect, they may call the match off. You have to do your part, you know. You can't do just as you please and expect to get a good husband."

This was a sobering thought. I was quiet for a moment. Then I said, "If I could choose a husband myself—"

"Hush!" exclaimed my grandmother. "You must put that thought out of your mind, Mariamne. Put it right out." She sounded almost as stern as my mother. "You'll make yourself miserable, thinking that way."

"I was only going to say, I would choose a man like Abba, but young."

"Ah, well." Safta's face mellowed. "My son Tobias is a dear man. The Lord blessed me when he gave me such a son. Tobias is not at all like his father, may the man rest in peace. Or like your uncle Reuben."

"Or like Alexandros," I added. It was true—my brother was more like our uncle than like our father.

My grandmother's advice made sense, so I tried my best to behave even more modestly. It wasn't easy. The very next day, my cousin Susannah sent a servant to invite us to meet a visitor. And what a visitor! She was a foreigner, a wise woman named Ramla of Alexandria, Susannah's servant told my mother.

Overhearing from the rooftop, I ran down the stairs to join my mother at the courtyard gate. Alexandria was in Egypt. I'd heard things about Egypt that were hard to believe. Egypt was a vast land, they said, with a single enormous river, as wide as our lake and so long that no one knew where it began. At the mouth of the river, where it met the Great Sea, they said there was a lighthouse ten times as tall as the one at Magdala, with a beacon brighter than the sun. The Egyptian kings had tombs the size of Mount Arbel.

Not only that, but the people worshiped outlandish gods, stranger than those of the Greeks and Romans. One god had a jackal's head. One goddess had the form of a hippopotamus. All this made me wildly curious to meet Ramla of Alexandria.

But my mother sent the servant back with a polite refusal. "Of course we can't go," said Imma. "It isn't seemly for Jewish maidens to show interest in Gentiles. Especially a Gentile who traffics with the occult."

"Oh, surely not the *occult*, Tabitha," protested my grandmother. "Our Susannah is a good, pious young woman, and she's receiving the Egyptian in her home."

"Still, Susannah is a married woman, and she doesn't

have to be as careful as a maiden. We can't have it rumored that Mariamne's family is careless about the company she keeps."

Ordinarily, I would have begged my mother to reconsider, and even burst into tears from disappointment. But with an effort, I turned and walked quietly back up the stairs. I was proud of my self-control, and that almost made up for missing the Egyptian wise woman.

A few weeks later, my family decided on a match for me. He was a young man named Nicolaos, of a family of dyers like Susannah's husband, Silas. On the next Sabbath, Imma pointed him out to me in the synagogue.

I could hardly believe my luck! Of all the young men I'd noticed, I liked the way Nicolaos looked the best. He had fine dark eyebrows that met in the middle, and curly dark hair with a short beard to match. Watching him talking with his older brother, I noticed that an endearing crease appeared in his cheek when he smiled.

Since I'd been on my best behavior lately, my mother was more relaxed with me. She chatted on, pointing out a woman sitting with Eleazar bar Yohannes. "That's Chava, Eleazar's widowed daughter-in-law. She must be glad that we didn't accept Eleazar's offer. Everyone knows that Chava wants him to marry her niece, that girl beside her."

I peered over at Chava, whose long face reminded me of

a sheep's. Her niece, a girl about my age, looked like a younger version of Chava. Maybe that girl wouldn't mind marrying old Eleazar. "Why doesn't he offer for her, then?"

"She has only a small dowry. Our family can afford much more, and of course, our sardine business would have been a profitable connection. And the girl herself is no great beauty." My mother gave me a glance, hesitated, and finally spoke again. "I shouldn't say this to you, and I don't want you to let it go to your head. Nicolaos's older brother told our people that Nicolaos thought you were quite pleasing to behold."

"Imma!" I hugged her, dizzy with excitement. This was such a new idea to me, that I was a maiden that a young man could be pleased—*quite* pleased—to behold.

"There, now." My mother seemed glad, but she disentangled herself and said, "As the proverb goes, 'Like a gold ring in a swine's snout is a beautiful woman without discretion.'"

If I hadn't been so excited, I might have resented that proverb. Pigs were disgusting, filthy animals. Gentiles like the Romans raised them and ate them, but Jews would have nothing to do with them. Pigs stank. They snuffled and rooted through garbage with their snouts.

Imma straightened her head scarf, then mine. "Shh. The lector's going to read."

I folded my hands in my lap and tried to listen while the

lector read from the Scripture scroll in Hebrew. But my skin tingled all over; my head buzzed. I could hardly pay attention, even when the lector translated the passage into Aramaic so that the congregation could understand.

Then a verse of a psalm sounded faintly through the buzzing in my head: "The earth is full of the steadfast love of the Lord." That was important. I needed to pay attention.

Gazing around the congregation, I was sure that most of them were not paying attention, either. They looked discontented, or worried, or even bored. I wanted to shout, "Listen! The earth is full of the steadfast love of the Lord!"

Of course, if I did shout out this good news, I would only disgrace myself and my family. Nicolaos's family would surely not want me for his bride. Nicolaos . . . Nicolaos thought I was quite pleasing to behold. The tingling crept over my skin again.

Soon after that Sabbath, a first meeting between Nicolaos's family and my family was arranged. One afternoon, we put on our best robes, as if we were going to the synagogue, and Imma carefully chose earrings for me and draped my shawl. We walked up the main avenue and through a maze of lanes to the dyers' neighborhood.

As Nicolaos's family welcomed us to their rooftop and seated us under the awning, I noted Nicolaos from the corner of my eye. I dared not look straight at him; I had to keep on behaving modestly, at least until we were betrothed. Nicolaos's mother sat down beside me and struck up a conversation. I tried to pay attention, although everyone else on the rooftop seemed small and far away compared with Nicolaos.

Across the rooftop, my father and uncle were talking to Nicolaos and his older brother, Thaddaios. Nicolaos seemed to be paying as little attention to them as I was to his mother. I was aware of him looking at me, then quickly looking away again.

I really have no idea what I said to Nicolaos's mother that afternoon, and no one told me what Nicolaos said to Abba and Uncle Reuben, either. But both sides must have been satisfied because the next day the marriage contract was drawn up, and shortly after that, we celebrated the betrothal. If I thought it was exciting just to be in the same room with Nicolaos . . . well, to stand right next to him! His eyes were hazel, I discovered, with long lashes. To look into those eyes . . . to drink from the same cup as we pledged our troth!

I felt my body glowing, so that I was afraid everyone in the room could see. Nicolaos's hand shook, and he sounded breathless as he pronounced the words. For just an instant, I noticed my brother's eyes on me, and I wished I didn't have to share this private moment of my life with him.

But then a cheerful thought flashed through my mind: after my wedding a year from now, I'll hardly have to see Alexandros at all. That made me feel almost kindly toward him.

Back home, my grandmother hugged me and whispered, "The Lord has blessed you, my dear. You and Nicolaos looked just like the devoted lovers Rachel and Jacob in the old story."

Two years before, when my cousin Susannah became betrothed to Silas, a screen had seemed to come between us, even before she left our family compound for her husband's house. Susannah was on one side of the screen, with all betrothed girls and married women. I was left on the other side.

But now I, too, had stepped through the screen of betrothal. The next time Susannah visited our house, she was eager to talk to me. Handing little Kanarit over to our grandmother, she sat down on the steps beside me. "Are you going to live with your in-laws before the wedding?" she asked.

"No," I said. "They suggested that, but Abba didn't want me to leave before I had to."

Susannah's eyes twinkled as she gazed at me. "Maybe *you* wouldn't have minded, though. Do you feel warm all over when Nicolaos is near? Yes, I know how it feels." She leaned close to me, whispering, "And the man feels the same way—even more so!"

"How do you know?" I asked in wonder.

Susannah giggled. "Silas told me. He says when he desires me, he feels as if he's on fire . . . there." She glanced down below the belt of her tunic, bit her lip, and burst out laughing. "Oh, Mari! I'm so happy for you."

As we talked on, Susannah showed me amulets that she'd bought for herself and her little girl from Ramla, the wise woman from Egypt. "I wish you could have met her, Mari. She's so . . . so different! She has a man as companion, and sometimes he seems to be her servant—her bodyguard, her musician—but sometimes he seems more like a husband. Oh—and guess what? Ramla has a bird, a parrot, that she talks to, and the bird *talks back*!"

"Really?" This was so amazing that for just one moment, I forgot about being betrothed. I also remembered something I hadn't thought about for a long time. "I used to talk to a sparrow," I mused. Susannah gave an astonished laugh, and I corrected myself quickly. "I mean, I used to pretend that the sparrow talked to me."

Then I forgot about the sparrow as Susannah turned the conversation to weddings, and to what happens in the bridal chamber when the bride and groom are alone.

FIVE

A LIFE OF BLESSINGS

Although my family's business was sardines, we also owned farmland on the plain of Gennesaret, north of Mount Arbel. We had a wheat field, a vineyard, and an apricot orchard. At harvest times, the whole family would camp out in the country-side to work—and play. Harvest was the happiest season.

During the year of my betrothal, Nicolaos's family invited me to their apricot harvest. Abba escorted me to an orchard on a neighboring hillside and left me with Nicolaos's mother, Lydia. I would spend the next several days with them.

"Welcome to our family, Mariamne," she said. She had a wide, generous smile and a soft, generous way of hugging. She showed me the tent where I'd sleep with the other unmarried girls.

As the days went by, the harvest proceeded much as it did in my family's orchard. The men knocked ripe fruit from the branches with poles. Women and girls gathered the fallen fruit into baskets and carried them down to the tents. There, other women pitted the apricots and laid them out to dry on cloths.

That whole week, I was in a constant flutter with Nicolaos so near. We couldn't be alone together, of course, but I often felt his gaze on me as I carried a basket out of the orchard. Any ordinary remark from him, such as "Let me lift that heavy basket for you," or "It's hot for this time of year, isn't it?" sounded like love poetry. We found many chances to "accidentally" brush against each other, gasping at the slightest touch.

I was a little shy with all these strangers at first, but Nicolaos's relatives were so welcoming that I soon felt at ease. I was glad to find out that Nicolaos's family, like mine, stayed up in the evening to tell stories. I thought this was the best way to listen to stories: tired after the day's harvesting, sitting in the shadows around the campfire.

The first night, Nicolaos's older brother, Thaddaios, told a story he'd heard from his father, who had remembered Herod the Great's reign. In old King Herod's day, Galilee was part of the kingdom of Greater Judea. But King Herod kept his power by pleasing the Romans, and there were many Jews who opposed him. The rebels hid in caves on the sheer north face of Mount Arbel.

Here, Thaddaios pointed to the bulk of the mountain, even darker than the night sky. Light flickered from a watch fire on the summit.

"Herod lowered his soldiers on ropes from the top of the cliff. They seized the rebels and hurled them off the mountain to their death. And their wives and children with them."

I shuddered, feeling with the rebels the panic in their bones, which were about to crack like sticks on the rocks below.

"But there was one rebel, a real hero, who threw his own family off the cliff," an uncle put in. "Herod thought he had this man cornered; he tried to make him surrender. But the rebel threw off his wife, then his daughters, then each of his three sons. Then he spit at Herod and leaped off himself."

"Thank the Lord that he didn't give *me* a 'real hero' for a husband," said Lydia dryly. There was laughter, especially from the other women. "Anyway," she added, "these are peaceful days around our lake, thank the Lord even more for that."

One of the young men spoke up. "Yes, we're as peaceful as oxen plowing the fields ahead of the farmer's whip. We peacefully pay and pay the taxes, like nanny goats giving milk."

"Hush!" said Thaddaios. "Do you want to get us into trouble? Herod Antipas has ears everywhere."

The young man was silent, but an old man's voice spoke out of the dark. "When, oh when, will the Lord send us his Anointed One?" There was a terrible longing in his voice, more frightening than the thought of falling off a cliff.

Nicolaos's brother seemed at a loss—he couldn't scold an older relative. But his mother spoke up to change the subject. "We Jews have faced terrible trials many times, and the Lord always sends help," said Lydia. "Do you remember Queen Esther? Instead of throwing her family off a cliff, she *saved* the lives of all her people."

This was one of the stories my grandmother told. It took place long ago when the Jews lived in exile in Persia, far to the east. The story began when the king of Persia, Ahasuerus, divorced his queen, Vashti.

Although I'd heard the story over and over, it struck me for the first time what a harsh man the king was. Why did he divorce Vashti? Only because she embarrassed him in front of his banquet guests. He summoned her to parade her beauty before his guests, but she refused. Surely divorce was too severe a punishment for that!

As the story went on, the king ordered a search for a new

queen among all the maidens of the kingdom. Mordecai, a
Jew who worked for the palace, turned in his own cousin and
ward, Esther. This part of the story, too, disturbed me now. I
couldn't imagine my father meekly delivering me to the
king's palace. He'd send me off somewhere, perhaps up in the
hills with my aunt in Arbel, until after the king chose a bride.

"Poor Esther!" I exclaimed. "Why didn't her guardian,
Mordecai, hide her? Didn't he care that Esther might have to
marry a Gentile?"

I'd spoken softly, but Lydia heard, and she gave me a tol-
erant smile. "You know it all comes out right in the end."

So I listened quietly to the rest of Esther's story. But to
tell the truth, I didn't think it was much more cheerful than
the story about the Galilean rebel who threw his wife and
children off the cliff to spite King Herod. Esther, beautiful
and charming, was chosen as Ahasuerus's new queen. She did
persuade him to spare his Jewish subjects from a massacre.
But first she had to risk death, just to approach the king without being summoned!

Nicolaos, as well as the other men, seemed the most interested in the end of the story, when there was a great battle.
King Ahasuerus decreed that the Jews in Persia could defend
themselves from the slaughter, set for the fourteenth day of
the month of Adar.

"And the Jews slaughtered their enemies instead, and

won a glorious victory," Lydia concluded. "And so we honor Esther when we celebrate Purim, to this day."

Good-natured repartee broke out as to whether Esther or Mordecai was the true hero of the story. While the others were talking, Nicolaos caught my eye. He smiled straight at me, and I dared to smile back as if the two of us were alone. It wouldn't be long before I could stroke his face, brushing my fingers right over those dimples. My bold thought made me blush and lower my eyes.

The next morning, gathering apricots at the top of the orchard, I shaded my eyes to gaze over the farmland to the lake. This was a good world: the blue water holding up our fishing boats, the golden wheat fields on the plain, and our prosperous town on the shore. It seemed that I was meant to spend my life in this fertile land, with this happy family. I murmured a prayer: "Praised be the Lord, who has chosen me for a life of blessings."

(Now I believe that demons must have overheard my prayer. They must have rubbed their hands in glee and remarked, *This one will be an easy target. Just wait.*)

At the end of the harvest, when the last fruit had been gathered and the apricot trees held only their dusty leaves, Nicolaos's brother walked me back to my family's orchard. I wore their gift, a costly silk scarf the color of apricots, orange blushing to pink.

"We would have been glad to keep Mariamne," Thaddaios told my father with a broad smile. "My mother wants her to come home and move in with us right now, rather than wait until the wedding."

My father smiled, not so broadly, and murmured polite thanks, but he put a firm arm around my shoulders. "The wedding will be time enough." When Thaddaios was out of earshot, he folded me in his arms, muttering, "Mari, my dear little daughter! How can I bear to see you go?"

My father's sorrow rushed from his heart into mine, and I clung to him. I'd hidden something from myself up until then: marrying Nicolaos would mean leaving my father.

Pulling back and taking both my hands, my father searched my face. Then he looked away, as if he was ashamed of what he was going to say. "I'm troubled." He sighed. "I have strange dreams. They seem to tell me it's not right for you to marry. But how could that be so? What kind of life could a woman have without a husband, without children?"

I had never seen my father look so distraught, and it hurt me that I'd been so happy with Nicolaos and his family while Abba was suffering. I lifted his hands to my face and kissed one hand, then the other, to soothe him.

"Lord forgive me," whispered my father. "I should not have told you of my perverse dreams. It must be my own selfish heart that wants to keep you with me."

I opened my mouth to protest, but my father added quickly, "We are *blessed* that you will leave us to join Nicolaos and his family. On your wedding day, I will release you to them with rejoicing."

SIX

THE MISSION

On the afternoon of my last happy day, Chloe and I sat in the courtyard at the bottom of the steps. The year of my betrothal had sped by; it was almost Tishri, autumn, again. Outside the kitchen shed, Yael laid a fire and set a pot to boil.

Chloe was finishing the embroidery on one sleeve of my wedding robe while I worked on the other. The robe was white linen, the fine goods that Magdala was famous for. We held the cloth carefully in our laps, away from the chickens pecking around the yard.

"I can't believe you're getting married tomorrow, can you, Mari?" asked my sister for the seventh time. She knotted a blue thread, the last stitch in the last flower, and bit it off. "You're so lucky. Nicolaos is so nice. Do you think they'll find someone that nice for me? Cousin Susannah's husband is nice, too."

"What do you think, that the marriage luck will be all used up by the time you're thirteen?" I teased. "Don't be silly; of course they'll find someone nice for you." But I, too, could hardly believe I was getting married. The biggest day of my life was rushing toward me, like a swift-sailing boat, to scoop me up and fly off with me.

"But after you leave, I'll be here without you for a long time," Chloe said sadly. "And you'll live on the other side of town, and . . ."

"You'll come visit me, won't you?" I asked. I was often impatient with Chloe's little fears and anxieties, but today I felt tender toward her. I wanted everyone to be happy.

"Of course, if you want me to." Chloe gave me a pleased glance. We stood to fold the finished robe. As we carried it upstairs and laid it carefully on a rack, she went on, "Imma's taking you to the *mikvah* tonight, isn't she?"

I nodded. This would be my first time at the women's *mikvah,* the ritual bath. Ritual purity is not the same thing as ordinary cleanliness. A person does not step into the *mikvah* to wash off ordinary dirt, as one washes a melon from the field before slicing it. The wedding was a sacred ceremony, and I must be pure of heart for it.

That evening, as I left the house with my mother, I was excited but nervous. I'd always thought the entrance to the *mikvah* looked something like a tomb. Past the synagogue and around a corner, a flight of black stone stairs led down to an archway.

Imma greeted the *mikvah* attendant, a woman she knew. The attendant smiled in a kindly way as she handed me a towel. "So tomorrow is her wedding day?" she asked my mother. "May the Lord shower blessings on both families!"

In the windowless chamber before the pool, I undressed by the light of a lamp and wrapped myself in the towel. I shivered— not because I was cold but because my first *mikvah* was such a serious occasion. I felt a building excitement . . . or was it dread? Just for an instant, I remembered Susannah's older sister, who had died in childbirth.

My mother led me into the next chamber. To my relief, this room was larger, and it was lit not only by lamps but also by the stars from a skylight over the pool. Handing Imma the towel, I walked down the steps into the water.

I was careful to keep my eyes and mouth closed, but my hands open and the fingers separated so that the water could touch me all over. I drew up my knees, floating free. The cool water flowed through my hair, lifting it and then pulling it down.

When I was sure I was thoroughly wet, I stood up in the pool and recited the prayer of the *mikvah,* as Imma had instructed me: "Who has sanctified us with His commandments and commanded us on immersion." Then I ducked under the water for the second immersion.

And then . . . I seemed to be raised up, although I was under the water; and bathed with light, although my eyes were closed. I understood that I was in holy water, in Miryam's Well.

Miryam. I knew that voice, clear and strong.

Miryam of Magdala, the woman's voice went on. *This day, if you choose, you are consecrated to a high purpose.*

I do choose it! I cried from my heart.

It is a steep and rocky way, said the voice. *It is lonely; it is perilous. You will need the courage of an eagle.*

I was afraid, but still my heart burned to set out on the way. I choose it, I responded.

"Mariamne." My mother was calling from far away. "Mariamne!"

I broke the surface, pushing my wet hair from my face. I felt such tenderness toward my mother. I saw that all her annoying work to turn me into a proper Jewish wife was done out of love for me. "Dear Imma!" I said.

"You aren't supposed to stay in all day," Imma said at the same time, holding out the towel. But she was beaming as I climbed the steps. She wrapped me in the towel and held me close.

In that moment, I felt that Imma and I understood each other perfectly. "Imma," I said, "I found Miryam's Well. With the ears of my soul, I heard her tell me my mission."

My mother smiled at me fondly. "The way you make such a story out of things! Those readings you hear in the synagogue, you know, they're very holy, of course, but you aren't supposed to take them literally. Isn't it exciting enough to get married?"

"But I truly heard Miryam's voice," I insisted as I pulled on my tunic. "She warned me that my way would be steep and rocky—perilous, she said."

Imma wound my wet hair in a scarf. "I see what it is. It's natural for a maiden to worry about the dangers of childbirth. Are you thinking of your poor cousin, may she rest in peace?"

"I did think of her while I was undressing," I admitted as we left the *mikvah,* "but that's not what I'm talking—"

"That was a completely different situation," my mother broke in. At the top of the steps, the manservant was waiting for us with a torch. As we followed him down the avenue toward home, she began to explain all the reasons why I wouldn't die in childbirth like Susannah's older sister.

I interrupted, trying to describe how it felt to be bathed

in light and hear the prophet Miryam's voice. But Imma made a joke of it. "I told you not to stay under so long—if you hold your breath like that, of course you'll start hearing voices. You've always let your imagination run away with you, even as a young child. *Ai,* that time you jumped off the top of the stairs, thinking you could fly!"

We entered the courtyard, lowering our voices so as not to disturb Abba and the rest, already in bed. "Imma, this was a real vision," I protested.

Stopping at the bottom of the stairs, Imma took me by the shoulders. "My daughter," she said kindly, "are you worried about the wedding night?"

It dawned on me that she meant, was I afraid of being alone in bed with Nicolaos. "No!" I exclaimed. I forgot to keep my voice down, and the chickens in the shed rustled and clucked. "Not at all," I whispered, feeling warm. I could have added, "I can't wait."

My mother seemed to understand my unspoken words because she chuckled and patted my shoulders. "Ah yes, I remember how it feels, to be giddy with love. . . ." Turning away with a sigh, she began to climb the stairs.

The next day, when it was near time to dress for the wedding, Imma discovered that my father was not in the compound. "He went to the waterfront," my grandmother told her. "Not to conduct business, of course. He's distributing gifts to the fishermen who work with him." Safta smiled. "My generous son! He wants them to rejoice with us on our happy day."

"That's all very righteous," my mother grumbled, "but he shouldn't keep the wedding party waiting." She ordered Yael to go to the waterfront and remind him to come home.

To add to my mother's irritation, Yael didn't obey promptly. She didn't actually refuse, but she twisted her head unwillingly. "Mistress, they say at the well that the Tishri fever's run right around the lake to Magdala. They say it's in the air down at the waterfront."

The fever? This was the first I'd heard about it. Of course, I knew that every few years in the autumn, the Tishri fever swept through town like an evil wind. When the fever was abroad, no one would go out on the streets if they could help it. All private celebrations had to be postponed. "Oh no!" I exclaimed. "My wedding!"

My mother frowned at Yael. "Nonsense. Just go straight to our warehouse, deliver the message, and come back. If you don't linger on the docks, talking to good-for-nothing idlers, you won't have anything to fear."

As Yael went out the gate, I climbed the stairs to the roof. There was nothing I needed to do just then, but I couldn't sit still. There was a pile of flax fibers under the awning, and I began to comb them.

As I worked, I thought of my vision while bathing in the holy well and Miryam's message of "a high purpose" for me. Imma must have been right, that those words were a poetic way to describe getting married and having children. It was a sacred duty and a privilege to be a wife and mother, to carry on the life of our people.

Still combing flax, I walked to the edge of the roof and looked over the low wall. There was Yael in the alley, not far from our house. She hadn't even reached the street that ran down to the waterfront!

I shook my head. Yael had a great talent for not quite disobeying orders. If she dawdled slowly enough, she might meet my father coming home. Then she wouldn't have to go to the docks after all.

Yael was annoying, but she was also a pathetic creature. People said that she had been the respectable wife of a landowner, but she'd done something to displease him. He'd divorced her, and her family were so ashamed that they'd refused to take her back. She had no choice but to join another household as a servant, grinding grain and washing feet. My grandmother felt rather sorry for her, but my mother said that Yael's troubles were her own fault.

My gaze shifted from Yael in the alley to a group of men climbing the street. They were moving as slowly as Yael, but for a different reason. They carried a man on a litter. I couldn't see their faces from this distance, but there was something familiar about them.

Yael emerged onto the street at last, and one of the men— now I recognized my uncle Reuben—called to her. She clapped her hands over her mouth and stood like that a moment. Then she whirled and ran back down the alley.

Something terrible had happened. With all my will, I tried to keep the bad news away. Instead of running downstairs, I stayed on the roof, watching the men struggle up the street with the litter. But I couldn't help hearing Yael's scream: "Mistress, the fever! The master—ah, woe!"

Of course, my wedding was postponed, but I hardly thought about that. The fever burned its way through our household. First Abba lay on his bed, shivering and sweating. My mother tended him, and I brought cool water and fresh cloths to lay on his forehead. We crept around the house with anxious faces.

Then my mother, then Chloe, and then I, too, sickened. In my delirium, I saw weird beings bending over my bed, sometimes one with a jackal's head and sometimes one with cow's horns. Then I would realize the phantom was only Yael, holding a cup of bitter medicine to my lips. Yael, in spite of her fears, somehow escaped the illness, and so did my grandmother.

I woke one day to see Safta's face near mine. "Thank the Lord, her fever has broken," said my grandmother. "Yael, hand me a fresh cloth."

Yael brought a cloth wrung out in cool water, and my grandmother laid it gently on my forehead.

Now I remembered the litter, and my eyes focused on my grandmother's robe. It was ripped at the neck, as in mourning. "Abba?" I croaked. "How is . . . ?"

My grandmother turned her face aside, and a tear ran down her wrinkled cheek. "Why did I live, to see my dear son die?" she muttered. "Why didn't the fever take me instead?"

"Abba!" I groaned. I tried to raise my hands to my neck, to rip my own tunic, but I was too weak.

During that day, I gradually became aware of what was going on in our house. My mother and Chloe lay in the same room with me, and each of them in turn woke and asked for my father. At the news of his death, my mother screamed out, "Why has the Lord done this to me? What terrible sin have I committed, that he's made me a widow?" She sat up in bed, as if struck by an even worse thought. "And Alexandros? What about my son? *Where is Alexandros?*"

I sat up, too, feeling guilty. I hadn't even asked about my brother.

"Hush, Tabitha," said my grandmother. "The Lord has spared Alexandros. He's at the packinghouse with his uncle."

With a deep sigh, my mother fell back on her bed. "Thank the Lord. We won't have to become poor relations in my brother-in-law's house." She closed her eyes. "Tobias . . . a good man . . ." Then suddenly she opened her eyes again and said, "There's something else, isn't there? What is it?"

I thought my mother's worn nerves were making her oversuspicious, but then my grandmother glanced sideways at me and said nothing.

"Is there something else, Safta?" I asked.

Safta swallowed. "Mariamne, dear, I didn't want to give you more bad news while you were—"

"The fever took Nicolaos, too!" interrupted my mother.

What a dreadful thing to say! Imma must be still feverish, I thought, but why does she always have to imagine the worst? I waited for my grandmother to deny it. But her eyes met mine, and she nodded.

"Life must go on," said Safta, although her tone was uncertain.

Nicolaos dead? Nicolaos gone—just like that? I'd been sure, even in my grief for my father, that a happy future lay before me. Now that future was gone, sheared off like a mountain meadow in an earthquake. I lay in bed stunned.

But the next day, I felt strong enough to get up, although still shaky. We sick ones had missed Abba's funeral, since by

Jewish law the dead have to be buried within a day after death. We'd also missed the first days of *shiva,* the week of mourning.

Chloe and Imma got out of bed, too, and we sat together in the upper room with Safta, Alexandros, and Uncle Reuben. I saw that my grandmother's eyes were red, as if she'd cried until the tears were gone. She'd been nursing us all the time she was grieving for her favorite son.

According to custom, Chloe and I wore the tunics, still stiff with sweat, from our sickbeds. My sister and I held hands like two little children, sobbing and comforting each other as relatives and friends came by to offer condolences. "Tobias was a good man and a righteous Jew," they told our mother and grandmother. To Alexandros they said, "Your father's sardines are known from Damascus to Petra. May you follow in his footsteps."

My chest ached, and it was hard to draw a deep breath. I had to be polite to our comforters, of course, but—sardines! I was glad to see my cousin Susannah arrive with Kanarit, toddling as she clutched her mother's hand. "Uncle Tobias was so good to me," said Susannah. "He was good to everyone."

As the people came and went, the meaning of their words to my brother sank in. With my father gone, Alexandros was now the head of our household. This made me uneasy, but I was too sad and weak that day to worry much.

My thoughts drifted back to my vision in the *mikvah*. It seemed like something that had happened a very long time ago, and I wondered what it could mean now. Did it only have to do with my future as Nicolaos's wife, which was gone forever? Or did it mean something else entirely?

As I grew stronger, the memory of Miryam and her words grew stronger, too. By the time the seven days of *shiva* had passed, I had an urgent sense that I should put everything else aside and try to discern the meaning of my vision. I went to talk to my brother. I would have preferred not to deal with him, but he *was* head of our family. Since Alexandros was young, Uncle Reuben would advise him, but I had no intention of dealing with my uncle.

I began, "Brother, about my future . . ."

My brother looked down on me, rubbing the sparse new beard on his chin. "Hmm. Yes, a new betrothal has to be arranged, but I'm not sure I can promise you . . . Speaking plainly, Mari, I doubt that Nicolaos was the best choice for you in the first place."

It was my brother standing before me, but it was Uncle Reuben's pompous voice coming from his mouth. Alexandros went on, "Of course, Nicolaos's family would have been a good connection for us, but . . . I'm afraid you need more guidance than a young, easygoing man like Nicolaos would give you."

"Nicolaos was our *father's* choice," I said, my voice trembling with anger. "You're not honoring his memory when you speak like that. But I was going to say something else."

My brother looked puzzled. "Well, then?"

"Listen to me, brother, I beg you," I said. "Before the fever struck, Miryam appeared to me and told me of a special purpose for my life. I'm not sure what she meant, but I believe that if I honor the vision, I'll be given some sign. So I ask you to wait before speaking to anyone else about my betrothal. If I could spend forty days in quiet, praying for—"

"Hold—who *is* this Miryam?" interrupted my brother. "Who let her in the courtyard? Or did you see her in the market?"

"No! I mean the prophet Miryam of ancient times—Moses's sister."

"Oh." He gave an annoyed laugh. "That story. You imagined her, you mean."

If Imma wouldn't listen to me, I realized, how much more hopeless was it to try to tell Alexandros of my vision? Angry tears stung my eyes, and I bit my tongue. It would only make matters worse if I spoke the words that sprang to my lips: Do you know how ridiculous you are, trying to talk like Uncle Reuben when you have such a scraggly little beard? With an effort, I asked instead, "May I have forty days, though, to pray and wait for guidance?"

My brother looked exasperated. "Pray as much as you like, but don't bother me about it." I had to be satisfied with that.

SEVEN

A NASTY JOB

Two years after James left, the Tishri fever struck Magdala. No one in Matthew's immediate family died, but commerce through the harbor slowed to a trickle for weeks. The customs taxes they collected didn't even amount to what they owed the Romans.

Alphaeus explained the problem to Quintus Bucco, the Roman official who came to town twice a year to collect from the collectors. The Roman, a man with sandy stubble on his chin and a weathered red face, was not especially sympathetic. "Bad luck about the fever," he told Alphaeus, "but that's your problem, not mine. We agreed on a set amount, not a percentage."

They were sitting in Alphaeus's upper room, with a

pitcher of wine and a plate of cakes on the table in front of Bucco. Alphaeus, as an observant Jew, did not eat with Gentiles, but he always offered refreshments to his Roman overseer.

At Bucco's answer, Matthew saw a flash of anger in his father's eyes, but the Roman didn't seem to notice. Leaning on one elbow, he drank deeply from his wine cup before going on in a genial tone. "Here's an offer for you: I've been thinking of replacing the highway-toll collector at the north end of the lake. We should be getting much more from the Damascus–Ptolemais route. An energetic man could double the take and do well for himself and us."

Alphaeus was shaking his head. "I have no wish to leave—"

"But I could do it, sir!" blurted Matthew. As the two men looked at him in surprise, he realized how much he wanted to get away from Magdala. He'd had enough of the unfriendly stares in the synagogue, of the Jews who exchanged greetings with Alphaeus and his son on the street but cursed them the instant they turned the corner. The Syrians, Phoenicians, and various other non-Jews of Magdala weren't much friendlier. Matthew wanted a fresh start for himself.

Quintus Bucco raised his eyebrows. "Your son seems capable and hardworking, from what I've seen," he said to Alphaeus. "What do you say?"

Alphaeus, although he was rarely at a loss for words, hesitated. It occurred to Matthew that his father didn't want to let his only remaining son leave home. He wished he hadn't suggested it so eagerly.

Recovering himself, Alphaeus nodded. "Maybe it would be good for Matthew to get some experience on his own. Then when I retire in a few years, he'll be ready to take over the harbor office in Magdala."

So it was arranged. "What have I always said?" Matthew's father commented after the Roman official had left. "Romans may be swine, but you can do business with them."

Bucco wanted the new toll collector on the job immediately, so Matthew had to make preparations in haste. He assumed at first that he'd rent lodgings in Capernaum, the Jewish community closest to his tollgate. But Alphaeus laughed at the idea. "You don't want to live in that stinking fishing village! Let's see, the city of Bethsaida-Julias would be a good place to live, but it's a little too far away. But we'll find a decent house for you. If you manage the tollgate as well as I expect, you'll easily be able to afford it."

Soon afterward, a Syrian acquaintance told Alphaeus of a comfortable villa to rent between Capernaum and the tollgate. The former renters had been Gentile, so Alphaeus sent servants ahead to clean the house thoroughly. Then Matthew hired a boat to transport himself and his belongings from Magdala to Capernaum. "You'll need more servants and more furnishings," said his father, "but you can get them in Bethsaida-Julias."

As they exchanged farewells on the wharf, Alphaeus gave his son a final lecture. "Remember what I've taught you about tax collecting. The main thing you have to keep in mind is very simple. If they think you might let them get away with paying less, or paying late, they'll give you all kinds of trouble. You might even have to hire some lads with clubs to rough them up. But if they know you won't stand for any nonsense, then most of the time they'll just pay up."

When Matthew arrived at the tollgate on his first morning, he didn't find anyone on duty. He'd brought two servants with him in case he needed help, but he'd expected that someone—maybe the outgoing toll collector—would show him the ropes for the first day or so.

The tollgate was a stone arch straddling the highway, with a booth for the toll collector built into the inside. The barrier stood at a logical place to collect tolls, shortly before the wealth from the Mediterranean city of Ptolemais was about to pour into the lakeside city of Bethsaida-Julias. The tollgate should have acted as a sieve, filtering out large clumps of money for the Romans and smaller clumps for the toll collector.

But the former toll collector must have allowed the traffic to beat down paths through the brush on either side of the tollgate. Even now, before the sun was fully up, the first travelers of the day were leading their donkeys and camels on those paths. Carts and wagons, which needed a level surface for their wheels, stayed on the stone-paved road, but they were rattling through the gate as fast as their drivers could urge the oxen or horses.

A few of Herod's soldiers were lounging on a rise overlooking the gate, and their blue-caped captain came down to meet Matthew. "You can see why they decided to replace the last toll collector, hmm?" He waved a hand at the travelers hurrying around the gate. "That fellow wanted everyone to like him."

But he laughed when Matthew suggested that the captain could help keep order around the tollgate. "Me, work for the stinking Romans? I'd rather eat donkey dung." As Matthew stared at him, he added in a friendly tone, "No offense meant. Everyone has to make a living." He explained that his patrol regularly checked this section of the highway for rebels. "So I'll be seeing you again—if you last at this job."

As the captain strolled off, Matthew cursed under his

breath. But there was no time to waste. He ordered his men to stop the traffic on either side of the gate while he stood in the gate itself and began collecting tolls.

An hour later, Matthew and his two men were soaked with sweat, dirty with road dust, and hoarse with shouting, but they hadn't managed to force more than a few unlucky travelers to pay tolls. The rest of them dodged the toll collector as skillfully as if they'd practiced together beforehand. First, one of the horses pulling a carriage dropped to its knees in the gate, blocking the entrance. When Matthew called his servants to help clear that roadblock, a whole camel caravan slipped around one side of the gate. When Matthew ran after the camels, a stream of heavily laden donkeys escaped the toll on the other side of the gate. Meanwhile, a flock of beggars ducked in and out of the traffic, adding to the confusion.

Matthew was getting really angry . . . and really worried. At this rate, he wasn't doing any better than the last toll collector. How was he going to pay for the rent on his villa, and his furnishings, and the extra servants?

Curse those lawless travelers! How dare they use this well-built highway without paying? Curse the Romans! If they expected him to collect their tolls, why weren't they here to back him up? Matthew thought of his father, and he knew how Alphaeus would solve the problem. He'd call up his thugs with their heavy sticks. Matthew pushed the thought away.

As Matthew stopped to mop the sweat from his forehead, an older man rode up on a donkey. "Good morning, toll collector." He gazed at the scrambling tangle of toll evaders, making *tsk-tsk* sounds with his tongue. His deep-set black eyes, above his trimmed gray beard, had a shrewd gleam. "What a disgrace! This generation has no respect for law and order."

"Good morning, sir," said Matthew. "You're so right. But if you'll excuse me, I'd better get back to work." He started to turn toward the gate.

"There's a simple way to stop the illegal traffic," said the man on the donkey.

Matthew turned back. He couldn't be rude to an older man, but he was losing patience. "And what way is that, sir?"

The man smiled in a kindly way. "Why, throw up a wall on either side of the gate to block the paths. The brush beyond the paths is so dense, they'll have no choice but to stay on the highway."

Matthew considered, squinting past the paths. The brush did seem thicker away from the road. If walls would do the trick, then there'd be no need for thugs with heavy sticks. "How much would that cost?"

The older man made a gesture to indicate how trivial the cost would be. "Just a rough wall is all you'd need. Five or six workmen could do the job in a day or so." He proposed a price.

Matthew exclaimed, "That's six times the going rate for laborers!"

"It includes labor *and* materials," said the other man calmly. "Nothing but the finest basalt rocks. And of course, I guarantee the work. I'll require only half the price now, and half when it's finished to your satisfaction."

Matthew bargained for a few moments, but he was eager to come to an agreement. As soon as the money changed hands, the older man beckoned to his crew, who had appeared out of nowhere.

For the rest of the day, the workmen rolled and piled rocks into two dark walls on either side of the tollgate. Matthew collected tolls as best he could, soothed by the sight of the stone wings rising quickly. By the end of the day, however, he'd rethought the price. "I don't owe you anything for materials," he told the contractor. He gave a short laugh. "You just used the rocks lying around on the ground."

"A bargain is a bargain," said the contractor. "My men can take walls down as well as build them."

Matthew cursed silently, but he paid the remainder.

For a few days, the walls worked fairly well to block the

paths and funnel traffic into the tollgate. Then new paths appeared, swinging around the walls in wider arcs. At first, only a few hardy travelers on foot could force their way through the brush. But gradually the paths widened.

Watching this happen, Matthew cursed himself for being such a gullible fool. Where was the contractor now who had "guaranteed" his work? Why had Matthew believed him about the brush being so impassable just beyond the old paths? Look, there: a fully loaded camel was squeezing through! Furthermore, now the detours were much farther from the tollgate, and therefore more trouble to guard. Matthew envisioned his father's face, one cynical eyebrow raised as if to say, What did you expect?

The next day, Matthew woke up before dawn and went down to the Capernaum docks. The first rays of sunlight flashed over the cliffs on the eastern shore of the lake, touching the sails of fishing boats returning from a night's work. "How was your catch?" he called out to the fishermen as they neared the dock.

"Lousy, to tell the truth," a man in the nearest boat called back. He was stripped for work, wearing only a loincloth. The sinews stood out on his arms and back.

"Then come and work for me," said Matthew. "I'll pay twice as much as you make on a *good* day. I need you and five others like you."

The men in the other boats heard him, and they hurried to tie up at the docks. "Count me in!" "Hire me, too, sir!" they shouted. Matthew was relieved to see that strongmen were just as easy to come by in Capernaum as in Magdala.

Pulling on his tunic, the first fisherman jumped onto the dock. "What kind of work would this be, sir?" he asked Matthew.

Matthew had gotten this far by pretending he was his hardened father, but suddenly he seemed to be himself again. "Some strongmen are needed up there," he muttered, nodding in the direction of the highway.

The fisherman's eyebrows pulled together in a puzzled frown. "Some kind of building going on?"

More fishermen joined the first one on the dock, their eager expressions turning suspicious. Matthew forced himself to say, "No. There's a problem with toll evaders. No one has to actually hurt anyone," he went on, talking faster and faster. "All you'd have to do is stand near the gate, carrying a stick— just *look* at them like you'd use it if they—"

"It's the cursed toll collector," said a man in the back of the group. "He moved into the villa up the hill."

Matthew backed away from the dock, suddenly uneasy. He'd come alone.

But the fishermen didn't threaten him. Some of them spit in his direction, and some said, "Roman lover" or "filthy vermin." Then they went about their business, lugging baskets of fish to the shore and spreading nets out to dry as if he weren't there.

Humiliated, Matthew was about to leave when he caught sight of a straggling fishing boat nearing the shore. "James!" he exclaimed. Could the man in the back of the boat really be his brother? He hadn't seen James for two years. "James!" He waved his arms.

The fishermen in the boat didn't seem to hear him. Now Matthew doubted that it was James after all; the morning light glittered blindingly on the water around the boat. And why would Matthew want to see James, even if it was him? He left our family, Matthew reminded himself. Why should I care about him?

Turning, Matthew walked quickly away from the shore. But he knew he was afraid that the man *was* James. What if James, too, shunned his brother the toll collector? That would be too painful to bear.

That very day, Matthew visited Bethsaida-Julias, where his father's contact lived, and brought back a team of tollgate guards. As soon as the travelers caught sight of these cold-eyed men with heavy sticks in their belts, they changed their minds about ducking the toll. Matthew imagined Alphaeus saying, Didn't I tell you?

On the second day, a caravan of merchants tried to go around the gate, perhaps thinking there were enough of them to brave the guards. But the moment the first camel was led off the highway, the guards jumped on the caravan with cudgels swinging. In a few swift, brutal moments, the camel stumbled, its left front leg broken, and the driver writhed on the ground beside it with a bleeding head.

Matthew turned away, sickened, and noticed the beggars at the gate. They were watching. The beggars were maimed, crippled, deformed, and clothed in filthy rags—but they stared at the toll collector with pure contempt.

Matthew started to call the guards off. Then he thought, *Isn't this what I hired them for?* He went back to taking tolls.

Clearly, the guards were accomplishing what he'd hoped, because there were no more toll-evasion incidents that day. Word of the new toll collector and his new policy must have traveled up and down the highway. Matthew avoided meeting the stares of the travelers, but he felt their hatred, like gravel flicking his skin.

Matthew had to give the guards room and board in addition to their wages, but he decided it was just as well to have them on his grounds. He needed bodyguards to protect himself and his strongbox, as well as the valuable furnishings of his villa, from thieves.

So Matthew's new life fell into a routine. Every morning

at dawn, he and the guards arrived at the tollgate with his brassbound collection chest. No one traveled at night, but caravans always got up at first light for a day of travel. Therefore, Matthew needed to be in place early to inspect baggage and take the tolls.

With guards controlling the traffic, Matthew could do his job. That, like Alphaeus's job at the Magdala harbor, was to check each merchant's cargo and assess its value. He was staggered by the wealth in some caravans: eastern silks and spices from Damascus, or the precious purple dye of Tyre from the west. After collecting the standard percentage for the Roman Empire, he could demand whatever he wanted for himself.

Matthew didn't have any qualms about taking money from these prosperous merchants. He had a good sense of how large a surcharge they'd bear. As Alphaeus had always taught his sons, set it high enough so that they hate you, but not so outrageous that they actually try to make trouble.

Matthew's problems came with smaller traders, such as a lone potter with his donkey almost hidden under a burden of bowls and jars. "Sir," he pleaded with Matthew, "if I pay what you ask, I can't make a profit from selling my pottery. Sir, I have five young children and an old, sick father at home. How will I feed them if you don't have pity on me?"

As Matthew hesitated, the traveler next in line spoke up. "That's a good story," he jeered. "Or is it five old, sick children and a young father at home?"

Matthew remembered Alphaeus's words: If they think you might let them get away with paying less, or paying late, they'll give you all kinds of trouble. Everyone within earshot was listening for his answer—the potter, the travelers behind him, the hired guards. This was no time to be weak.

"Pay up," Matthew barked. He kept his eyes on the coins dropping into his hand, but he saw the man's shoulders sag as he led his donkey through the gate.

EIGHT

LIKE QUEEN ESTHER

Although Alexandros had refused to take my vision of Miryam seriously, I chose to believe that he'd granted me the forty days I'd asked for. In any case, I hoped it would take him at least forty days to arrange a betrothal.

I wasn't sure how to go about seeking a sign from heaven, but I had the impression that praying and fasting might help me recognize it. So I kept a regular time for prayer. I fasted during the day, eating sparingly only before dawn and after sunset.

But it wasn't easy to stay alert for a special sign. There was so much coming and going in the compound, and I didn't want to ask Imma or Safta or Chloe to do my share of the chores. When I sought out a quiet corner for prayer, my grandmother and sister tried not to disturb me. But my mother made it clear that she thought I was behaving in an odd and rather selfish way.

Alexandros seemed very busy at the sardine-packing works—too busy, I assumed, to arrange a new marriage for me. I went to talk to him one evening, thinking he was alone on the roof. I intended to ask his permission to visit my aunt in Arbel for a month of peace.

As I reached the top of the stairs, I realized that Imma and Uncle Reuben were with Alexandros. Pausing in the shadows, I listened to a whispered argument. I couldn't make out what they were discussing, but my name was mentioned over and over.

The next day, my mother took me aside. I had a bad feeling even before she spoke, and I burst out, "They haven't chosen a husband for me already, have they? Alexandros might at least have honored my request for more time!"

Imma frowned and folded her arms, as if to say she was not to blame. "I did remind them that you had some idea of waiting to discern something. But the men judged that it would seem ungrateful not to accept such a good offer at once."

Distressed at the idea of having to drop my search for a sign, it took me a moment to sense that there was more bad news. I stared at my mother. "Who is it?" She hesitated, and I exclaimed, "Not Eleazar bar Yohannes!"

"It was a *very* good offer," she said.

"No!" I exclaimed. "How could Uncle Reuben . . . ? How could Alexandros . . . ?" They knew I'd asked Abba to refuse the old man's offer the first time. "Doesn't my brother care how I feel?"

My mother didn't answer my questions. "Mariamne," she said, "I had my heart set on Nicolaos for you; that was such a happy match. But that's water under the bridge. Now your father's gone, Nicolaos is gone, and everything's different."

"I know it's different! It's dreadful. Why do they want to make it even worse for me?"

"Hush, Mariamne!" Imma's eyes flashed. "It's time you grew up. Life isn't all honey cakes and jasmine for any of us. Think, for a moment, what the fever did to the rest of us, not just you." She spoke faster and faster, her words pouring out. "Think about Alexandros: young as he is, he has to take on the burden of being the man of the family. Think about Uncle Reuben: he's lost not only his brother but also his business partner. Our business isn't doing well—many of the workers caught the fever, and several of them died. On top of that, the household taxes will be due soon!" She paused, then added in a low tone, "And I . . . I am . . . a widow."

My mother hardly ever cried, but now tears shone in her eyes. I was shocked and ashamed. "I'm sorry, Imma."

"True, this new marriage isn't what you expected," she went on, blotting her tears quickly with her sleeve. "But your uncle and your brother are using their best judgment. Eleazar is a respected member of the synagogue. And your brother agreed to provide you with a generous bride-gift; I insisted on that."

"A generous bride-gift?" Forgetting about being unselfish, I snorted. How would a bride-gift make up for being married to an old man?

"Try to think about what's best for the whole family." My mother's tone turned stern again. "After you're betrothed to Eleazar, you see, Eleazar will sell only our sardines. He's the supplier for Herod Antipas's palace in Tiberias, as well as for Herod's troops."

"Sardines," I repeated.

My mother ignored that remark. "You're not the only one who needs to marry, you know. Chloe will be of age in a year or so, and she'll have no chance for a good match if our business fails. And even more important, your brother needs to marry well."

Ah yes, I thought. Alexandros, even more important.

"If you're betrothed to Eleazar," Imma explained, "then

Eleazar's cousin Thomas—Thomas the Elder; you've seen him in the synagogue—will allow Alexandros to marry *his* daughter Sarah. That'll be an excellent connection for our family. Of course, the girl's only twelve, but they can be betrothed now, and we'll have her come to live with us until she's of age."

As my mother talked, I realized that there was something much more at stake than whether I liked Alexandros's choice of a husband for me. "Imma, all this doesn't matter. What I really need is time to seek a sign—to meditate on the meaning of the prophet Miryam's words to me."

Imma sighed and pressed her lips together. "Back to what you imagined in the *mikvah*? Don't you see it's time to give up on that?" She put her hands on my shoulders, looking into my eyes. I was surprised to realize that we were now the same height. "You *must* do your part, Mari! I'm afraid your father— may he rest in peace, the good man—indulged you."

"My father was a righteous man!" I retorted. "He would not force me to marry against my will." Desperately I wished for Miryam to appear to my mother, right then. Why didn't the prophet help me if she expected me to follow such a hard path? I exclaimed, "I will not do it. Hang a millstone around my neck and throw me into the lake if you like—I will not marry Eleazar bar Yohannes."

"Selfish, selfish daughter!" My mother tightened her grip on my shoulders, as if to shake me. Then, throwing up her hands, she walked away.

Imma must have told Chloe what I'd said, because a little while later my sister came and sat down beside me. "I don't blame you, Mari," she said. "It would be better for the whole family to starve than for you to marry unwillingly."

I glanced sideways at her. Was she being sarcastic? No, my sister didn't know how to be sarcastic. "No one is going to starve," I said uncomfortably. Did Chloe realize that her own marriage depended on mine? If she did, she didn't mention it.

At least my grandmother would understand my point of view, I thought, even if she had no influence over my uncle and brother. I went to Safta and told her about meeting Miryam in the *mikvah*. I thought it would bring my vision back afresh, but to my dismay, it now sounded to my ears like something I'd made up.

Safta listened with a wondering smile. "What a marvelous story, my dear! I must remember that one. I never thought of meeting Miryam in the *mikvah*, but yes—it makes perfect sense."

"But what about the mission Miryam spoke of?" I pleaded. "Shouldn't I try to understand what she meant?"

"Oh yes . . . let's think about this together," agreed my grandmother. "A 'steep, rocky way,' Miryam said to you? Requiring 'great courage'? Do you know what that reminds me of, Mari dear? It makes me think of the story of Queen Esther."

By the end of the day, I felt confused and miserable. As I lighted the lamps, Alexandros appeared at my side. Of course, Imma had told him my answer, too, and he wouldn't be as sympathetic as Chloe or Safta. I returned his greeting, but I kept my eyes on the lamp wicks.

"Mari," said Alexandros. "I don't know what to do." His tone of voice was reasonable, and I turned to look at him. "When Abba was dying," he went on, "he told me to take care of the family. And I promised him, as was my duty. But now I can't fulfill my promise."

"What do you mean?" I asked. "Abba left you the sardine business. Aren't there still sardines in the lake, and people waiting to eat them?"

Alexandros shook his head. "That's not the point. Abba left us . . . in debt. He didn't even tell Uncle Reuben how much he was borrowing. If you'd married Nicolaos, his family would have paid what we owed. But now, just to pay Herod's taxes, we'll have to sell this house that our grandfather built. We'll have to move into rooms above the packinghouse."

This was a shocking thought. "Poor Safta!" I exclaimed. Our grandmother loved her well-made stone house. She had ornamented it with fine pillows and hangings that she'd woven and stitched, and she kept the house fragrant with sweet herbs. I shrank from the thought of her in the ugly, smelly packinghouse.

Besides, how could she bear the shame? It had broken her heart to see her favorite son die. To know that he hadn't provided for her after all would kill her. "No . . . that mustn't happen."

"We'll have to give up our seats in the synagogue," my brother went on. "We'll have to let the servants go." A note of impatience came into his voice. "You must see the wisdom of my choice for you? This marriage will save everything. It will save the honor of the family."

I remembered something Imma had said, and I narrowed my eyes at him. "Aren't you going to mention the fine marriage Eleazar promised you, to his cousin Thomas's daughter?"

"That's only as it should be!" exclaimed Alexandros. "You seem to forget who I am: the firstborn, the only son, the head of the family."

My heart hardened and blasphemous thoughts entered it. Why not just send me to the Temple in Jerusalem and let me be sacrificed with the lambs and the doves? It amounted to the same thing. "No! Never!"

Alexandros's face hardened, too. He stalked away, muttering, "Foolish to think she would listen."

No one spoke much during the evening meal, and I felt that they were all trying not to look at me. Afterward, when I carried the leftovers down to the kitchen, Yael was waiting for me. She took the pot from me and set it aside. "Wait, Miss Mari." She seized my hand and kissed it. "Have pity on me!"

"What in the world is the matter?" I tried to pull my hand away.

"Oh, young mistress, if this family falls upon bad times, I'll be turned out into the street! What will become of me?" A sob burst out of her mouth with the words. "It was only by your father's kindness that I escaped the brothels." She sobbed more violently. "I swear, I'll hang a millstone around my neck first, and throw myself into the lake!"

That was almost exactly what I'd said to Imma. But I'd worked myself up into a frenzy, trying to sound even more desperate than I was. Yael truly meant what she said. Imagining her trudging into the lake with her millstone, I felt a queasy dread.

"Please, leave me alone." I pulled away my hand, which was wet with Yael's tears, and wiped it on my tunic.

That night, I lay on my bed in a strange state of mind. I

don't know whether I was dreaming or awake, or somewhere in between. I was gazing at the dark sky, where one star shone brighter and brighter as it neared me.

Behold Queen Esther, the star.

I smelled perfume, and I heard the rustle of silk. Then a young woman stood before me, dressed in a foreign style. Her robes were stiff with embroidery, encrusted with gold ornaments. Her earrings were woven from gold wire and hung with tiny gold bells, and she wore a gold crown on her oiled curls.

Mariamne, she said. *Mariamne, you know my story. I, too, was afraid of marriage to an older stranger—I, too, shrank from my destiny—but I chose to save my people. Think of* your *people, Mariamne. You can save your people, too.*

The vision of Queen Esther faded, but her message sank in. There was no longer any mystery about what I should do next, or why. This must truly be the rocky path intended for me: to become a heroine like Esther.

Eleazar was eager to marry as soon as possible, and I was almost fourteen. So my family agreed that the wedding could take place after a thirty-day mourning period for my father, instead of our waiting the usual year after a parent's death. They applied to the council of the synagogue, and (with

Elder Thomas's influence) an exception was made. Also, my family agreed to skip the preliminary meeting and go straight to the betrothal.

When Eleazar entered our courtyard with his family, my heart sank. But I tried not to show my feelings, partly because I felt sorry for him. He seemed in high spirits as he exchanged courtesies with Alexandros and Uncle Reuben. I thought it would be cruel to let him see I was unwilling. I told myself, "You can see he's pleased with you. Surely he'll be a kind husband, and what more could you expect?"

As Eleazar and I drank from the same cup, I kept my eyes cast down. I tried not to remember Nicolaos's clear eyes and sweet breath, and especially not the disturbing, delightful glow that Nicolaos had caused in me. Eleazar still had most of his teeth, unlike many old men. True, his eyelids reminded me of a lizard's. His tongue flicked out like a lizard's, too, at the end of every other sentence.

After the ceremony, I was presented to Eleazar's various relatives, including his important cousin, Elder Thomas; his unimportant half brother, Hiram, who lived with his wife and children in Eleazar's compound; and his widowed daughter-in-law, Chava, who was also Eleazar's housekeeper. Chava gave me the expected kiss on the cheek. "Welcome to our family, Mariamne," she said without smiling.

After the guests had left, I sat down beside my grand-mother and leaned my head against hers. "Oh, Safta! I'm confused. . . . It doesn't seem right."

"I know." There was an odd tone in her voice, almost as if she were talking in her sleep, and I pulled back to look at her. Her eyes were fixed on the livestock shed across the courtyard. "Your father is absolutely against this match. For one thing, no good will come of the business connection with Herod Antipas's city, Tiberias."

"You mean my father *was* against this match," I corrected her gently. "Did Abba tell you he didn't want me to marry Eleazar?" I thought she meant that my father had discussed the matter with her the previous year.

"Oh yes." Safta nodded several times. "Only this morn-ing, he came to me as I was picking over the lentils."

The back of my neck tingled, and I stared at my grand-mother. "You saw him . . . today?"

As if I hadn't spoken, she went on, "Tobias said, 'I'm very displeased, Imma. This isn't the marriage I imagined for my darling Mari.' And I said, 'I know, Tobias, but they wouldn't listen to me. Perhaps you could speak to them.'"

At the thought that my father was still trying to protect me, tears stung my eyes. I ached for him to be with us again, a shield between bad fortune and me. But I also saw a ray of

hope. If Abba appeared to Alexandros, too, he might frighten
my brother into obeying him. "Did he say he would speak to
Alexandros?"

"Mm . . . did he?" said Safta vaguely. "I can't say that he
did. He wanted me to tell him the old story of Miryam's
Well." She smiled fondly. "Tobias loves to listen to my stories."

During the weeks before the fever, my wedding to Nicolaos
had glided toward me like a sailboat. Now my wedding to
Eleazar rushed at me like a boulder bouncing down the cliffs
of Mount Arbel. The thought of my wedding day made me
feel like screaming and running out the gate. I wondered if
Esther in the story had felt like this as her cousin Mordecai
delivered her to the king of Persia's palace.

The only thing that steadied me was the way my family
treated me now. They didn't speak directly of the sacrifice I
was making, but they were respectful and gentle with me.

The night before the wedding, my mother took me aside.
"Do you understand, Mariamne, that you must submit to
your husband?"

"Yes, yes," I said, looking at the floor. "I won't argue with
him. I'll control myself."

Imma sighed. "Pay attention," she said sharply. "This is

important. I'm talking about the marriage bed. A wife must not refuse her husband, whatever he wishes to do."

The strange tone in Imma's voice made me look at her. She seemed distressed, as if she were commanding me to jump off a cliff. "What will he do?" I asked. That was a willfully ignorant question; after all, I'd had a good idea what Nicolaos would have done.

"It will be unpleasant," Imma went on without really answering me. "Try to think of it as bitter medicine. When we had the fever, Safta gave us medicine, and we drank it down, didn't we?"

I nodded. I remembered the vile taste of that herbal brew, even though I'd been delirious at the time.

"Yes," said Imma. "So just remember that you're doing your duty as a wife, and surely the Lord will reward you. As the saying goes, 'A good wife makes a good husband.'" The tender tone in her voice made me tremble. If my mother felt sorry for me, my sacrifice was even greater than I'd thought.

NINE

BITTER MEDICINE

The morning of the wedding, Susannah came to take part in the preparations. She and Imma, Safta, and Chloe all helped me dress. I sat numbly on a stool while my grandmother combed my hair over my shoulders. The locks hung down to my waist.

"Look how Mari's hair shines!" exclaimed Susannah. "It's like polished acacia wood against the white robe."

"Yes, how proud we are of our bride!" said Safta. "She's as beautiful as Queen Esther."

My mother set the pointed headdress on my head. "Mari is a good, good daughter," she said, "and that makes her beautiful in my eyes."

Chloe lifted a veil bordered with flowers over my headdress. "Wear this with my loving wishes, sister." She looked at me with awe, as if I were indeed a queen and she my grateful subject.

"There, now," said my mother, pushing bangles onto my wrists and ankles. "The wedding litter is waiting in the court-yard."

At her words, something roused in me, and I clutched the stool with both hands. *No. No!* I felt as if I'd been sleepwalk-ing and awakened to find myself teetering at the edge of a cliff.

"Mariamne," said my mother. "Come . . . it's time to go."

"No!" I burst out. I would not, *could* not marry that hideous, smelly old man. "Don't make me go!"

"You have to go." Imma grabbed my arms and pulled me off the stool. "You are betrothed in the sight of the Lord. Think of your family's honor. Do you want your mother to be ashamed that she ever bore such a willful, wicked daughter? Do you want to dishonor your dead father, may he rest in peace?"

I collapsed at Imma's feet, hugging her ankles. "I *love* my family!" I sobbed. "Just let me stay—even as a servant in this house! As a slave!"

"Oh, Mari," said Chloe in a shocked tone. Susannah stared with one hand over her mouth.

My mother glared down at me for a moment, but then she said briskly, "Talk is useless. She needs something to calm her down." Prying my hands away, she went into the kitchen shed.

But Safta stooped beside me and laid her cool hands on my cheeks. "Mari, Mari, Mari. Shh, little lamb. It's a terrible shame, but try to see the bright side. I predict that this marriage will be only the hard shell of a sweet almond for you."

Surprised, I lifted my tear-streaked face. "What do you mean, Safta?" Was she hinting that I'd come to love Eleazar bar Yohannes?

"What I mean," said my grandmother cheerily, "is that old men don't live forever. Did you know that my own sister's first husband was older than our father? He died before they even had children."

"Mother-in-law!" exclaimed my mother, reappearing with a cup of dark liquid. "What kind of talk is this?" She held the cup to my lips.

I sipped cautiously. It was strong and sweet, and I drank it down.

Ignoring Imma, my grandmother went on, "She was left with her bride-gift, and then she married a younger man, someone almost as nice as your father."

At the mention of my father, my eyes filled with tears again. Abba! How could he have died and left me to pull the family out of debt and disgrace?

Safta squeezed my hand with both of hers. "Take heart, Mari."

Gulping a last sob, I nodded and stood up. As the honeyed

wine rose to my head, it seemed that perhaps Imma was right. The honor of my family was at stake. Eleazar could be worse. And perhaps Safta was right, too. Maybe I wouldn't have to put up with my old husband for long. But aside from that, how could I have forgotten my higher purpose? Like Queen Esther, I was saving my people from disaster.

They wiped my face and straightened my crumpled robes. I left my family's house with my bridal jewelry jingling.

On my wedding night, I didn't sleep well. You may think I mean because of my husband's attentions, and indeed that was unpleasant. I tried to take my mother's advice. Lying with this stranger, this old man, I told myself, was only a cup of bitter medicine.

But the worst part was afterward, when Eleazar fell asleep and I lay awake. I longed to creep out of my husband's bed and somehow find myself back in my cot next to Chloe.

Eleazar's bedchamber felt strange, even in the dark. His snores echoed from the walls, and the stuffing in his mattress smelled—not bad, exactly, but different from mine. I couldn't sink into sleep the way I used to at home, as if I were sinking right through the bed into the dream world. I lay on the surface, trying not to wiggle and wake my husband.

Thinking again about my mother's advice, something disturbed me. My mother had spoken as if the wedding night would naturally be "bitter medicine" for the bride. Did that mean that she, too, had lain sleepless and miserable on her wedding night? Could lying with my father have been bitter medicine for her?

I'd known, of course, that my father was several years older than my mother, but I'd never wondered what she'd thought of that. Now I remembered her remark, after my first *mikvah*, about young love—she hadn't been talking about my father. Somehow, it made me feel even worse, the possibility that young Tabitha, my imma, had been as unhappy about marrying Abba as I was about marrying Eleazar.

The next morning, I did my best to find my place in Eleazar's household. I helped him dress; I followed him downstairs, intending to set breakfast before him. As I peered into the unfamiliar pantry, Chava appeared at my elbow.

"Good morning, Daughter-in-law," I said politely. Strictly speaking, Chava was only my husband's daughter-in-law, not mine, but it seemed friendlier to greet her that way.

Chava squinted at me as if she couldn't imagine whom I was talking to. Then she replied, "Good morning, Father-in-law's wife." Reaching past me into the shed, she nudged me out of the way, filled a plate with bread and olives, and took it to Eleazar.

Eleazar didn't seem to care, or even notice, who brought

him his breakfast. He ate quickly and went out the gate, leaving me to wonder why Chava was so unfriendly to me. Maybe she thought I wouldn't be willing to do my part in the household work? To show her that I was, I followed her around the house, watching her polish brass and swat flies and cut up meat for a stew. But each time I tried to help, Chava waved me away.

So it went until noontime, when Eleazar returned. Of course I knew that the master's feet must be washed, but I expected that one of the serving women would do it, as Yael did in our household. Then, when Eleazar sat down on a bench, I realized that none of the servants were in the courtyard; Chava had managed to send them away just as Eleazar walked through the gate.

I supposed then that Chava would wash Eleazar's feet, since she'd been taking chores away from me all morning. But after greeting Eleazar, she busied herself with something in the kitchen shed.

Eleazar looked at me as if he was trying to be patient. "Wife, bring the basin," he said. I opened my mouth to answer that I didn't know where it was kept, but Chava handed it to me. With a prim expression, she also gave me a pitcher of water and hung a towel over my arm.

I knelt in front of Eleazar and untied his sandals and set

them aside. The sandals smelled as if he'd been walking in the gutter. As I placed the basin under his feet and poured the water, I tried not to stare at his toenails. They were as yellow as chicken feet. I poured more water over his hands, offered the towel to dry them, and dried his feet.

Chava then stepped forward to serve Eleazar his midday dinner of stew and bread. He looked pleased, and as he ate, he said, "Wife, listen to Chava. She knows how the household should be run."

After all had eaten and taken midday naps, Eleazar left again. Chava brought out a handloom and began to thread it. The other women of the family appeared in the courtyard. The wife of Hiram, Eleazar's half brother, came out with her two smaller children and a nursemaid. And there were two women I had only glimpsed at the wedding: Eleazar's widowed cousin and her slow-witted daughter, who was carrying a spindle and a basket of wool.

This felt a little more comfortable to me. In my family, too, the women gathered in the courtyard in the afternoons to do handwork and chat. I fetched my embroidery basket and took out a partly worked scarf. As I stitched, I gazed around the compound. Two smaller dwellings formed the second and third sides of Eleazar's courtyard, and the private *mikvah* and the livestock shed made the fourth.

The women began to gossip among themselves. At first, I

asked a question or made a remark now and then. But each time I spoke, the slow-witted girl laughed. Chava raised her eyebrows, looking at us as if we were two of a kind. She exchanged knowing smiles with Hiram's wife and the cousin. Following Chava's lead, the other women ignored me or replied in an off-putting way.

I gave up on trying to join the conversation. Poking my embroidery needle back and forth, I ached to be in my family's courtyard with Chloe and our grandmother. I was no more part of this family, I thought, than was the lizard on the courtyard wall. Even the slow-witted girl seemed to be at home here, busily spinning her wool. I noticed glumly what a nice, even thread she was able to spin, though her mouth hung open and she breathed noisily.

It dawned on me that Chava might have told the other women something to make them dislike me. Recalling how I'd come here thinking of myself as Queen Esther, I felt hot with anger and shame. Instead of the queen in Eleazar's house, it seemed, I was the new hen in a flock of chickens. Chava, the chief hen, led the others in pecking me.

That was my first day in the house of Eleazar bar Yohannes. Each day that week went on in much the same way, except that one afternoon Chava's niece, Daphne, came to visit. As Chava and her niece embraced, their sheeplike faces looked almost attractive.

The other women smiled at Daphne and included her in their chatter, and I wished for some friendly company of my own. Why didn't Chloe visit? When it was Nicolaos I was going to marry, she'd been so eager.

The afternoon before the Sabbath, Hiram's wife brought news from the market about a storm on the lake the previous night: "They say several fishing boats went down." Forgetting to ignore me, she asked a direct question. "Did your family lose any boats, Mariamne?"

"I don't know," I said. I was worried. As part of their sardine business, my family owned boats. They rented the boats to fishermen, and the fishermen turned over a portion of their catch in payment. Each boat was an expensive piece of property, protected by good-luck herbs tied to the mast and lucky pebbles in the ballast. Losing even one of those boats would hurt the business.

I was seized with longing to find out what was happening with my family. They seemed so far away although they were only on the other side of town. I beckoned to the servant by the gate. "Go quickly to the house of Alexandros bar Tobias and ask if they lost any fishing boats in the storm."

"What!" exclaimed Chava. "We can't be sending the servants here and there on every whim. They have work to do, and we'll find out about the boats when the men come home." She made a shooing gesture at the servant, who was now looking from Chava to me. "Shovel out the shed, as you should have done this morning."

I felt as if she'd yanked a mat from under my feet and I'd landed hard on the floor. I started to repeat my order, but then I bit my tongue. The servant had already disappeared into the animal shed.

I bent over my handwork again, angry and bewildered. Why does Chava hate me? I asked myself. What have I done to her? Am I so unlikable? Nicolaos's mother, after all, had taken to me right away. My father had *doted* on me. As I imagined my father's fond gaze, my heart ached.

For some reason, I remembered the time I'd fallen down the stairs when I was three. I wasn't expecting to fall down the stairs and hurt myself; not at all. I was balancing on one foot at the top of the stairs, entranced by the way I could lean on the air, or so it seemed. For a moment, I was sure that I could fly.

And then I toppled off the top step and tumbled all the way down. It seemed to take a long time, but there was nothing I could do to help myself. Each time I hit another stone block, it felt as if the step were hitting *me*. I was shocked that they wanted to hurt me so much, that they really would break my bones if they could. Finally, as I sprawled on the courtyard flagstones, fighting for the breath to start screaming, Alexandros laughed at me.

Now I thought that the last few months had been like

falling down the stairs. First the fever struck me. *Whack!* But that was only the first hard bump. *Whack!* Your father and your betrothed are dead, their dear bodies wrapped and stored in the cemetery outside town. *Whack!* Your family is on the brink of ruin. *Whack!* You must give yourself to a repulsive old man. *Wh—*

Chava's sharp voice pierced my thoughts. "I call her Weepy," she remarked to Hiram's wife with a chuckle. She was pointing to the tears rolling down my face. Hiram's wife laughed, and the cousin and the slow-witted girl joined in.

That night, I didn't ask Eleazar about the boats after all. Somehow, I no longer felt like one who had a right to ask questions. I felt like "Weepy," whose place it was to wash dirty feet and take bitter medicine.

On the Sabbath, I went to the synagogue with Eleazar and his household. Since Eleazar's cousin Thomas was one of the elders, we were seated in the second row. That didn't mean that I personally was honored, though. When Chava's niece joined us, Chava nudged me almost off the bench to make room for her.

Craning my neck, I found my family in the assembly by spotting Alexandros, the tallest. I was seized with longing to be back among them—even with my brother. If only Safta's wish for me would come true and Eleazar would die . . .

Then I seemed to hear my mother uttering one of her favorite sayings: "Wishes won't fill a basket." Eleazar seemed perfectly healthy, aside from some rheumatism and flatulence. I must pull myself together and make the best of the way things actually were. Surely, as the wife, I didn't have to let Chava push me around—surely I had some rights? Queen Esther had risked death to approach the king—couldn't I be brave enough to approach my husband?

That evening, as I helped Eleazar undress for bed, I tried to tell him about my problems with Chava. "I don't want to complain, Husband," I said with downcast eyes, "but I don't think she's treating me fairly. She's not helping me learn the ways of your household, as you wished. She seems to be trying—"

Before I was finished speaking, Eleazar put up his hand. "Women's squabbles! I don't want to hear about it." He gestured for me to lie down on the bed. It was not an inviting gesture but a command.

I obeyed, but still protesting. "She seems to be trying to make my work difficult for me!" Eleazar climbed into bed without answering. Angry tears came to my eyes. *Bitter medicine, bitter medicine,* I repeated over and over in my mind like a prayer.

TEN

CAGED

Although I'd gotten no help from Eleazar, I resolved not to let Chava make me miserable. The next afternoon, as Chava and the other women gossiped over their tasks, I wound a scarf around my head and neck. "I'm going to my mother's house to get an embroidery pattern," I told Chava.

Chava leaned back in exaggerated astonishment. "You're going out? With so much work to be done?"

"What difference does that make?" I answered. "Whatever work I do, you do it over again. You watched me sort those beans, and now you're re-sorting them."

Going out the gate, I heard the women murmuring. Chava's voice rose above the others: "You see what I have to put up with?" Then, in a lower voice, she muttered something about a "bad bargain."

Taking a deep breath of the air outside Eleazar's compound, I walked down the alley to the avenue. I crossed the street to avoid the loiterers outside the men's *mikvah*. A woman by herself, even a married woman in broad daylight, had to be careful to behave properly. Farther up the street, I crossed again, to avoid the men standing in the synagogue's porch. One of them was Elder Thomas; he might recognize me and mention it to Eleazar.

As I hurried across town, I decided I wouldn't bother my family with my problems. I'd just enjoy their company and lift my spirits a bit.

Yael, opening the gate, told me that Imma and Chloe were at the market, but my grandmother was home. Before the serving woman had finished speaking, Safta appeared behind her with open arms. I forgot my resolution and fell on her neck, sobbing.

Safta patted my back and made clucking noises. "Hush, hush, little bird." She wiped my wet face with a corner of her shawl. "So marriage isn't like the story of Rachel and Jacob, after all. Those unfriendly spirits lurk under the bed, making trouble. But I can give you something to ward them off. . . . And remember, Nicolaos is a good young man. Give him time."

Nicolaos. I couldn't believe what I'd heard. My tears dried up. "Not Nicolaos. You mean Eleazar, Safta."

"No, no, chick," she said with a vague smile. "I mean your husband, Nicolaos." Hobbling to the basket where she kept her belongings, she brought me a linen-wrapped packet of herbs. "Hide this in your mattress. It'll keep spiteful spirits away—you'll see."

"Thank you, Safta," I said slowly. Now I felt worse than before, and I wished I hadn't come. "I'd better be going back." I hugged her and turned away quickly before I could start crying again.

Outside the gate, I was thankful to see Imma and Chloe coming home from the market. I rushed down the alley to embrace them, squeezing Chloe so hard that she squeaked. "What's the matter with Safta?" I asked. "She doesn't seem quite right."

My mother and sister looked at me strangely. "No . . . she isn't right at all," said Chloe. "She won't eat more than a few bites."

"She hasn't been right since your father died," said Imma. "Hadn't you noticed that her mind was wandering? Sometimes she thinks she talks to her dead son. *Ai,* with all our other troubles!"

"I . . . I suppose I thought maybe she *was* talking to him," I admitted. I sensed I should ask my mother, What other troubles? But I was bursting with my own woes. I described how Chava had been treating me, and how Eleazar sided with her. "Aren't I the wife?" I demanded. "*I* ought to be in charge of the house, not the daughter-in-law!"

My mother nodded, her lips tightening.

"Then can't you ask Uncle Reuben to speak to Eleazar?" I pressed on. "For the honor of our family, at least."

Imma sighed, and she turned her face away. "Yes, our honor . . . But it's not so simple. Reuben isn't in a position to make demands of your husband just now. You see, two of our fishing boats were lost in that storm last week."

"Oh, the storm!" I exclaimed. I was shocked that it had slipped my mind.

"And we're still shorthanded at the packing works," continued my mother. "In fact, we couldn't supply the full number of jars that Eleazar was supposed to deliver to Tiberias. He had to scramble and pay a high price to another supplier, or he would have lost his arrangement with the palace."

I began to understand. That must have been the reason for Eleazar's curtness with me, as well as for Chava's remark about the "bad bargain."

"So it's still sardines," I said.

My mother shrugged helplessly. Chloe exclaimed, "Oh, Mari!"

"You aren't the first young wife who had to knuckle under to another woman," said my mother, recovering her usual tartness. "How do you think it was for me, coming into your grandmother's house?"

"Safta?" I exclaimed. "Dear, sweet Safta treated you the way Chava treats me?"

"She wasn't always so sweet," answered my mother.

Walking slowly back to Eleazar's house, I brooded over what I'd learned. First, my grandmother was not in her right mind. Second, I couldn't expect my family to intervene with Eleazar for me. And third—if Imma spoke the truth—even my dear grandmother had once been unkind to the homesick young woman in her household.

As I entered the courtyard, Chava remarked to the other women, "That one's used to having plenty of spare time."

I was so downhearted from my home visit that I didn't try to argue or answer back. Remembering the herb packet Safta had given me, I went upstairs to tuck it under the mattress. As I knelt on the floor, a picture flashed in my mind of Nicolaos, my first betrothed, lying on such a bed, holding out his arms.

Was that what my grandmother meant by "spiteful spirits"? I pressed the packet to my face and breathed the scent deeply to chase them out of my mind. Then I pushed the packet under the mattress, jumped to my feet, and hurried out of the room.

***

One day, Eleazar's cousin Thomas, the synagogue elder, came
to dine with my husband. His ornamental belt with its heavy
silver clasp, as well as the large, silky tassels on the corners of
his coat, announced his importance. Eleazar was boyishly excited and pleased, more pleased than he'd seemed at our wedding.

As Chava and I served the men in the upper room, I listened to their talk. Mainly, it was Elder Thomas giving his
opinion about this and that and Eleazar listening respectfully,
even if it was about his own business. But when Thomas
mentioned the last wave of Tishri fever, Eleazar groaned. "It
robbed me of my son, Abram," he exclaimed. "Why couldn't
my daughters have died instead?"

Elder Thomas shrugged sympathetically. "Who knows?
We can't see the world the way the Lord does."

But I have seen the world that way, I thought. The elder's
words sparked a flame in my mind, lighting up a precious
moment in my life that had been dark since my betrothal to
Eleazar.

I remembered the time on Mount Arbel with my father
when my soul spread its wings and flew like an eagle. Now I
felt close to another such moment, when I would understand
through and through why I was here instead of married to

Nicolaos. Miryam had warned that my path, if I chose it, would be steep and rocky. And indeed . . .

"Wife," said Eleazar sharply.

I glanced down at the platter in my hands. It was tilting, and I righted it just in time to keep the broiled fish from sliding into Elder Thomas's lap. Eleazar smiled apologetically at his cousin.

Setting the platter down, I hurried from the room and leaned against the wall outside. *I,* see the way the Lord does? What monstrous self-importance—worse than my idea that I was like Queen Esther.

Still, the very next day, I felt that I was on the brink of recovering another precious moment. It was my first time to bathe in Eleazar's *mikvah,* and I plunged in eagerly. As I stood in the middle of the small pool and said the prayer for immersion, I trembled with hope. Would Miryam speak to me again? Oh, I longed so badly to find myself in Miryam's Well, to be bathed with light, to be assured of my high purpose!

I held my breath under the water for as long as I could. But it was only ordinary water, and rather stagnant at that. When I stepped out of the pool, I found no one holding out a towel to help dry me; Chava must have called the serving woman away.

I was chilled, and I did not feel clean, inside or out. Now

I doubted that I'd ever received a commission from the prophet Miryam. Certainly, no one else would believe it. But even if I had once been consecrated to a high purpose, that could no longer be. Surely such a mission would have to be carried out by someone fresh and pure, not a used rag like me.

Months went by. With the winter rains, the hills below Mount Arbel turned green. Weeds sprouted in Eleazar's courtyard, too. Most of them were quickly pulled up and tossed out the gate, but I found one growing unobserved.

This plant appeared in the crack between two paving stones, in the corner formed by the courtyard wall and the kitchen shed. Some seldom-used tools leaned there, and I noticed the two round new leaves the size of my little fingernail, only because I was looking for a flax flail. I almost pinched the sprout out of the ground, but then I stayed my hand. I was curious to see what kind of plant it would turn out to be, and so I left it.

When I looked in the corner a day or so later, the seedling's first true leaves had appeared. I thought they looked like the leaves of a mustard plant—one of the serving women must have dropped a seed from a pouch of spices. Sure enough, with each new leaf I was more certain it was mustard. By this time, I no longer wanted to pull up the plant. In fact, I moved some of the tools to shield it from view while still allowing enough sunlight for it to grow.

I got in the habit of looking in on the mustard plant each morning—greeting it, so to speak. If the dirt between the stones looked dry, I would dribble some water on it. But I was careful not to let the others see what I was doing. The seedling seemed like a secret message to me from the One who creates all things: *Look! I'm making a tiny, dry seed turn into a fresh green plant, just for you.*

On the day that I found a yellow blossom on my plant, my heart leaped. I hadn't thought the plant was large enough to bloom; in the fields, mustard plants are waist high by the time the flowers appear. But there it was, tiny but bright.

Footsteps came up behind me, and Chava snorted, "Weeds!" Reaching past me, she yanked the plant up.

I smothered my cry of distress. I watched her drop the plant on a trash heap by the gate, but I waited until she was busy somewhere else. Then I picked up the mustard plant, which was already limp. Lifting it to my face, I sniffed its sharp scent. It seemed unbearable that its life was over, and I shoved it into the middle of the trash, out of sight.

I found many excuses to go out of the house. It cheered me a little to visit my family, although for pride's sake I tried not to go there every day. Chloe always looked glad when I walked in the gate. As for my grandmother, I resigned myself to the fact that her words might not make sense. It was still wonderfully sweet, sweet as honey, to feel her tender gaze on me.

One day, as I helped Eleazar pack for a business trip to Tiberias, he said abruptly, "People tell me you're spending all your time at your brother's house. They're beginning to wonder."

My heartbeat sped up. Surely Eleazar wouldn't take this little pleasure away from me. Then I felt a flash of anger. "Did Chava say that? It's not true! She doesn't like me; I tried to tell you. Can't I see my own mother and grandmother and sister now and then? Please—"

"This idle visiting must stop," he cut me off. "You belong to this house now."

I was trembling, but I dared not protest anymore.

After Eleazar and the servant carrying his pack had left for the docks, Chava handed me a market basket. "Where is your head scarf?"

"I didn't know we were going to the market today," I said.

She rolled her eyes. "I would have thought that a girl's mother would have taught her to notice when the pantry supplies were getting low."

I would have thought that if she expected me to watch

the supplies, she'd let me look in the pantry. But it didn't
seem worth squabbling with Chava, and besides, if I annoyed
her, she might make me stay in the compound. I followed her
out the gate with my basket.

The crowded, noisy market would be something different, at least. There was always plenty to look at, especially
among the Gentile vendors. Last time we'd been in the market, for instance, I'd noticed a booth of pottery figurines.

Chava had noticed them, too, and said aloud to no one in
particular (she didn't address me directly if she could help it),
"They're lucky the elders haven't noticed these abomina-
tions."

Images were forbidden by Jewish law, and the town elders frowned on any images in public, even if they were dis-
played by non-Jews. They'd certainly be angry if they saw
those little statues of Artemis, a Greek goddess. I thought she
was fascinating, in a disgusting kind of way, covered with
dozens of breasts.

That day, when we reached the corner where the alley
met the avenue, I hesitated. Chava turned downhill to the
market, not looking back to see if I was following. What if I
walked up the avenue, away from the market? What if I
walked out the west gate, into the hills, and just kept walking?

Then I was truly frightened. Was I going mad, like my

grandmother? There was no safe place for a lone woman in the hills. Savage animals lived there, and savage people. One of them was related to me on Imma's side, as a matter of fact: the son of a cousin. The boy suffered from violent fits, and he was too wild to keep at home. They put him in a hut in the hills and paid a shepherd to bring him food.

There were also rebel bands hiding in caves in the cliffs, people said. Herod Antipas sent a troop of soldiers up the mountain every once in a while to root them out, but the rebels always returned. I wouldn't want to meet any of those desperate men—or Antipas's soldiers, either, for that matter. With a shudder, I turned down the avenue and hurried to catch up with Chava.

Outside the market, Chava met an acquaintance and stopped to chat. She kept her back turned to me, and the neighbor glanced at me curiously but didn't greet me. I stood there behind Chava like a servant.

Nearby, a woman squatted on a tattered cloth. She must not have been able to afford even the small fee for a vendor's space in the market. She had a wicker cage of sparrows for sale. Only poor people who couldn't afford a chicken or even a dove would buy such a pathetic little mouthful, hardly worth plucking and roasting. "Sparrows, plump and tasty, only a sestertius," she called.

The birds were strangely still, with only their heads

turning this way and that. Then one sparrow, as if realizing where it was, fluttered up from the floor of the cage. In an instant, every bird in the cage was frantic, beating its wings against its fellow prisoners and the wicker bars. And then, just as suddenly, they all gave up at once and huddled on the bottom of the cage.

I couldn't bear to look any longer. "I'm going into the market," I muttered to Chava, and I hurried into the maze of booths. But the sight of the cage seemed to follow me. I walked faster and faster.

Rushing past a glassblower's booth, I became aware that someone was calling my name. "Mari. Mari!" It was a young woman with a round, shiny face and merry dark eyes. I'd walked right by my cousin Susannah.

As we hugged, Susannah mock-scolded, "Why haven't you visited me? Doesn't your husband let you see your kinfolk?" She pulled back and looked at me more closely. "What's the matter, Mari? You look upset."

I cast around for some more or less believable answer, but instead the truth came tumbling out. "Susannah . . . the sparrows for sale outside the market . . . it broke my heart to see them trying to escape. . . ." I was horrified at myself, but it was too late.

Susannah didn't look shocked, as I feared; she squeezed

my hand. Taking my arm, she spoke quietly in my ear. "I was going to send my servant to your house and tell you to come to me this afternoon. You know the wise woman from Alexandria? She's our guest now."

With an effort, I calmed myself enough to pay attention to her words. "Oh yes—the Egyptian." I dug into my memory for more. "You invited us to meet her before, but Imma wouldn't let us go. I thought she'd left for Tiberias."

"She did," said Susannah, "but she came back. And Silas said I could invite Ramla—that's the wise woman's name—to stay with us." Her eyes sparkled as she put a hand on her belly. "Have you heard that I'm with child again? We're hoping for a son."

"I'm so happy for you! May the Lord grant you and the child the best of health." I spoke the expected words and hugged my cousin again, although in my misery I felt she ought to be satisfied with the good fortune she already had. But, of course, Susannah and her husband, after having a daughter, wanted the next baby to be a son. Wise women were said to be especially helpful with such matters.

"Come to see Ramla, Mari," said Susannah. "She truly is wise. She foretells the future, and she counsels people in . . . in difficulties. She said it would be no extra trouble to advise my friends."

I felt my face grow hot. So Susannah had already known that I was unhappy. Maybe everyone in our congregation was watching Eleazar and me, talking about how miserable I was. Pitying me.

Chava appeared beside me, and she and Susannah exchanged cool greetings. Susannah hesitated, and then I suppose she thought Chava might make trouble for me if she wasn't invited to Susannah's gathering. "If you, too, wish to see Ramla of Alexandria this afternoon," she said, "you would be welcome a thousand times."

Chava thanked Susannah with barely concealed distaste. "That Egyptian woman, back again?" She clucked her tongue. "Did she ever receive permission from the council of elders to practice in Magdala? I'm not sure Father-in-law would approve of us consulting her."

"I'm sure he *would*," I snapped, with something like my old spark. Of course, I wasn't sure at all, but Susannah's presence gave me a little courage. I straightened my back and forced a smile. "I don't know that I need advice," I told Susannah, "but I am curious to see the Egyptian. I'll come this afternoon."

ELEVEN

THE WAY OUT

Chava didn't try to stop me from going to Susannah's, but she did almost spoil my afternoon. As Chava watched me cover my hair with a scarf, she remarked to her niece, "See, Daphne, she's going out *again*. Most young wives would be eager to prove their worth at home. But she's used to idle entertainments, I suppose."

I left without answering, trembling with anger. I no longer wondered why Chava hated me, because I hated her. I wished the earth would split open under her feet, then close up again with a clap, squeezing the bile out of her. The evil wish satisfied me for a moment, but then it made me feel disgusted with myself.

After I sat down on a cushion in the upper room of

Susannah's house, it was several minutes before I began to enjoy myself. It helped to be in a room full of friendly women; it helped to sip my cup of cool pomegranate juice. It helped most of all when little Kanarit ran over to me, lisping, "Cousin Mari!" and snuggled down beside me.

Wistfully I thought it must be sweet to have a baby, and I wondered if Eleazar had lost his power to beget children. Then immediately I recoiled from the thought of bringing a helpless child into that household. Heaven forbid!

I hoped that Ramla's performance would take my mind off my troubles, and I was glad when the Egyptian wise woman appeared at the sound of a gong. She made an exciting entrance, standing in the doorway with the light silhouetting the crescent on her headdress and the large bird on her shoulder. Yes, she had a talking bird, just as Susannah had promised. "Greetings, ladies," it said in a cracked but distinct voice.

Ramla took a step into the room, and now I saw that her parrot was gray with a scarlet tail. The young woman next to me whispered nervously, "What if . . . what if it's a *demon* speaking through the bird?" I thought that was a silly idea, but I patted her arm.

"Honored ladies," Ramla intoned, "last night I kept a vigil to watch the stars. Know that we are in a time of new beginnings."

New beginnings. The words called up a reading from the

prophets at last Sabbath's synagogue meeting. I'd hardly listened to the reading at the time, but now the Scripture came back to me: "New things I now declare; before they spring forth, I tell you of them."

The wise woman went on, "As the great lighthouse at Alexandria guides ships on their voyages, the light of hidden wisdom can direct your journey." She gestured with a scroll. "The Scroll of Wisdom holds a message for each one in this room."

My journey? A new beginning for me? What a mockery! My journey through life had ended in a cage.

With an effort, I turned my attention back to Ramla as she proceeded to impart special advice from the spirit world to each of us. Staring upward as if the ceiling would dissolve before her gaze, she pronounced the name of one of the women in the room. Next, she raised her scroll in the direction of her gaze, as if to receive some kind of power. Then she opened the scroll and read from it. When she was finished, the parrot squawked, "Ramla has spoken."

The talking bird reminded me of the sparrow I'd named Tsippor. I thought my sparrow had more intelligent things to say than the Egyptian's bird, though. I'd had long conversations with that sparrow.

I was intrigued by Ramla's scroll. I'd never seen such a fine scroll, with carved and polished handles, except in the synagogue. Furthermore, I'd never seen a woman hold one. In fact, I didn't know any women who could read more than a few words.

As Ramla read out a passage for each of us, I tried to guess whether the advice really fit the person. I didn't know most of the guests well, but I knew that Susannah's husband's aunt was concerned about her share in a caravan from Damascus. Ramla's reading assured her: "A venture is bound to be successful." Susannah's reading hinted at a baby boy to come, which, of course, was what Susannah and Silas hoped for.

Then Ramla spoke my name. Immediately I wished I'd asked her *not* to read for me. Nothing could help me. Besides, I didn't want the other women thinking and speculating about me as I had about them.

The Egyptian went through her motions of gazing upward, raising the scroll, and unrolling the parchment. "It is written: 'Lo, the iron bars will melt away, and the prison door will gape open. Trust, and the way out will be revealed to you.'"

Ramla's bird companion cocked its head to look at us with one pale eye and then the other. "Ramla has spoken," it said.

The way out? A way out for me? I didn't really believe it,

but I felt a painful surge of hope. To hide my feelings, I bowed my face over my cup.

After giving each guest a reading, Ramla offered amulets for sale, and some of the women bought them. They were small pouches of colored linen, strung on cords and smelling of herbs. "Nothing the Jewish elders could disapprove of," Ramla assured us. "No graven images or unclean ingredients. This one protects against fevers. This one ties an unfriendly tongue. This one prevents accidents by fire." I thought the one to tie an unfriendly tongue would be useful against Chava, but I had no money.

Then it was time to leave, and each woman presented Ramla with a gift: a dish of stuffed dates, a carved and painted comb, a little jar of scented oil. I waited until the others were gone to give her my gift, a string of crocheted flowers. "Thank you," croaked the bird, and leaned from her shoulder to accept my flowers with its beak.

The Egyptian woman nodded a gracious dismissal to me, but I didn't go. No one could hear us, since Susannah and her departing guests were down in the courtyard. I blurted out my question: "Is there truly a way out for me? How long do I have to wait?"

Ramla gazed at me with a puzzled frown. "Ah yes. You're . . . Mariamne?" She smoothed back a lock of hair that had escaped from her headdress. Her expression, too, smoothed into one of dignity. "I cannot answer your question, how long," she intoned, "but I can help you bear the time of waiting." As she spoke, her Egyptian accent thickened. "I will teach you a charm so that you can slip into the spirit world now and then, and come back refreshed and rested."

I felt a chill. "Into the . . . spirit world?" It was one thing to listen to a wise woman but quite another to cast a charm myself.

"It's nothing to worry about," Ramla answered. "It's only as if you discovered a private garden, a place you can steal off to from time to time. No one else can see it, no one else can know about it."

This wasn't what I wanted, but at least it was something. I nodded. "What is the charm?"

First, Ramla instructed, I must close my eyes and breathe slowly until I feel calm. If troubling thoughts come to me, brush them away. "Then, to get into the spirit world, say 'Abrasax, I enter.' You will step through a doorway into a garden, the loveliest garden you can imagine."

"Abrasax," I repeated.

"And when you wish to leave the garden," Ramla went on, "you will say 'Abrasax, I leave.' You will open your eyes, and you will find yourself back in this world."

"That's all there is to it?" I asked.

"Yes," said Ramla. She yawned as she spoke, and I saw that two of her teeth were missing. I hadn't thought of Ramla as being any particular age, but she must have been as old as my mother. "Now I go to rest and restore my powers."

On my way home, I thought over the words from the scroll. What way out of my cage could there be, other than Eleazar's death? But that solution couldn't be "revealed" to me, because I'd already thought of it. I supposed it would make my plight less miserable if Chava died, but that wasn't the same as escape.

A grim thought struck me: I might die myself. That would be a way out, all right, a nasty fulfillment of Ramla's prophecy.

By the time I walked back into Eleazar's courtyard, my pleasure in the afternoon had dissolved like morning mist from the lake. Chava and the other women were there, watching and criticizing everything I did. That night, although I had the bed to myself, I was tempted by Ramla's idea of a hidden garden.

As Ramla had told me, I closed my eyes. I let my breath slowly in . . . slowly out. Slowly in . . . slowly out. Thoughts swam through my mind like fish, nibbling at me: Had Susannah told her other guests how unhappy I was? Would the elders of Magdala disapprove of what I was doing? Pronouncing magical words by myself seemed like crossing a line, a line maybe as important as the one between a maiden and a married woman.

I brushed the thoughts away. Slowly breathe in . . . slowly breathe out. Gradually I felt that I was floating free. I whispered, "*Abrasax,* I enter."

Immediately an archway appeared in my mind's eye. It was like the entrance to the *mikvah,* only the steps leading down were white marble. And the space I glimpsed beyond was not dark but sunny. It was frighteningly real.

"*Abrasax,* I leave!" I gabbled, and my eyes flew open in the dark. My heart tripped. There *was* a private garden, and who knew what else, in the spirit world. I felt that I'd made a narrow escape.

The next day, Eleazar returned, and that night it was bitter medicine as usual. I was tempted to say the charm again, but I had promised myself that I would not. I sensed danger. Was it the danger of being discovered practicing magic, or of the hidden garden itself? I wasn't sure, but I was afraid.

I thought I would only do the slow breathing, clearing my mind and letting myself float. Surely there was no harm in that much. Breathe slowly in . . . slowly out. By the time I was calmed and drifting, the magical words didn't seem so dangerous. "*Abrasax,* I enter."

My foot seemed to meet the cool marble step, and I felt a jasmine-scented breeze on my face.

No, I must not go there! Again I was frightened, as if I'd walked right to the edge of a cliff. "*Abrasax,* I leave."

By the time three days had passed, I felt myself back in the cage. I longed desperately to be with my grandmother, who would simply give me loving looks and speak kind words. Putting on my head scarf, I picked up a basket and told Chava, "We need fresh herbs. I'm going out the west gate to gather them."

Chava looked sincerely shocked. "Outside the town by yourself? Unheard of!" She added grudgingly, "If we really need herbs, we'll all go together when Daphne arrives this afternoon."

"No. I'm going now." I paused just long enough to make up a plausible lie. "I'm not going alone. Susannah is going, too."

On my way through the alley to the avenue, I wondered if I should change my mind—if I should actually go to Susannah's house. I knew I was risking trouble, deliberately disobeying my husband. But I was ashamed to have Susannah see me in such a pitiable state.

When I stepped into the familiar courtyard a short while later, the first thing I saw was Chloe sitting with another girl. Their heads were together, and they were laughing about something.

"*Shalom,* Mari!" exclaimed Chloe. She jumped up and kissed me. "Look, this is Sarah, Alexandros's betrothed. She's come to live with us." The other girl smiled shyly at me.

So this was my brother's bride-to-be, paid for with my marriage to Eleazar. I managed to say, "*Shalom,* Sarah."

"Who's there, Chloe?" called my mother from the rooftop. She started down the stairs, with Safta following more slowly. Halfway down, my mother caught sight of me and halted. "Mariamne. What are you doing here?"

That was not a welcoming question, and I couldn't answer. Imma hurried down to the courtyard, took my arm, and pulled me aside. "You mustn't come here again," she whispered.

"What do you mean—I'm not welcome in my own home?" I tried to speak calmly, but my voice came out in a wail.

"Not for now, at least." She sighed heavily. "Mariamne, get it through your head that your home is your husband's home. Eleazar has spoken to your uncle Reuben, and Reuben has spoken to Alexandros, and Alexandros told me: Your husband does not wish you to keep coming back here. He says you're neglecting your duties. He says you quarrel with the other women in his household."

"That's not true!" I exclaimed. "*They're* unfriendly to *me.*

Eleazar must have heard those lies from Chava, and that woman hates me! She—"

"Go . . . now!" My mother spoke sharply and gave me a little push toward the gate.

But I turned aside instead, falling into my grandmother's arms. "Safta, Safta!"

My grandmother felt scrawnier than I remembered, but she patted my back and murmured, "There, there, little bird." Ah, her sweet voice! This was what I had come for.

Closing my eyes, I felt for a moment like a much younger girl. Plaintive words came out of my mouth, as if I really were a forlorn child: "Safta, do you like Sarah better than you like me?"

My grandmother pulled back, looking bewildered, and she had me repeat my question. Then she said, "You mean my aunt Sarah? No, I can't say I liked her very well, may her soul rest in peace."

I smiled meanly to myself, pleased that my grandmother didn't even know who the new Sarah was. But then Safta went on, "I'll tell you who I do like—that nice girl Mari." She nodded toward the bench where Sarah sat with Chloe. "She came to live with us. They say she's betrothed to Alexandros."

TWELVE

OUTCAST IN CAPERNAUM

Business was brisk at the tollgate, and the strongbox where Matthew kept the toll money filled quickly. If he didn't think too much about how he'd gotten all that money, it was very satisfying. Matthew was proud, too, that he had servants doing his bidding at home and guards following his orders at the tollgate. And the house he lived in, though it was only rented, was finer than his father's house.

On the first Sabbath morning, Matthew decided to leave the leader of the guards in charge of taking the tolls. The man didn't have Matthew's expertise in judging merchandise, but there would be less traffic than usual. Only Gentiles traveled on the holy day.

Matthew walked downhill to the synagogue in Capernaum. It was easy to see, he thought as he neared the village, that none of that river of wealth on the highway trickled down into Capernaum. Most of the houses were humble one-room huts, and there were none of the spacious compounds such as those owned by the prosperous families of Magdala. The Jews of Capernaum had little to do with highway commerce; they were fishermen and small farmers. Travelers on the highway didn't seek lodging in Capernaum but went on to the caravan stops and inns at Magdala or Tiberias.

Matthew found the Jewish assembly in Capernaum under an open-sided shed near the shore. They must be too poor to have a proper synagogue hall, he thought. Perhaps he could help pay to have one built—the idea pleased him. In Capernaum, he realized, he would be one of the more well-to-do members of the assembly.

But as Matthew stepped onto the black stone floor, a circle of empty space appeared around him. Rough-clad laborers, who must have had to take their Sabbath-eve baths in the lake, pulled their coats aside to keep from touching him. How did they know who he was?

Matthew realized that some of the men looked familiar although their faces were shaded by prayer shawls. They must be the fishermen he'd tried to hire. And then there was a cluster of beggars on the edge of the assembly, some of the same ones as at the tollgate. There was his answer.

Matthew realized that day that Capernaum was a

completely Jewish village; there was no section of Syrians and Phoenicians as in Magdala. On the streets of Magdala, there had always been someone to give Matthew a courteous greeting, even if it was only because they were afraid of his father. But when Matthew walked through Capernaum, no one so much as nodded to him. Women turned their heads and crossed to the other side of the street, and men didn't wait until his back was turned to spit. Even the Jewish beggars dropped their outstretched hands when they saw him coming; they didn't want his filthy money.

Matthew could have traveled to Bethsaida-Julias for Sabbath prayer meetings, but he stubbornly kept coming to Capernaum every week. Wasn't it his right, as a Jew? After all, he kept many parts of the Law. He didn't associate with Romans, except on business. He kept the dietary laws, and he didn't eat with Gentiles. He didn't work on the Sabbath.

The other Jews didn't try to stop Matthew from entering the synagogue, but they always left an empty circle around him. When the shed was full, they'd rather suffer in the noonday sun than stand next to Matthew in the shade of the thatched roof.

One especially hot Sabbath, Matthew noticed in the middle of a reading that an old man was looking unwell. He'd been in the shade at the beginning of the service, although keeping a careful distance from Matthew, but now the sun beat down on his head. Matthew thought he'd wait until the reading of the prophecy was over and then let the man have his place. But in the next moment, the old man crumpled to the ground, his face as gray as his beard.

The old man's relatives carried him out, looking at Matthew with loathing. "Wait till Simon returns," one of them muttered. "He'll get rid of the . . ." The voice trailed off, but Matthew could imagine the rest of the sentence.

As Matthew monitored the tollgate week after week, he felt as if his father and his brother were arguing in his head. Every time a hard-luck case approached the stone arch, Alphaeus and James clamored for his attention.

Let that woman leading her blind brother go through free, James would demand.

Make her pay, barked Alphaeus. If she can't pay like everyone else, she shouldn't be using the highway.

Like everyone else? repeated James. Like the landowner's steward who just went through free, with a wink from Matthew? Besides, the blind man needs a smooth road to walk on.

Matthew wanted to shout at both the voices for silence. But he followed his father's rules, charging as much as he judged each person could pay, allowing for how important they were. Some travelers couldn't pay the toll at all, and they simply turned back. Some looked at him reproachfully and said, "The last toll collector had a heart—he let me go through for half the fee."

All this put Matthew in a bad temper. He became quicker and quicker to beckon one of the guards, and he learned that just a glance in the direction of a guard with a cudgel would usually put an end to any complaints.

The incident that bothered him the most was the woman with the blind brother. She didn't argue, but she didn't pay or turn back, either. She stood still in the shadow of the arch, her eyes pleading under her worn and mended scarf. Her brother's sightless eyes seemed to gaze past Matthew, focused on something no one else could see.

As Matthew looked around for a guard to prod them with a club, the traveler behind the woman and her blind brother spoke up. "Here—I'll pay their toll as well as mine." He was obviously not a wealthy man, a dried-fruit seller with only one servant boy and two donkeys. The woman tried to kiss his hand, but her benefactor waved her off with a laugh. "Did you think I'd stand here waiting for you all day? I'm expected in Gennesaret tonight!"

Taking the coins from the generous man, Matthew met

his eyes for an instant, then dropped his gaze. He felt a surge of unreasonable anger, and he was tempted to order a guard to beat this man. "Move on!" he said roughly.

After that, Matthew added a rule of his own to his father's list: was the traveler polite and friendly to the toll collector, or did he make him feel ashamed? Matthew gave a discount to people who treated him with respect.

Alphaeus hadn't taught his son the last rule because Alphaeus didn't care about respect or friendship, real or pretended. "Just assume they'd all knife you in the back if they got the chance," he'd told Matthew more than once. "You'll be right most of the time. Trust only your own kin. Even with them, count your change."

As time went on, Matthew felt leathery layers growing over his feelings. He was becoming more and more like his father: tough as a camel's toe. Still, there was a difference: his father didn't seem to need other people's company any more than a camel needs to drink water during a scorching day in the desert. But Matthew felt parched for companionship, living by himself on the outskirts of Capernaum.

Gradually Matthew came to know a few of the regular travelers who appeared at his tollgate. These men were Jews, but like Matthew, they understood what a man had to do to get along in the real world. They didn't mind chatting with a toll collector, or even accepting his hospitality. Matthew suspected things would have been different if he'd lived in their hometown, but he didn't dwell on that.

One of these acquaintances was a silk merchant from Sepphoris who traveled regularly to Damascus. Another was an officer of Herod Antipas's army, the one with the patrol looking for rebels. When he saw these men, Matthew always invited them to stay overnight at his villa. He wished they'd come around more often. They were his only friends, if you could call them that.

On a visit to his father in Magdala, Matthew blurted out something about how lonely his life was now. Alphaeus gave a harsh laugh. "What did you expect? What have I always told you? You can't count on anyone except family. You need to start a family of your own. I'll look for a wife for you."

THIRTEEN

CROSSING A LINE

For several days after the upsetting visit to my grandmother, I moped around my husband's house. I heard Chava refer to me again as Weepy and the other women in the compound laugh at her wit. The insult didn't even make me angry now; it was only one more drop falling into my lake of misery.

Then Eleazar left on another trip, and the misery lifted a little. I felt angry as well as unhappy. That night in bed, I spoke the charm defiantly.

"*Abrasax,* I enter," I whispered. I ducked under the arch, brushing aside a sprig of jasmine, and descended the marble steps to a paved path. Boldly I imagined a splashing fountain, and behind it a bay tree with rustling leaves.

Excited, I imagined the garden in more and more detail:

an awning on the south wall, painted tiles decorating the walls, even a line of ants crossing the paving stones. I fell asleep smelling fragrant herbs—perhaps the imaginary bunch hanging from a pole in the imaginary awning. Or perhaps the real packet my grandmother had given me for my marriage bed.

I awoke refreshed, as Ramla had promised, and almost cheerful. I put on a clean tunic and combed my hair. That day, Chava was as unpleasant as ever, and Eleazar returned home as usual to have his ugly feet washed. But I felt different, knowing that I could escape to my garden again when the day was done.

You see? I told my mother—and all of my faithless family, who had so easily replaced me with this girl, Sarah. Their sweetness to me had been nothing but honey to mask a paralyzing poison. Even my father, although he called me "dear little Mari," had abandoned me by dying.

I don't need you, I told them all. I don't even want to visit your house. I have someplace better to go.

The Passover holidays came and went. I didn't try to visit my family, but I heard from Susannah that Alexandros had taken them to Jerusalem to celebrate the Passover. The summer sun baked the hills above Magdala until the grass turned brown.

In Eleazar's house, we settled into an arrangement—or so I thought. Eleazar possessed a young wife. Chava was allowed to run the household, just as she had before I arrived.

As for me, I didn't bemoan my lot any longer. I learned to simply make myself absent from the dreariest parts of my life: the afternoons with the other women in the compound, Eleazar's feet, Eleazar's bed.

Lying with my husband, like washing his feet, didn't take long. As soon as I heard his snores, I closed my eyes and whispered, "*Abrasax,* I enter." And I was free.

Now and then I stayed in the garden until I fell asleep so that I didn't have a chance to say "*Abrasax,* I leave." This worried me at first, but then I decided it didn't matter. With each visit, the garden became more vivid. The rest of my life took on a faded quality, bleached out like a scene in full sunlight after a dark room.

Sometime that summer, I had the idea of imagining my old friend the sparrow, Tsippor, in the garden. He fluttered up to my shoulder and perched there, as Ramla's parrot did with her. Shalom, *Mari! Where've you been so long?* We talked and talked. He was eager to know my thoughts, he was indignant when I was mistreated, and he made me laugh.

There came a night when I dared to imagine my first betrothed, Nicolaos. I allowed myself to feel his arms around me and the warmth between us glowing hotter and hotter. But it was too much for my imaginary garden. Without uttering any secret words, I was back in bed with Eleazar, twisting and moaning.

"What is it, woman?" grunted Eleazar. He nudged me with an elbow. "Can't a man sleep peacefully?"

That incident frightened me, and I didn't permit myself to bring Nicolaos into the garden again.

As Susannah became more awkward and heavier with child, I visited her often to see if I could help. When Susannah's baby was born—a boy, just as Ramla had promised—I spent even more time with my cousin. Often I took care of Kanarit, playing singing games and telling her stories while Susannah nursed the baby.

Chava's niece, Daphne, now visited her almost daily. She spent as much time at Eleazar's house as I did, during the daylight hours. If I was performing a task when she arrived, I'd find some reason to go to another part of the house. Daphne would take over my task, which suited me.

Now and then I observed Daphne as she crossed paths with Eleazar. At these times the girl would simper, always with properly downcast eyes. Chava would watch from the background.

One day when I arrived at Susannah's house, my cousin complained about Ramla. The Egyptian wise woman was still living in Silas's apartment. "I don't want to offend her," said Susannah, twitching her shoulders, "but she won't take a hint. When I said we needed to rent out the apartment, she started paying rent herself!"

Susannah's tone made me uneasy, since I'd benefited from Ramla's advice. "Are you worried about her traffic with the occult, so close to your family?"

"I'm more worried about her traffic with the real world," Susannah snapped. "Too many people come into our compound to consult her, and we have no privacy. And her parrot has learned to bray like the donkey, and they both bray and wake up the baby. Besides, my neighbors ask me about the man with her. Is he her bodyguard? Then why does she spend time alone with him? Or is he her husband? Then why doesn't she show him proper respect?"

Thinking that was the end of her complaints, I started to say something sympathetic, but Susannah wasn't through. "Also, that parrot eats our pomegranates and flings the rinds around."

Eleazar said nothing about my absences now. I thought he must not mind, as long as I was there at noon and in the evening to wash his feet. Or perhaps Chava had stopped reporting my activities to him. She was civil to me, or at least not unfriendly.

One evening, Eleazar, Chava, and I were on the rooftop. I was lighting the lamps while Eleazar finished supper and Chava hovered over him. I started down the stairs with the oil, and for some reason, I halted halfway down.

Chava was talking in a low tone. Eleazar's responses were curt at first, but as she persisted, they became more thoughtful. He asked a question. Chava answered, "They say that madness runs in the family."

I was fairly sure she was talking about me, although it was ridiculous to say that madness ran in my family. At first, I took it as merely another of Chava's belittling remarks. But later that night, as I was about to pronounce the magic words and enter my garden, I hesitated. I'd always had a lively imagination, like my grandmother. What if imagining so much had caused her to forget the difference between imagining and the real world? I did not say the words that night after all.

The next day was unusually hot, even for the season. Although Eleazar was in town, I decided to visit the Egyptian woman again. I hoped she would calm my fears about imagining, but I also hoped she might give me a healing charm for Safta.

I put a market basket on my arm. I told Chava, "I'm going to the market for . . . for millet."

Chava looked at me with that way she had of seeming surprised to see me and disappointed that I was still there. "To the market?" she said in a disbelieving tone. "We still have half a large jar of millet. Millet gets worms if it's kept too long—surely your mother taught you that much."

Not answering, I went out the gate. Chava couldn't upset me the way she used to. It was as if she were making her unfriendly comments through a wall, and I hardly heard her.

At Silas's compound, Ramla sat under the awning, sharing a pomegranate with her parrot, and Ramla's bodyguard (or was he her husband?) lay sleeping under the fig tree. I told her about my grandmother's fading mind. "Do you know of something that could be done for her? I don't have anything to pay you with," I added quickly, "but maybe I could perform some service for you."

Ramla regarded me thoughtfully, then nodded. "Yes, you could do something for me. You might remind your cousin of how much I have helped you and her both. Lately she has made some uncivil remarks—I almost begin to think she would like me to leave. I cannot commune with the spirits in an atmosphere of criticism."

"I'll talk to Susannah," I promised. Remembering my cousin's complaints, I picked up scraps of pomegranate rind from underneath the parrot's perch and tucked them into my sleeve.

"And I will teach you a spell for healing," said Ramla. She recited it, and then she had me repeat the phrases until I knew them by heart.

"Understand," she warned, "the words do nothing by

themselves. Their power is released and channeled by the circumstances. The spell for good health must be uttered at dawn, facing into a breeze, and you must name the part of the body to be strengthened. If the words were pronounced in the dead of the night and the dark of the moon, they would have the opposite effect. Do not use them carelessly!"

"I would never use them carelessly," I assured her. "To tell the truth, I'm a little worried even about visiting my garden now."

"I see," said Ramla with a wise smile. "You are troubled, and not only for your grandmother. You wonder, Did Safta begin by merely imagining?"

"That's it," I said quickly. "What if madness does run in the family? Could it be dangerous for me to imagine so much?"

Ramla put out her hands in a calming gesture. "It's not imagining, in itself, that causes madness. Your poor grandmother has let the unseen world master her. To protect yourself, you must disguise yourself when you step into the spirit world. Then any spirits you meet there will be afraid to harm you. And they will not follow you back into this world."

"Follow me?" I repeated with a shiver. I hadn't thought of that.

"Oh yes. They can do all kinds of mischief if you let them out. And they're harder to get rid of than ghosts, which can be driven away with wormwood and gall."

Ramla's warning frightened me, and I wondered if it wouldn't be better to give up dealing with the unseen world entirely. But she insisted that it was perfectly safe as long as I took sensible precautions. "You wouldn't go on a journey by yourself, would you? Of course not—you'd go with the men of your family, or with a bodyguard, as I do. The words of disguise are a kind of bodyguard, except they fool unfriendly spirits into thinking that *you* are powerful."

"Can they be fooled so easily?" I asked.

"More easily than you think, my dear Mariamne. That is why I wear the moon headdress and moonbeam robes when I do readings. If I stepped into the spirit world as myself, the spirit powers would not obey me. But when they see me dressed like the goddess Isis, they tremble; they do my bidding."

That made sense; I remembered how grand Ramla had appeared the first time I saw her.

After Ramla taught me the words of disguise, I left her and went to see Susannah. I found my cousin sitting cross-legged at her loom while Kanarit plucked at her robe and the baby slept fretfully in a basket nearby. Kanarit stopped bothering her mother and tried to climb into my lap, but I put her off with a kiss. "It's too hot for cuddling. Sit by me here."

I chatted a few moments with Susannah, and then I began to praise the Egyptian wise woman, as I'd promised. "I

feel so grateful that you introduced me to Ramla," I said.
"She's helped me so much! And of course, she also helped
you." I nodded toward the baby's basket.

Susannah, shoving the shuttle through the threads,
glanced at me unsmiling. "I wouldn't say she 'helped' me
with the baby. Surely that's close to blasphemy. It's the Lord
who forms the child in the womb."

I stammered something, startled at her tone. Susannah
added, "To tell the truth, I suspect Ramla is an imposter. Did
I tell you that before you and the others came to my house for
the readings, Ramla got me to talk quite a bit about all of
you? Foolish me, I didn't think anything of it at the time; she
was very clever about seeming interested in a kindly way. But
later it dawned on me that she'd learned enough to have special advice ready for each guest."

Ramla, an imposter? Taken aback, I tried to remember
that afternoon more exactly. Surely it couldn't be a trick that
Ramla had looked into my heart?

"And you?" Susannah went on coolly. "How has the
Egyptian helped you?"

I hesitated, afraid now that Susannah might disapprove
of the magic Ramla had taught me. "She . . . she explained to
me how to soothe myself when people are . . . unkind to me."

"Hmph," snorted Susannah. "Maybe she should go dwell
in your house, then."

We sat in silence for a short while. Susannah knew quite well that Eleazar would never welcome the Egyptian wise woman into his house. Finally, I patted Kanarit, stood up, and left. I felt guilty that I hadn't carried out my part of the bargain with Ramla, although I'd tried.

Back in Eleazar's house, it was a day or so before I found a private moment at dawn to say the healing spell for my grandmother. In the following days, I wished I could visit Safta to make sure she was getting better, but I was afraid to defy Eleazar's order. I looked forward to the Sabbath, when I would see my family across the synagogue.

I didn't forget the protection words that Ramla had given me, but I felt uneasy about using them. Whenever I found myself on the threshold of my imaginary garden, I pulled back. If I didn't enter, I wouldn't need protection.

But I missed my retreat so badly! I began to dwell on the caged sparrows again. Finally, one night after Chava had been especially spiteful, and Eleazar especially brusque, I was frantic to escape.

As soon as Eleazar was snoring, I whispered the words of power beneath my breath. "I am Queen Mariamne. Beware, any spirits who try to threaten me!"

Immediately I felt a surge of strength. I almost laughed out loud with the pleasure of it. Why had I waited so long?

"*Abrasax,* I enter," I uttered, and I stepped confidently through my secret doorway. My sparrow friend lighted on my shoulder. I had a sense of many other beings present but just out of sight—no doubt waiting to serve me, like attendants in a palace.

Early the next morning, as I tidied the bedchamber, I heard Eleazar reciting morning prayers on the roof. The air was already hot and damp, as if the lake were a cauldron of boiling water and we were living in its steam. While I listened to my husband droning, I felt a light touch on my shoulder. *It's very different from the way your abba used to pray, isn't it?* said a sympathetic voice.

I started, turned to look behind me, and glanced around the empty room. I pinched my arm to wake myself up, in case I was dreaming. "Who's that?"

Come, you know me! The voice chuckled in my ear, as if some creature were sitting next to my head. *I'm your old friend, Tsippor.*

The sparrow. I turned my head again, and I thought I caught a glimpse of a gleaming eye and a short, thick beak. "You're supposed to stay in the garden," I hissed. "Go back. I command you."

What's the harm? chirped the voice. *Don't worry—I won't*

*talk to anyone but you. By the way, Eleazar doesn't sound like
he's praying to the Lord, does he? It's more like he's counting the
packs on his camels.*

I giggled in spite of myself. No, Eleazar's prayers were
nothing like the heartfelt prayers my father used to recite.

Although Ramla had warned me against letting anyone
out of my private garden, I decided the sparrow couldn't hurt
anything. Besides, he was good company. Throughout the
day, whenever Chava made one of her slighting comments,
he chirped a saucy reply in my ear.

The next Sabbath morning, as I dressed to go to the synagogue, I opened my jewelry basket to get a bracelet. Immediately I had an uneasy feeling. Nothing was missing, but the
things in the basket seemed disarranged. Or, rather, not disarranged but arranged differently. Had someone been going
through my things?

I told Chava my suspicion, watching her to see if she
would react in a guilty way. Her bland expression didn't
change, and she actually answered me civilly. "I'll speak to
the serving woman," she said. "I caught her trying on my jewelry once."

Later as we entered the synagogue, we passed my family,
and I paused to give them a hurried greeting. My grandmother looked much the same, I thought; was she getting

better? At least, she didn't seem worse. Maybe the healing charm worked slowly.

In the following days, I was glad for the sparrow's company, and I quickly got to depend on it. One morning, I came down the stairs chatting out loud with Tsippor, thinking the courtyard was empty. Suddenly I realized that Chava was standing there in the shade, watching me.

She didn't seem disturbed, and she didn't say anything, but the incident made me remember Ramla's warning about letting spirits follow me into our world: They can do all kinds of mischief. Probably Ramla didn't mean a harmless spirit like the sparrow, but maybe I needed to ask her.

By that afternoon, I'd decided to go tell Ramla about the sparrow spirit and ask her advice. On my way to Susannah's house, though, I kept changing my mind. What if Ramla urged me to banish the sparrow, even from my private garden? He was an old friend. These days, I didn't have such a great crowd of friends that I could afford to lose one.

Intent on talking to Ramla, or maybe deciding to go home without talking to her, I wasn't expecting to talk to Susannah. She surprised me by greeting me at the gate. "*Shalom, Mari*," said my cousin without smiling. Kanarit was beside her and tried to take my hand, but Susannah pulled the child back. "Go—help the women with the bread. Quick now."

"*Shalom,* Susannah." I realized that I'd seen that troubled expression on my cousin's face recently, and more than once. "What's the matter?"

"Cousin . . ." Susannah usually came straight out with whatever she had to say, but now she hesitated. "Has Eleazar said anything . . . Did you know that your husband is not satisfied with you?" She bit her lip, as if to punish it for saying something so harsh.

"What?" I tried to laugh. "Eleazar isn't satisfied with anything. He grumbles about the heat, the cold; the lentils undercooked, the lentils cooked mushy; his relatives bothering him with their company, his relatives never visiting him. That's just the way he is. I'm not surprised if he complained to someone about me."

"Mari, listen! I'm afraid for you. Silas's aunt told me she overheard Elder Thomas talking to her brother, another elder of the synagogue. She said that he said Eleazar had asked Thomas's advice about . . . about divorcing you."

FOURTEEN

WORSE THAN DEATH

My breath was taken away. In a flash, I saw that my life could be much worse than it was now. Divorce! It was better for a woman to die than to be divorced. I would be disgraced forever, like my family's servant, Yael.

"Silas's aunt was worried for you," Susannah was saying. "She thought it might not be too late, if you went to Eleazar and begged him for forgiveness. Tell him you'll do anything to please him."

"But I haven't done anything wrong!" I said with a flare of anger. "The elders wouldn't let him divorce me for no reason at all—would they?"

Susannah shrugged. "I don't know. I've heard some terrible stories." She caught my hand. "Oh, Mari, I'm afraid it might be my fault, for introducing you to Ramla. Eleazar could claim you were practicing witchcraft with her. Silas says the assembly is considering complaints against her."

"Witchcraft! The assembly!" The Jewish leaders in Magdala tolerated minor kinds of magic, like telling fortunes or casting healing charms. But practicing witchcraft was a serious crime. "Does Ramla know this?" I took a step toward Ramla's apartment.

Susannah pulled me back. "Don't. I'm going to talk to her myself. Silas says we have to tell Ramla to leave our compound. You're in enough trouble, Mari. You'd better go home."

I walked back to Eleazar's house with my scarf pulled well over my forehead, brooding about the one divorced woman I knew: Yael. Although she'd come from a respectable family, after her divorce she was lucky that my father had hired her as a servant. A divorced woman was more likely to end up in the brothels down by the docks.

It's true, little sister, chirped a voice from my shoulder. *Right now you may be unhappily married, but at least you can show your face in the market without shame.*

Yes, now I could greet my cousin as one married woman to another. If Eleazar divorced me, no one would respect me, not even my own family.

But if Eleazar was thinking of divorcing me, why hadn't I heard anything about it? Something was going on behind my back. Or . . . maybe it was going on in front of my eyes, but I'd been blind to it.

Now that I thought of it, Chava had been observing me closely recently. There was the time she'd seen me come down the stairs chatting with my invisible sparrow. Maybe there were other times, too. Had she reported them to Eleazar?

And was Chava the one, after all, who'd been pawing through my jewelry basket? I went over each bracelet and earring in my mind, wondering if there was something about one of those pieces that could be criticized.

At Eleazar's house, Chava and the other women were doing handwork and chatting in the upper room since it was too hot in the courtyard. I murmured the usual greeting and sat down. They returned the greeting, but then the group was silent. I caught Hiram's wife looking sideways at me. The half-witted girl, on the other hand, stared openly at me until her mother nudged her and spoke sharply. What had they been saying about me just now?

When the light from the high windows softened to late afternoon, the women gathered their handwork and left to prepare their evening meals. I went into the bedchamber I shared with Eleazar. In this sweltering weather, his bed, as well as Chava's couch and the servants' sleeping mats, had been moved to the cooler rooftop. It was my task to put the bedcover away each morning lest the sunlight fade its colors, and put it back at the end of each day.

I carried the folded coverlet up to the roof and spread it over Eleazar's bed. *Look under the mattress,* chirped a voice in my ear.

"Be quiet, sparrow!" As soon as I spoke, I was afraid, and I glanced around to make sure no one had heard me.

You'd better look under the mattress, he sang.

I reached under the mattress. "There's nothing there but the packet of herbs Safta gave me."

The packet, chirped Tsippor. *Take a close look.*

I pulled out the packet of coarse linen. It was heavier than I'd expected. I held it up to the light. The stitches closing the packet were not in Safta's style, or Safta's thread. Cutting the stitches with a small knife, I dug a pottery figure out of the dried herbs.

It was a woman in ornate dress except for her naked torso, clustered with breasts like grapes. My heartbeat sped up. This was an image of the goddess Artemis of Ephesus, like the figurines I'd seen in the market.

My first thought was to get rid of the nasty thing.

Lunging at the railing, I flung the pottery figure over the rooftops as far as I could. Then I wondered who'd hidden it. Could it have been Eleazar? Surely not, a respectable member of the Jewish assembly! But maybe he was desperate for a son to replace the one he'd lost. I hadn't become pregnant yet, and Artemis was a fertility goddess.

Down in the courtyard, the gate opened and the servant said, "*Shalom,* master." Eleazar was home already, and I hadn't filled the basin to wash his feet. I hurried down the stairs.

Sweating and panting, Eleazar sank heavily onto a bench. Even in the shade, the black paving stones of the courtyard seemed to breathe heat like the inside of an oven.

Chava sat down beside Eleazar and kissed his hand. "Welcome home, Father-in-law. I'm afraid you've overexerted yourself in this heat."

Eleazar grunted and waved his other hand. "I had to consult with Elder Thomas again, and Elder Thomas lives at the top of the city, so I had to exert myself. I'll soon be in my grave—not that it matters."

"How can you say such a thing, Father-in-law? If you left us, my suffering would know no bounds." Lifting his fringed robe from his shoulders, Chava folded it reverently. "I'll bring a fresh tunic."

I knelt in front of my husband to untie his sandals. The paving stones scorched my knees through my robe. I washed the grime from his feet, dried them with a towel, and carried the basin away.

Meanwhile, Chava returned with the clean tunic and helped Eleazar change. "I've been wondering, Father-in-law," I heard her say. "You must have good reasons for allowing magic to be practiced within your walls."

About to pour the dirty water into the alley, I paused at the gate. Why was Chava hinting about magic? Did she know about the Artemis figurine hidden under the mattress? If Eleazar had put it there, how would he explain that to her?

"Eh?" Eleazar sounded annoyed, not guilty. "What are you talking about—that my brother's wife casts little charms to prevent gray hair? It's too hot for your gossip and women's squabbles!"

"I'm only thinking of you, Father-in-law, and your standing in the assembly," Chava said in a hurt voice. "Maybe the elders wouldn't consider a heathen Egyptian amulet as real magic."

Eleazar scowled. "Amulet? What amulet?"

"The amulet in your wife's jewelry basket." Chava's voice sank to a whisper, but I understood her words perfectly well.

And suddenly I understood her plan. I turned and stared across the courtyard at her.

"Look in her basket for yourself, if you don't believe me," Chava went on.

Eleazar puffed his lips out impatiently. But he said, "Very well, bring the basket. Wife," he called to me, "come here."

"If anything's in my basket, it's because Chava put it there!" I protested. But Eleazar beckoned without answering. I crossed the courtyard again, still holding the basin of dirty water. Meanwhile, Chava hurried up the stairs and returned with my jewelry basket. "Look under the lining, Father-in-law," she urged.

"Don't you see what she's doing?" I exclaimed. "How would she know what to find, unless she put it there herself?"

Paying no attention to me, Eleazar lifted the lid of the basket. He pulled the cloth lining away from the basket and picked up a beetle the size of an apricot half. It wasn't a real insect—this beetle was carved in polished green stone.

Eleazar's jaw dropped, showing his yellow lower teeth. He looked as frightened as he did angry, and I was glad in spite of the trouble I was in. He shook the amulet at me. "What is this unclean thing you have brought into my household?"

"Ask *her* that question!" I snapped.

Then my hands, acting by themselves, tilted the basin. They flung the gray water in Chava's face, drenching her head and shoulders. I let out a horrified giggle.

"Are you possessed?" Eleazar shouted at me.

Chava, sputtering and wiping her face with her shawl, shot me a look of hatred. She said, "Father-in-law, I fear she *is* possessed. I didn't want to worry you, but this isn't the first time she's attacked me."

The lie struck me speechless, or so I thought. "It won't be the last time, you snake-woman!" The words seemed to chirp in my ear, but by the expressions on Eleazar's and Chava's faces, I knew that I'd spoken them myself.

In a panic, I seized my jewelry basket and ran up the stairs to the roof. I cowered against the railing, my heart pounding so hard that it seemed to push me away from the plaster with each beat. What would Eleazar do to me now?

Down in the courtyard, Chava's voice went on. "You see, Father-in-law? I'm worried for the honor of your house. As I told you, I've noticed other signs. Often she seems to be absent in spirit, or communing with unseen beings. She stares into the air and talks when no one is there."

"This is not the kind of wife I bargained for," Eleazar agreed. After a moment's pause, he said, "Elder Thomas advised against putting her aside, although I have the right. But he might change his mind if he saw this"—he must mean the scarab—"and knew of her uncontrolled behavior."

"There are families with more suitable girls," said Chava.

"But *ai!*" sighed Eleazar. "What a lot of trouble! And her

uncle and brother would be angry. Not that they have any right, after all I've done for them. Besides, they'd have to hold their tongues if they wanted to keep the sardine business in Tiberias."

I felt sick. Susannah's rumor was true—Eleazar had been thinking of divorcing me. So Chava had been civil to me only to keep me in ignorance while she plotted. My visits to the house where the Egyptian woman lived made it easy to cast suspicion on me.

I felt small claws clutch my shoulder, and the invisible sparrow chirped, *Yes, you could become a pitiable creature, like Yael. But you don't have to let them do this to you. Remember, you have power.*

"Quiet!" I muttered. The sparrow said no more, for the time being.

After my outburst, the household was ominously calm. Eleazar called me to serve the evening meal as usual. We ate on the rooftop, where the air was a little less steamy. Then we prepared for bed. Chava pretended to fluff up Eleazar's mattress, but I saw her poking under it. "What's this?" she asked loudly.

"Well, what is it?" I asked even louder. I knew what she was looking for, and I knew it wasn't there. I smiled as she drew out the packet of dried herbs and felt for the figurine—

which, of course, lay shattered in a nearby alley. It was good to see her blink in disappointment and shoot me an angry glance.

"Will you women never stop bickering?" Eleazar demanded. "I need my rest. In the morning, I'll decide what's to be done."

So all of us went to bed. I suppose I was worn out, because I had barely time to quiet myself and enter my secret garden before I fell asleep. As I drifted off, I seemed to see a group gathering around me, talking among themselves. *This is our chance,* I heard one say.

Sometime later, I opened my eyes. Judging by the stars, it was the middle of the night. I edged off the bed, where Eleazar lay snoring. Chava, too, looked fast asleep on her couch.

A plan was laid out in my mind, fully formed:

If Eleazar were struck with a malady, he wouldn't have the strength to divorce me.

I knew a curse for bringing on illness. Ramla had explained it to me because it was close to the charm for healing, and you had to be careful not to mix up the two procedures.

The curse was supposed to work best on a moonless night—like tonight.

So I crept down the stairs from the rooftop to the

courtyard. It seemed natural to hear a woman's cultured voice speaking Greek (which, somehow, I understood perfectly) in my ear. *First, you'll need a doll.*

Lighting a little lamp with a coal from the hearth, I found a greasy rag. I rolled and tied it into a figure with a head, two arms, and two legs.

I propped the rag figure on the bench where Eleazar usually sat to have his feet washed. I pronounced the curse: "*Abrasax*. Let the words of his mouth forsake him."

That was all I meant to say, but then the voice asked, *What if Eleazar writes out his wishes? Chava couldn't read them, but Elder Thomas could.*

My voice whispered on, "*Abrasax*. Let the strength of his right hand also forsake him."

The dirty rag figure pitched forward off the bench, as if an unseen finger had pushed it, and landed on one side. Drawing in my breath sharply, I put a hand to my mouth. What had I done?

Quickly I picked up the rag, untied it, and tucked it into its corner by the oven. Then I hurried up the stairs. On the rooftop, nothing seemed different. Eleazar was snoring as loudly as before. Chava, too, was still asleep. Somewhere in the neighborhood, a rooster crowed.

I waited for a moment, then unrolled a mat and lay down

beside Eleazar's bed. The woman's voice that had directed me through the curse was silent. As far as I could tell, nothing had happened.

"Father-in-law! What is it? Speak to me, dear Father-in-law! What's the matter?"

Chava's cries woke me up from strange dreams. In the light of dawn, I saw Chava bending over Eleazar's bed.

My husband was making donkeylike noises. "Aa-ee. Eh-oh-a." Waving one arm, he repeated the noises, louder, as if he expected Chava to understand him.

I scrambled to my feet. At a gesture from Chava, I helped her raise Eleazar to a sitting position. His eyes rolled, and he kept trying to speak, but only donkey noises came out of his mouth. The right side of his face sagged, and his right arm—the one I was holding—hung limp.

"Let him down gently! Bring water!" cried Chava. "Run, tell Hiram!"

FIFTEEN

A WIDOW AT LAST

Eleazar's cousin Thomas, the elder of the synagogue, came as soon as he heard the bad news. His silver-clasped belt was on crooked, and the silk tassels of his coat were tangled. I was surprised to see him distressed; I hadn't thought he cared much about Eleazar.

Now I was sure that this wise, pious, important man would know at once who was to blame. When his glance fell on me, I felt sick with fear. But Elder Thomas paid no further attention to me, except for a general nod of greeting to all us women. After questioning Hiram about what had happened, he climbed up to the roof, where his cousin lay in bed.

Eleazar tried to speak, but Elder Thomas hurriedly hushed him. "Rest, cousin! Save your strength, and soon you'll be hopping around again like old times, when we were boys playing by the lake." He recited the prayer for the sick: "May the One who blessed our ancestors, Abraham, Isaac, and Jacob, bless Eleazar bar Yohannes with healing. . . ."

As he left, Elder Thomas seemed more worried than before. He muttered to himself, "Shame on me, for letting the old man climb the hill in the heat! It was too much for him." To Hiram, he pronounced, "I will send my physician."

I was frightened all over again when the physician, a learned Greek, arrived. Surely he would detect the signs of a curse on Eleazar. But the physician only questioned Hiram about Eleazar's activities the day before. When Hiram told how his half brother had walked all the way to the top of the city in the heat, the physician shook his head gravely.

Like Elder Thomas, he ignored us women, except to prescribe broth ("I knew that already," muttered Chava) and absolute quiet for the stricken man. For now, Eleazar was not to be moved, so the serving man adjusted the awning on the rooftop to shade his bed. The Greek also advised Hiram to take his brother to the mineral springs at the Tiberias spa, when he was well enough to travel in a litter.

After the physician left and Hiram went off on a matter of business, I wandered around the house in a daze. No one had any idea how powerful I was! Elder Thomas, the

Greek physician, Hiram, even Chava, who'd accused me of witchcraft—none of them realized that I'd actually harnessed the forces of the unseen world! The idea made me giddy. I wanted to laugh out loud.

All that day, Chava hardly left her father-in-law's side. Hiram's wife and the cousin tiptoed up to the roof, offering to help, but she waved them away. Chava sponged Eleazar's forehead, adjusted his pillows, and lifted his head to spoon broth into the good corner of his mouth. Every once in a while, I climbed to the top of the stairs to observe them. My husband, struggling to move, reminded me of a crushed wasp flailing its legs.

At first, my only thought was to reassure myself that Eleazar was still half-paralyzed, that he couldn't declare himself divorced from me or write an order to that effect. As the day went on, though, I began to feel sorry for Chava. I'd thought she'd only fawned on "Father-in-law" and fussed over him to get his favor. But there was real tenderness in the way she touched Eleazar, stroking his limp right hand or wiping his chin.

I began to wonder if I'd been hasty in casting the spell. Maybe Eleazar wouldn't really have divorced me. Chava wanted him to, but he didn't necessarily do what she wanted.

After the midday rest, a rabbi from the synagogue arrived.

He sat by the sick man's bed for a long time, reciting psalms. Eleazar kept his eyes on the rabbi's face and made noises as if trying to repeat the words.

One verse in particular seemed to be aimed at me:

> *Let them be put to shame and dishonor*
> *who seek after my life!*
> *Let them be turned back and confounded*
> *who devise evil against me!*
> *Let them be like chaff before the wind,*
> *with the angel of the Lord driving them on!*
> *Let their way be dark and slippery,*
> *with the angel of the Lord pursuing them!*

I couldn't bear to listen any longer, and I went downstairs again. I devised evil against my husband, I thought. I am a wicked person, and surely I will be punished. Unless I made amends—yes, I could do that. I would cast a second spell, this time for healing instead of illness. But I'd have to wait until morning because now the western sky was pink with the sunset.

Going back to Eleazar's bedside, I urged Chava to let me tend Eleazar so that she could rest. She shook her head. Did she suspect me?

I lay down on the far side of the roof, outside the light cast by the lamp at Eleazar's bedside. Chava hummed a lullaby to the sick man, as if he were a baby. She spoke to him in a broken voice, between sobs. "Forgive me, Father-in-law. I brought this upon you. I meant to help . . . but I should not have brought in the unclean images. Forgive me."

I should have been glad that Chava blamed herself for Eleazar's seizure, but her guilt only made my guilt weigh more heavily on me. I wanted to get away from the sound of her voice. At the same time, I was afraid to enter my private garden.

Finally, I couldn't stand it. Only for a moment, I told myself. "*Abrasax*, I enter," I whispered into the sleeping mat.

As soon as I set foot in the hidden garden, the fear and guilt drained out of my heart. A woman stepped forward to greet me. *Hail, Mariamne! I am Phomelei, your friend and guide.* I recognized her voice, still speaking Greek; somehow, I understood her as if it were Aramaic.

"You're the one who helped me cast the spell on Eleazar," I said. I liked her looks: fierce eyebrows and a strong nose, and red lips against white teeth.

Phomelei acknowledged what I said with a modest nod of her head. *But the honor goes to you, for choosing your own destiny! I knew you had the strength and courage to do it.* She added, *When you choose your own destiny, you can't help choosing the destiny of others, too. That's the way it is.* She shrugged and smiled.

I knew she meant that Eleazar had stood in the way of my destiny, so he had to be pushed aside. I shrugged and smiled back. Another voice, a smooth male voice, agreed with us: *No one could be expected to bear such a miserable fate, married off to an old lizard!*

Arising the next morning, I found Chava asleep by Eleazar's bed. She was kneeling on the floor with her head resting against his side, like a lamb nestled up to its mother. Eleazar was not sleeping, though. He lay on his back with eyes and mouth open. He was dead.

My heart soared. I was a widow at last! I was free!

I felt a breath tickle my neck, and a soft, slick voice whispered, *Yes, he's dead as a salted sardine! But careful—no one must find out. Take Aiandictor's counsel: You must seem to be sad.*

Aiandictor? That was the same new male voice I'd heard the night before. Who was he?

I am your counselor, came the answer in a voice as mellow as the first pressing of olive oil. *My only wish is to serve you. Don't you judge my counsel sound?*

Of course he was right. A wife couldn't openly rejoice at her husband's death, no matter how he'd treated her. I ripped the neck of my tunic in the traditional gesture of grief. At the sound, Chava raised her head, and I put on a serious face for her. "Husband's daughter-in-law . . . he has departed to his ancestors."

Chava's eyes flew wide open. Her next breath came out in a wail, cutting through the air, bringing everyone in our compound running.

Since a person must be buried within a day after death, we women got to work. Hiram's wife and cousin went to the market and bought spices while Chava and I washed Eleazar's body. As I wiped Eleazar's yellowed toenails, I thought, I will never have to wash these feet again. I felt a burst of triumph.

While we anointed the body with spices mixed with oil and wrapped it in linen, Chava spoke in halting phrases about Eleazar's thoughtfulness to her. For instance, one time he'd given her a pot of ointment, for rubbing on sore muscles, that he'd bought on his travels. He'd bought two pots of ointment, actually, but he let her have the one that had turned a bit rancid.

I kept my head bowed over the cloth I was tearing into strips, relieved that no one expected me to talk. I was surprised at the tears in the others' eyes, at their voices choked with feeling. I hadn't thought Eleazar was especially kind to any of them, but they all managed to remember some miserly favor of his. It seemed that only I was glad he was dead.

When the body was prepared, the men, led by Elder Thomas, lifted Eleazar onto a litter. They processed through the town, out the south gate, and into the cemetery to the family tomb. The women followed, wailing. The day was as hot as the previous day and the one before, and the sun glittered on the lake.

As the procession passed my family's tomb, the oily voice of Aiandictor spoke to me again. *Think of your father; they'll assume you're grieving for your husband.* So I pretended that this was my father's funeral, the one I'd missed.

At once, tears stung my eyes, and I began sobbing out loud. I felt alone, unprotected, and I missed my father as if he'd died only yesterday. I heard neighbors telling each other, "How she grieves for her old husband!"

For the next week, a stream of people came through the house to offer condolences. My cousin Susannah, one of the first, knelt down beside me and took my hand. "Cousin Mari, what a terrible sorrow!" She lowered her voice, glancing over at the corner where Chava huddled, red-eyed, with her niece. "At least, for her."

I nodded; Chava was pitiable. The compound belonged to Hiram now, so Hiram's wife was the new woman of the house. Chava wasn't an important mourner, and most of the visitors greeted her last, even after Eleazar's widowed cousin.

"It must be bitter for Chava to be a poor relative in the house where Eleazar let her be mistress," I said. "But I suppose she doesn't have any place else to go."

"And you?" asked Susannah. "I suppose you'll return to your own family?" It was a reasonable question, since normally a young widow returns to her birth family until she remarries.

But at the very thought, I began shaking with rage. Return to those people, who had fed me poisoned honey to make me marry a loathsome old man? Susannah drew back, frightened, and I realized my face must have shown my feelings. I managed to turn the snarl coming out of my throat into a coughing fit.

"You know," I explained quickly, "I never got along with my brother, and now he's master of that house. But I don't want to stay here, either." I nodded toward Hiram's wife, who wore a look of satisfaction under her mournful expression. "She offered to let Chava and me share their old apartment."

Susannah made a face of horror. "No! You didn't marry *Chava,* thank the Lord! Mari . . . I've been thinking: You could live with us! We have extra space, now that Ramla's gone. Silas agrees."

Phomelei's amused voice spoke: *You see how it goes, when you use the power that's yours? Whatever you want, it falls into your hand like a ripe fig.*

"I'd be so grateful, cousin!" Aware of the room full of solemn mourners, I tried to keep the excitement out of my voice. "You know, I have some money of my own—my bride-gift. I would pay rent."

"Then it's settled. Kanarit will be so happy!"

I wasn't sure it was settled, though, as far as Alexandros and the rest of my family were concerned. They arrived not long afterward—all, that is, except my grandmother. "Safta is too feeble to leave the house, but she sends her love," said my mother. I nodded, although I suspected, with a pang, that it was my grandmother's mind that was too feeble for visiting.

When I told them I planned to live with Susannah, Imma's brows drew together. "Think how it will look," she protested, "a young woman living alone. People will talk."

"I won't be *alone*," I argued. "I'll be in Silas's compound, under his protection."

Alexandros was also frowning. "To be frank, I doubt that I could approve of such an arrangement."

"You don't have the right to tell me what to do," I said. "I am no longer a member of your household." Immediately

Aiandictor warned me, *Don't defy him! If Alexandros objects,*
Silas might feel reluctant to take you in.

Indeed, I saw at once what a mistake I'd made. Imma,
Sarah, and Chloe were all watching, expecting my brother to
show that he was in charge. Alexandros drew himself up. In
his most pompous tone, he said, "Perhaps my father-in-law
should be consulted about this matter." He nodded across
the room, where Elder Thomas was talking to Hiram.

As Aiandictor poured smooth words into my ear, I repeated them to Alexandros. "Brother, I apologize. I know
you are weighed down by all your responsibilities: the family,
the sardine business, your important role in the synagogue.
But there's no need for you to feel responsible for me any
longer; you have done your duty by me. You chose a husband
for me, and you gave me a generous bride-gift."

I said all this without a trace of sarcasm. As I spoke,
Alexandros's offended expression faded. I went on, "I don't
wish to crowd you and your growing family." I gestured
toward Sarah, who blushed and put a hand on her belly.
"How much better for me to move into Silas's empty apartment!"

Alexandros gave his young wife a satisfied glance. He
nodded. "Perhaps. I'll have a word with Silas."

After the visitors had left, I was convulsed with giggles.

Did Alexandros really think he was so important? Did he not even remember that my mother had had to talk him into giving me a decent bride-gift? I noticed Chava staring at me, and I pretended to sob into a corner of my shawl. But in the back of my mind, it was chuckles and snickers.

When the thirty days of mourning for Eleazar had passed, I moved to Silas's compound. That Sabbath eve, I held the baby for my cousin while she lighted the Sabbath lamps. I sat with Susannah's household as Silas blessed the bread and broke it, and little Kanarit beamed at me.

I beamed back triumphantly. In time, I thought, I'd remarry and light the Sabbath lamps in my own household. I'd endured a miserable year, but now all my troubles were behind me.

SIXTEEN

SUMMONED BEFORE
THE COUNCIL

That very night, though, I dreamed that Eleazar appeared at the door of my bedchamber. "I thought you were dead," I blurted. He didn't speak, but he frowned impatiently and beckoned. I realized that I would have to go back to his house and lie with him again as his wife. Only—the horror of it!—he *was* dead.

The dream woke me up. It was the middle of the night, but I couldn't go back to sleep. When morning finally came, I thought of Ramla—perhaps she could help me drive off such dreadful dreams. I went to Susannah and asked where Ramla had gone.

Susannah said she thought the Egyptian wise woman had taken a room at a Syrian inn, in the neighborhood of the boat builders. She looked at me sharply. "You aren't thinking of bringing her here, are you?"

I *had* been thinking that, but I could see that my cousin wouldn't allow Ramla there, even for a short visit. Wondering what to do, I sat Kanarit down to comb the snarls from her hair. Did I dare go see Ramla by myself? I wouldn't want anyone in our Jewish congregation to know that I'd visited a Gentile inn. Also, the street of the boat builders had a bad reputation. On the other hand, I'd be afraid to go to sleep that night if I might dream of Eleazar again.

Why do you need to seek out Ramla? asked a cultured voice. *I, Phomelei, am your friend and guide, and I am right here with you.*

"Then how can I keep that man—that thing—out of my dreams?" I asked.

I'd spoken out loud without thinking, and Kanarit wiggled around to see who I was talking to. I quickly made a funny face, as if I'd been talking silly to entertain her.

Phomelei answered me, *First, understand that Eleazar's spirit has no right to trouble you. You filled your wifely duties better than he—*

A harsh, ugly voice broke in. *We taught that man a lesson, didn't we? Wasn't it fun to watch him twitch and mumble, his face sagging lopsided?*

A grating laugh burst from my mouth, and Kanarit turned again. "Don't do that, cousin Mari," she begged. "I don't like that voice." Susannah, who had been washing her baby's face, looked up with a frown, but then he cooed and drew her attention back.

Shaken, I tried to soothe Kanarit while Phomelei took charge again. *Never mind that brute, Odjit; I have him under control now. As for the bothersome spirit of Eleazar: if you believe what I say, this recipe will bar him from your home.* She advised me to brew a mixture of wormwood and gall and smear it on the lintel of my door.

I did so, and sure enough, I had no more dreams about my dead husband. Susannah asked me about the stain on the door frame, but I told her it was a substance to keep out biting insects. Luckily, Susannah didn't notice how little effect the mixture had on the wasps that swarmed around the fig tree by my door.

A few days later, as I chased a wasp around my apartment, a man appeared at the courtyard gate and asked the serving woman for Silas. I recognized him as a scribe from the synagogue.

After a moment or two, Silas came to my door with a serious expression. The visitor was a messenger from the council of elders. They were holding an inquiry, and they wished to ask some questions of Eleazar's widow.

"It's just a matter of a few questions, they say," Silas tried to reassure me. "I'll come with you."

Silas was being kind, but fear put a sour taste in my mouth. Did they suspect me?

Don't be afraid, chirped a familiar voice in my ear. *No one knows what you did to that old lizard, except us friends of yours. Just do what we tell you, and you'll be safe.*

So I covered my head and walked with Silas to the assembly hall. It seemed strange to climb up the broad stone steps on an ordinary day. I'd never been in the synagogue building for anything but Sabbath prayer meetings.

On this day, Silas and I were shown to a chamber off the main hall. The usher waved Silas to a seat against the wall and showed me to a bench facing a table with three empty chairs behind it. Another woman already sat on the bench, and although her back was to me, I recognized Chava's shawl. Sure enough, it was Chava who turned to glance at me. She looked frightened, too.

I sat down on the bench, as far from Chava as possible, and then we had to rise as Elder Thomas and two other men from the council entered. One elder, wrinkled and white-bearded, walked with a staff. The other, a stocky man with a bald head, was dressed in even finer robes than Elder Thomas. The scribe who'd summoned me came with them, carrying tablets and stylus, and took his place standing at a high desk. The elders sat down in the chairs.

"Peace to all," said Elder Thomas briskly. He turned to Silas. "This is only an informal hearing, but understand that our questions must be answered fully and honestly. We who lead the Jews of Magdala are troubled that some of our community are disobeying the Law against images. This is not a private matter, you understand. If one in the group sins, the whole group is affected. As it is written: 'Did not Achan the son of Zerah break faith in the matter of the devoted things, and wrath fell upon all the congregation of Israel?'"

The elder then spoke to Chava and me. "Widow of Eleazar bar Yohannes, and daughter-in-law of Eleazar bar Yohannes. It has been reported that heathen images appeared in the house where you lived with the aforementioned man." He placed a pouch on the table, opened the drawstring, and picked out the green scarab with wooden tongs.

"His brother and heir, Hiram bar Yohannes, found this"— he held up the scarab—"in Eleazar bar Yohannes's chest. And this image of a heathen goddess"—he held up a piece of broken pottery, again using tongs, and grimacing at the clusters of breasts—"was discovered in the alley behind the deceased man's house, evidently thrown off the roof." He looked straight at me. "What do you know of these?"

My knees, already watery, began to tremble. How would

the elders punish idolatry—by flogging? Then I heard Phomelei's firm, cool voice: *Say: "I did not bring the heathen images into
the house of my husband. Perhaps Chava, who ran his household,
knows where they came from."* I kept my eyes downcast before
the elders, but I repeated the words in my own firm, cool voice.

"Well?" asked Elder Thomas, turning to Chava.

I expected her to accuse me in turn, but Chava seemed to
have lost her nerve. "If only dear Father-in-law"—her voice
broke with emotion—"were here to tell you what a disgrace-
ful excuse for a wife—"

"Stop!" Elder Thomas leaned forward, frowning
solemnly from Chava to me. "Can't you see, the important
thing is, our Jewishness is at stake? We're ruled by Gentiles;
we're forced to live cheek by jowl with Gentiles—and all you
women can think about is your petty grudges!"

I was afraid they would punish both Chava and me, just
to punish someone. Then the bald, stocky elder spoke up.
"Yes, it's deplorable how these women behave, but it seems
they know nothing of the images. Isn't it more probable that
the Egyptian is to blame? Let Ramla of Alexandria be
brought before us."

This made no sense; as far as I knew, Ramla had never
even set foot in Eleazar's compound. I stole a glance at
Chava, who also looked puzzled. But then she burst out,
"The Egyptian did visit Father-in-law, now that I think of it."

I stared at her. Chava stared back, as if daring me to defend Ramla. *Say nothing,* counseled Aiandictor. *You'll only cause trouble for yourself. The elders want to blame the Egyptian, not one of their own.* I said nothing.

An assistant to the elders led Ramla through the doorway. This day, she was dressed like any ordinary respectable woman of Galilee, in a long-sleeved tunic, robe, and head scarf. The only unusual thing about her appearance was the parrot perched on her wrist. Her husband/bodyguard followed her into the room and stood against the wall near Silas.

Bowing to the elders, Ramla spoke in a shrill voice. "Sirs, I must protest this high-handed treatment—forcing me to appear before you, even searching my dwelling! The Jewish council has no authority over an Egyptian such as myself."

"The evidence, revered elders," said the assistant. "This item was found in her room at the Syrian inn." He put a scroll, which I recognized as Ramla's Scroll of Wisdom, down on the table.

Elder Thomas frowned at the scroll before he turned to Ramla, still frowning. "You are correct, woman of Egypt, in that this council has no right to punish you ourselves. But the civil magistrates listen carefully to our recommendations."

Ramla sat down on the bench between Chava and me.

She took hold of my hand, and I felt her trembling. She must be imagining, as I had, how it would feel to be flogged. The parrot squawked, "*Shalom,* Mariamne."

The elders are watching you, cautioned Aiandictor's smooth voice. I didn't answer the parrot, and I pulled my hand out of Ramla's.

The elders seemed glad to turn from Chava and me and our family quarrel to Ramla, a foreigner and a known dealer in magic. Elder Thomas began with a stern lecture. "Ramla of Alexandria, you realize that we only tolerate your presence in Magdala. If we find that you have tempted any Jews to take up heathen practices, we will use our influence with the civil authorities, and you will find yourself very unwelcome in this town. And if your actions have caused harm to one of our synagogue, we will turn you over to the courts for punishment."

Elder Thomas went on in that vein, and the other two elders added their comments, throwing in quotations from Scripture. Ramla sat silent and shaking, but the parrot squawked out one of its senseless remarks: "Adjo loves Naomi." Meanwhile, the scribe picked up the scroll and began to read, moving his lips silently. As he unrolled the parchment, his expression turned from a frown into bafflement.

Finally, the eldest of the council suggested looking at the

new evidence. Elder Thomas nodded to the scribe. "Have you examined the scroll of magic spells found in this foreign woman's dwelling?"

The scribe cleared his throat in an embarrassed way. "Yes, revered elder, I have examined the entire document."

"Well?" asked the aged elder.

"It is written in common Greek," said the scribe.

"What?" exclaimed Elder Thomas. "I can see from here that the handles are carved with Egyptian hieroglyphs."

"They are," admitted the scribe, "but the parchment doesn't match the handles. It's coarsely finished, and it seems to have been glued onto the handles rather inexpertly."

"Yes, yes, never mind," said the bald elder. "Tell us the contents of the scroll."

The scribe coughed gently. "Revered elders, this scroll is . . . a bill of lading." He bent his head over the scroll and began to read. "Received by Kronos, captain of the ship *Dolphin,* of Apollodoros, merchant of Cyprus: Two hundred amphorae of olive oil. To be delivered unbroken and full to the warehouse at Joppa." He glanced up. "It goes on like this."

The elders looked dumbfounded. Then Elder Thomas asked, "Could this not be a kind of code for magic spells?"

The scribe shook his head. "Revered sirs, this is certainly a bill of lading."

The elders all turned toward Ramla. "Ramla of Alexandria, explain yourself," ordered Elder Thomas.

Ramla answered in an unmystical tone with no trace of her Egyptian accent. She admitted that she'd filched an old bill of lading from a merchant's storeroom. Her husband/ bodyguard had carved the handles for the scroll, inscribed them with hieroglyphs copied from a public obelisk, and glued the bill of lading onto the handles.

Elder Thomas gave her a piercing look. "You are not actually from Egypt, are you?"

Ramla said with lowered gaze, "No. My father was Jewish, from Joppa; my mother was Phoenician. They named me Naomi."

"Naomi," echoed the parrot.

"In other words," said the bald elder, "you are a fraud."

The elders conferred in whispers for a moment. Then Elder Thomas announced their decision: for the offense of bringing Gentile images into Jewish households (Ramla/ Naomi protested here, but at a threatening look she fell silent), Ramla was to leave Magdala at once, taking her parrot and husband (or was he her bodyguard?), and never return. Chava and I received a lecture on our selfish and quarrelsome hearts, but we were free to go.

Back home, Susannah brewed me a cup of calming mint

tea. She let Kanarit carry it to me. "The child was so worried about you," Susannah whispered to me. "So was I." She added to Kanarit, who was watching me solemnly, "You see? Cousin Mari is fine after all."

I gave the little girl a secret smile and wink, and then I told Susannah what had happened at the council. "I *knew* she was an imposter!" exclaimed my cousin. "Ramla of Alexandria, indeed!"

"Well, as a name for a wise woman, Naomi of Joppa doesn't have quite the right ring," I said. We laughed and laughed.

After the first thrill of relief, though, I had troubling thoughts. That night, I entered my private garden with many questions. Was Ramla truly a fraud, or had she pretended to be a fraud in order not to be punished? If Ramla was a fraud, then how could the magic she'd taught me work so well? What of my sparrow companion, and my invisible guides and counselors? What of the spell I'd cast against my husband?

Wings brushed my hair as the sparrow lighted on my shoulder. *Don't you understand? You're the one with magical gifts, not Ramla! You, not she, can enter the spirit world at will. You, not Ramla, commune with powerful spirit advisors. You, not Ramla, cast potent spells.*

It must be true! My mood soared, and I laughed out loud.

Phomelei, also laughing, was waiting to greet me with a slim, winsome young man. *I am Aiandictor, my lady,* he said, bowing, and I recognized his smooth voice. I'd expected those two, as well as the sparrow on my shoulder.

However, there were also several other beings in the garden. I could only glimpse them from the corner of my eye, but there seemed to be something strange about each of them. I thought I saw ears like a donkey's, and someone else's skin seemed to shimmer like scales—or was it only brocaded cloth? "Who are these others?" I asked Phomelei.

Why, these are your attendants, my lady, said the Greek woman. *Behold those whose only wish is to serve you! Dionesiona. Odjit. Zaphaunt. Panhasaziel.*

I was reassured, although I still couldn't see them clearly. Crowding around me, they placed a laurel wreath on my head and seated me on a gilded chair. *Hail, Mariamne, sorceress of great power!* said Aiandictor. *Aren't you pleased with us? We turned the elders' suspicions to Ramla! We confused those old hypocrites!*

I took the jeweled goblet they pushed into my hand and drank the sweet, spicy drink. It made me giddy. "Yes," I giggled, "I *am* well pleased with you!"

SEVENTEEN

A FREE SPIRIT?

The next morning, I woke up to hear Silas saying his daily prayers. He recited them in a comfortable, sturdy drone, and the meaning of the words didn't penetrate my mind until he was in the middle of chanting a psalm:

> *Happy are they who trust in the Lord! They*
> > *do not resort to evil spirits or turn to false*
> > *gods.*
> *Great things are they that you have done,*
> > *O Lord my Lord! How great your wonders*
> > *and your plans for us!*

The Lord's plan for me . . . I tried to grasp the thought, but it slipped out of my mind like a small fish through a net.

Only a dull sorrow, as if I'd lost something precious, was left. In a short while, that was gone, too.

With the exception of that fleeting qualm, I was in high spirits for the next few weeks. Protected by my invisible allies, I felt sure that no one could harm me. I was safe from the council of elders, safe from even Herod Antipas and his army if they took a notion to come after me! Herod himself in his walled palace couldn't feel any more secure than I did.

Then, early one morning, another messenger came to the gate. It was Yael, my family's serving woman. She brought the news that my grandmother had died.

Once more tearing my clothing to show grief, I left with my cousin for my brother's house. Susannah tried to comfort me on the way: "Our Safta was a dear woman, and I know how much she loved you especially." Putting her arm in mine, she patted me. "But maybe this is for the best, Mari. She was confused in her mind; she was unhappy. She'd become such a worry to your mother."

What Susannah said was true, but she didn't know what really troubled me: my healing spell for my grandmother had not worked after all. What did that mean?

It means that you can work magic for dark purposes, but not for good, brayed a voice. It sounded like Eleazar trying to talk on his last day, except that somehow I understood the words.

"No!" I screamed. "That's horrible!" I clapped my hands over my ears, as if I could shut off the voice that way.

Susannah drew back from me, looking hurt. "I'm sorry," she said. "I was only trying . . . I'm sad, too."

My cousin had thought I was screaming at her. I couldn't explain, so I hugged her wordlessly. Susannah was one person who truly cared about me.

But she wouldn't, if she knew your secrets, brayed the hateful voice. *Remember Safta's story about Miryam's Well? You have a gift for finding the opposite kind of well: one that poisons all who drink from it.*

I would have screamed again and run blindly through the alleys, except that Phomelei's cool voice broke in. *Silence, Zaphaunt! No one asked you. Lady Mariamne, pay no attention to the donkey-headed one. He has his uses but no manners.*

During our period of mourning for our grandmother, Susannah gently suggested that I should think about getting married again. "You can start over, as if the last year hasn't happened."

But it had happened, I thought with a pang. I could never be the same young girl who'd thought she was offered a life of blessings. And beyond that . . . My mind groped to remember something further that was missing, something even deeper. . . . It was gone.

However, Susannah's advice was sensible. After the time of mourning, I approached Alexandros and explained that I wished to remarry.

My brother looked down on me. "I'm very busy these days," he said. "I don't see how I can do anything for you right now. Uncle Reuben has to mourn a full year for Safta, his mother, of course, and I can't make any important decisions without him."

"But you're arranging Chloe's betrothal," I said. "She told me."

"Ah . . . yes, I am negotiating a match for Chloe," he admitted. "That's why I don't have time to look for a new husband for you."

"You don't want to help me, do you?" I said. *He wants to make you grovel,* said Phomelei.

Alexandros stroked his beard, not so straggly anymore, before answering, "Frankly, I wish I could help you. But I have to consider my position as Elder Thomas's son-in-law. Everyone knows that you were called up before the council and reprimanded—naturally that makes people wonder if you'd be an obedient wife."

I wonder if you'll be an obedient son, Phomelei shot back. I spoke her words, and added, "Didn't Abba make you promise, on his deathbed, to take care of your sisters?"

Alexandros flinched at that, but he recovered quickly. "I

tried to bring you home, but you refused my protection," he said piously. "Uncle Reuben says you're really Silas's responsibility now."

Fury rose in me, and Zaphaunt's bray formed in the back of my throat. But Aiandictor quickly put smooth words in my mouth: "You're right; I apologize for troubling you about this matter. Silas will make a better match for me than you could have, anyway." It was gratifying to see Alexandros's offended look, but I also thought what I'd said was true. Silas listened to Susannah, and my cousin would advise him about the kind of man I would be happy with.

When I asked Silas to negotiate for me instead of my brother, he seemed reluctant at first. Susannah, too, looked troubled. But Silas agreed: he would investigate the husband prospects among men of our class in Magdala.

Meanwhile, the real world grew less vivid to me as I spent more and more time with my invisible allies. "I wish *you* could arrange a new marriage for me!" I exclaimed to them one night. "Can't you? Let Silas think he's doing it."

Leave it to me, my lady, said Aiandictor with a sly smile. *I'll use my connections to find you a prince.*

Phomelei gave a scornful laugh. *Connections! Don't listen to Aiandictor, my lady. First of all, you need an ordinary husband, and we don't arrange ordinary matters. Let Silas find you a match for your humdrum life. Then*—her red lips trembled with amusement—*I'll present you to your real consort. Yes, a prince.*

Aiandictor contradicted her indignantly, and other voices chimed in, including a brassy female voice and a braying male voice. They all argued at once, until I had to order them to be silent. But I was filled with almost unbearable excitement. One way or another, I would have a prince. How could I wait?

In fact, I waited for more than a month before I asked Susannah if Silas had made any progress in finding a husband for me. My cousin shrugged and murmured something vague. She added, "Silas wondered if you might consider taking a husband in another town."

"Perhaps, if it was a nearby town, and if I could visit here," I said. "Which town does he have in mind?"

"Oh yes, it's nearby," said Susannah. "Matthew—the man Silas has in mind—lives outside Bethsaida-Julias, not far from Capernaum. And his father lives in Magdala, so you'd come here often." She didn't seem to know much more about this Matthew, except that he was young and prosperous. "Silas will see if he can arrange a first meeting, then."

EIGHTEEN

THE PROMISING
YOUNG WIDOW

Managing the tollgate month after month, Matthew stopped feeling anything about the travelers streaming under the stone arch. Most of them came to seem like walking money pouches, not human beings. His only interest in them was transferring coins from the pouches into his collection box. His feelings were not exactly tough, like his father's, but numb, like a foot sat on for too long. Matthew's occasional smile, when he recognized one of his few acquaintances approaching the tollgate, stretched his face in an unaccustomed way.

After the harvest season, Alphaeus made a visit to Matthew's new home. Alphaeus hadn't actually seen the house he'd found for Matthew, and he was pleased. "Just what I was told, a comfortable villa. You don't have any trouble paying the rent, do you? No? Good."

As Matthew showed him around the house and garden, his father mentioned that he'd found a promising prospect for a wife for his son. "I don't suppose you'd object to a young widow, eh? I've heard of someone in Magdala—good family, and she has some money of her own."

"I wouldn't mind a young widow at all," said Matthew, his heart leaping hopefully. He'd feared that no respectable Jewish family would even discuss marriage with the tax collector's son.

"Apparently she's a *little* peculiar." Alphaeus waved his hand as if it was nothing to worry about. "And there were some rumors about her keeping Gentile amulets, but you could put a stop to that. I'll arrange a first meeting, then."

Leading his father on through the house to the dining hall, Matthew imagined this young widow very close to him. He would feel her warmth, breathe in her perfume. There would be a pink flush on the curve of her cheek as they sipped from the betrothal cup. . . .

"Even a dining hall, eh?" said Alphaeus. "You must have fancy dinners here!"

His father's comment jerked Matthew out of his daydream. The large, airy room was ideal for fancy dinners: open on one side, with a view of the lake through the pillars. Matthew didn't tell his father that he had trouble filling his fine dining hall with guests. In Capernaum itself, there were only two kinds of Jews who might accept an invitation from the toll collector: his colleagues, the harbor-tax and house-tax collectors; and the brothel owner and his prostitutes. Not such a fancy dinner party.

At the tollgate, Matthew met some interesting travelers, some of them wealthy, important people. But most of them were Greeks, or Phoenicians, or Syrians, or Chaldeans—in other words, Gentiles. Matthew was determined to keep at least the Jewish law against eating with Gentiles. When Quintus Bucco, his supervisor, came by to collect the chest of tolls, Matthew offered him refreshments, as his father did. He sat politely with the Roman while he ate and drank. But after the Roman left, Matthew made sure the servants threw all his dishes (now unclean) on the trash heap.

If it hadn't been for the few Jewish travelers he'd gotten to know, Matthew would have been miserably lonely. Travelers tended to have a more liberal attitude about associating with tax collectors, especially when they were away from home. Such was the case with Philip the salt trader, a short, genial man and Matthew's favorite of these acquaintances. He was well-known around Lake Gennesaret, where he traveled in a slow circle through Galilee on the west side of the lake, Gaulanitis on the northeast, and the independent cities of the Decapolis in the southeast.

Philip had a talent for gathering the latest news from each place and turning it into dramatic stories for the next town. He loved dinner parties, with their natural audience for his storytelling. Matthew looked forward to Philip's visits, not only for his own company but also because the trader attracted other guests. No one wanted to miss such an evening's entertainment.

On the salt merchant's recent visit, he'd told a story about a wandering preacher named Yeshua. The story began as the preacher arrived on the other side of the lake, in some Gentile town above the cliffs. Rabbi Yeshua discovered a poor lost soul, infested with demons, howling naked in the cemetery. The man's family had tried to keep him at home by chaining him, but he'd broken loose and escaped to live among the tombs.

The townspeople warned the rabbi not to go near the wild man. His demons made him bash himself, and anyone else nearby, with stones. But Yeshua went right up to the possessed man and began giving commands to the demons.

Matthew, listening to the story, thought of the rabbi who'd taught him and his brother to read and write. He had a meek manner except when he saw any wrongdoing, such as the older boys bullying the younger ones.

Philip continued with his story. "It was a terrifying scene." He described the townspeople watching from behind the tombs, fearful but fascinated. Confronted by Rabbi Yeshua, the demons threw the possessed man on the ground. He writhed and foamed at the mouth as the unclean spirits spoke through him: "What have you to do with us, Yeshua of Nazareth?"

The rabbi demanded to know the demons' names. They cried out, "We are legion!"

At this point in his story, Philip winked at Matthew and looked around the dining room, making sure everyone got the joke. " 'Legion'—meaning 'many,' but also meaning a legion of the Roman army, see?"

The guests snickered at the suggestion that Roman soldiers were demons. Matthew smiled, too. Any joke on those self-appointed masters of the world was a good joke.

The story continued: The demons bargained with Yeshua. They'd leave the possessed man quietly if only the rabbi wouldn't banish them to the pit of everlasting fire.

But where else could they go? asked Yeshua. They couldn't expect him to allow them to possess someone else.

Desperate, the demons noticed a herd of pigs on the

hillside. "Let us possess the pigs!" they begged. So the rabbi gave permission, and instantly the legion entered the pigs.

Philip paused again, savoring the roars of laughter. A legion of Romans as not only demons but also a herd of unclean animals!

"And now the pigs were as wild as that poor fellow used to be, and they rushed down the cliff and drowned in the lake," continued the storyteller. "Meanwhile, the man freed from demons put on his clothes and told everyone he knew, in a perfectly sane voice, how he'd been saved." Philip looked around the room with a little smile, signaling a final joke. "And then, you'd think, they all flocked to this rabbi, this holy man of great power, for healings and blessings?"

"But they didn't?" prompted Matthew.

"Not at all!" said the storyteller. "They didn't want anything to do with that Rabbi Yeshua! The townspeople begged him, very politely and sincerely, to please leave and never come back again. For they all had large herds of pigs." The dining room rang with more laughter and applause.

A fine story, thought Matthew. It insulted the Romans and made fun of the Gentiles. It also showed the rabbi's cleverness. He'd tricked the demons into leaving the possessed man. The rabbi had had a good idea how the pigs would react to being possessed. And once the pigs were dead, of course the demons had nowhere to go.

As the laughter died away, a woman at the back of the room spoke up. "I wonder where all those demons went?"

There was an uneasy silence, and several of the guests made the sign against the evil eye, to ward off any stray demons that might have drifted across the lake. Matthew, eager to keep the party going, clapped Philip on the shoulder. "Tell us some more news, my friend!" So the salt merchant launched into a description of the magnificent public square that Herod Antipas was building in Tiberias.

A few weeks later, after the rainy season had begun, Matthew received a message from his father: the first meeting in Magdala with the young woman and her family had been arranged. Her name was Mariamne, widow of Eleazar. Her father was no longer living, but her cousin's husband, a well-thought-of cloth dyer, was negotiating for her. She'd been married only briefly before; her old husband had died of a stroke, and there were no children.

Again Matthew imagined the beautiful young widow close to him, and he caught his breath. He quickly made arrangements to leave the tollgate in charge of his guards for a few days.

On the appointed day, Matthew and his father put on

their best striped coats and hurried through a downpour to the house of Silas, Mariamne's cousin-in-law. The host himself met them at the gate and showed them to the upper room, where a young woman with a round, cheerful face took their wet cloaks. Matthew liked her on sight, and a picture flashed in his mind of her tenderly washing his feet at the end of a long day's work.

"Welcome to our home," Silas said to Alphaeus and Matthew. "This is my wife, Susannah. And this is her cousin, Mariamne." He motioned to a tall girl standing behind Susannah who bowed to them.

So *this* was Mariamne. She was pretty enough, thought Matthew. But her cool way of looking at him, as she helped her cousin serve refreshments, made him uneasy. After they were all sitting on the cushions making polite conversation, he noticed that her slim hands moved restlessly. She kept touching her left shoulder, and at times she seemed to be listening to faraway sounds.

Aside from that, Matthew thought there was something familiar about this girl. Of course, he may very well have seen her in Magdala sometime or other. Perhaps in the synagogue, in the years when Alphaeus and his sons were still attending.

It was pleasant for a tax collector to be welcomed into a respectable Jewish home so cordially, even though Matthew had been told why Silas and Susannah were eager to promote this match. According to a reliable source, Alphaeus said, Silas had taken a bad loss on a shipment of cloth to Sepphoris. The entire shipment had been stolen on the road by bandits.

Matthew glanced at his father. Alphaeus was saying to Silas with a meaningful smile, "I wouldn't be surprised if your cloth could slip out of the harbor from now on without paying any customs tax." He nudged Silas to make his meaning clear.

Silas nodded, looking embarrassed. "Most gracious . . . most appreciated," he muttered.

"Please take another spice cake, sir!" Susannah put in, offering the platter again. "I baked them just this morning."

Matthew caught Mariamne staring at him with a slight frown, and he realized that he'd been looking at her the same way. Suddenly an expression of disgust and contempt came over her face. In that same moment, he knew where he'd seen her before, with exactly that same expression. "You're the girl who spit on our doorway," he said in an undertone.

"And *you* are the tax collector's son!" Mariamne didn't bother to lower her voice. She turned on Susannah. "How could you possibly think—" Jumping to her feet, she backed toward the wall. In a different, imperious voice she declared, "I was promised a prince. I deserve a prince! I spit again, on you and your offer of marriage."

Mariamne seemed ready to actually spit on Matthew, except that her cousin leaped up, grabbed her arm, and turned her aside. Still, Mariamne continued to speak in a queenly voice that was interspersed with chirps uncannily like a bird's.

The rest of them jumped up, too. Silas was talking quickly, making soothing motions, but Alphaeus cut him off. "A *little odd,* you told me," he accused Silas. "Odd! This girl is out of her mind. She imagines she's some kind of a princess, or is it a sparrow? You thought you'd fob her off on us . . . oh yes, good enough for the tax collector. Maybe she has leprosy, too?"

A wave of fury and shame swept through Matthew. How could a shrewd businessman like Alphaeus have been deceived? He was almost angrier for his father's sake than for his own.

"Your business isn't really in trouble, is it?" Matthew demanded of Silas. "That was just a cover for the truth about her. And the truth is, you'd better take her to an exorcist. After that, maybe someone else will have her!" Grabbing his still-damp cloak from a peg, Matthew stamped out into the driving rain.

Alphaeus followed his son down the stairs, flinging over his shoulder, "And don't expect any customs-tax breaks from me!"

NINETEEN

THE TOLL COLLECTOR PAYS

The first morning after his return from Magdala, Matthew rode up to the tollgate in a gloomy state of mind. So much for his bright marriage prospects with the suitable young widow. "A little peculiar," his father had told him! Completely deranged was more like it.

To add further insult, the demented woman had scorned *him*. She might be stark, staring mad, but she wouldn't sully herself by marrying a toll collector. Matthew laughed hollowly. He supposed it was good that both he and the young widow, although shunned by the rest of the Jewish community, still had their shreds of pride left.

Matthew squinted into the morning sun. A group was approaching the tollgate from the east, the direction of

Bethsaida-Julias. It wasn't a merchant's caravan, or a train of cushioned wagons bearing wealthy travelers, or farmers with carts full of produce. Just a group of men on foot. Judging from their rough, worn clothes, their cloaks had to double as their blankets at night.

There were about thirty in the group, but as they approached the gate, several dropped away. These laborers couldn't afford to pay the toll, even the small fee for travelers on foot without merchandise. Instead, they'd hike over the rocky hillside and rejoin the road farther south.

Matthew expected the whole group to peel off—why should any of them pay just to walk through his gate? But the core of the group, led by a tall, long-faced man with an easy stride, kept coming. As they neared the gate, Matthew heard the others arguing with their leader. "Rabbi, why not turn aside? Why should we pay the toll? We need to save the money. Simon can't feed all of us."

"That's right, Rabbi," said the biggest man in the group. "On this road, we always cut across the hill back there, to duck the toll."

Since they were calling the tall man rabbi, Matthew guessed that he must be one of the many wandering preachers who led disciples here and there around Galilee. Matthew glanced up at the ridge to see if Herod's soldiers were keeping watch—although this ragtag band didn't look like much of a threat.

Their leader held up one hand to answer his followers. "It's important to walk through the tollgate," he answered. "I have business there." The others fell silent.

What possible business could a wandering preacher have at the tollgate? wondered Matthew.

The rabbi stopped in front of him. "Peace, Matthew bar Alphaeus."

Matthew was startled. The rabbi had called him by name. Of course, he might have found out Matthew's name from another traveler. What was much more surprising, a holy man was greeting a toll collector as if he was a decent human being. Matthew felt confused. "Peace, rabbi," he mumbled.

The rabbi caught Matthew's gaze and held it. "I've been looking forward to meeting you," he said.

What! Matthew was too amazed to answer. He glanced at the rabbi's disciples to see if this was a joke. But they looked as surprised as Matthew felt.

Finding his voice, Matthew was further surprised by the words he spoke: "Let's see—ten of you would be four sestercii—I'll give you a break and call it only three sestercii. Wait . . . only two sestercii."

The rabbi nodded and gestured to one of his followers to pay the toll. But he didn't gush with gratitude, as Matthew expected. He looked at Matthew encouragingly, the way a patient teacher looks at a pupil who has learned *aleph,* the first letter of the alphabet.

Then the rabbi walked through the stone arch, and his disciples followed like ducklings after their mother. They took the branch of the highway that wound down toward the lakeshore, and soon they were out of sight.

One of the guards said to his fellows, "Now that's a new trick, the way that rabbi got his whole gang through the gate for half the toll!" The other guards didn't look openly scornful—Matthew paid their wages, after all—but Matthew knew he'd lost some of their respect.

Strangely, Matthew didn't feel tricked. He felt as if a new possibility had opened up for him. He watched the rabbi and his disciples reappear farther down the hill, turning off on a dirt road that led to Capernaum. Matthew went over in his mind how it had felt when that man met his gaze. When he said, "I've been looking forward to meeting you."

He really did want to meet me, thought Matthew. The rabbi was a working-class man for whom even two sestercii was a price to be spent carefully. Rabbi Yeshua must have thought it was worth the price, to meet Matthew. To get his attention? Matthew was mystified but at the same time filled with hope.

Matthew's hopeful mood grew during the rest of the day.

He gave a reduced rate to several travelers, none of whom could do him any favors. He restrained his guards from beating an olive oil merchant who tried to sneak around the tollgate. He didn't overcharge anyone, not even the obviously wealthy trader with the Persian rugs.

At home that evening, however, Matthew began to worry a little. The tolls he'd collected that day didn't even add up to the Romans' portion. He had to take a few coins from his own money chest and put them in the Romans' strongbox. Well, it was all right to be generous at the tollgate for one day. He'd make up for it the next day.

But in the next days and weeks, generosity became a habit with Matthew. He got a secret thrill out of seeing travelers react to his unexpected kindness. Some of them looked as if they hadn't expected any good surprises for the rest of their lives. When their eyes widened and their faces lifted, Matthew felt his own heart lift. It was like the satisfaction he used to feel for protecting his brother from the bullies at synagogue school, and now he seemed to sense James's approving gaze on him.

Matthew began attending the Sabbath prayer meetings in Capernaum again. He still got a chilly reception at the synagogue, but it was worth it on the days that the rabbi was there. Rabbi Yeshua, as he was called, apparently traveled a good deal; the rest of the time he lived in Capernaum with Simon, one of his disciples. Whenever Yeshua caught sight of Matthew at the Sabbath meeting, he nodded and said, "*Shalom.*" No one else did, not even Yeshua's followers.

Yeshua's followers. How had the rabbi chosen them? Matthew wondered. Most of them seemed to be peasants— fishermen or other laborers—but each of them had an air of confidence that didn't fit with their low class.

There were even *women* among Yeshua's disciples! It took Matthew a few weeks to come to this conclusion because, at first, he naturally thought the women in Yeshua's following must be either wives of the disciples, or prostitutes. But these women did not act meek, like wives, nor did they have the come-hither manner of prostitutes. Like the men, they seemed confident in themselves. Furthermore, Rabbi Yeshua spoke to them as if he hadn't noticed they were women.

After a Sabbath meeting, Rabbi Yeshua would lead a crowd out of the village to the hillside. They sat down there to listen to him speak. Matthew came, too, but he stood at the back of the crowd, so as not to make people shrink from him. He listened to the rabbi like a dog gobbling scraps.

"Blessed are the merciful," said Rabbi Yeshua one day, "for they shall obtain mercy."

"Yes!" Matthew exclaimed, causing people to turn and

stare at him. But didn't they see? It was just simple arithmetic, like "two and two is four." When Matthew went easy
on a poor traveler at the tollgate, he could feel his own mercy
reflected back on himself.

At the end of the month, the Roman overseer came by to
collect the take from the tollgate. Matthew noticed that
Quintus Bucco looked weary. "I hope all's well with you and
your family," said Matthew.

Bucco shot him a puzzled look. "My family? I suppose
they're well. I don't see much more of them than I see of you.
They're at the main garrison in Caesarea, and my route cov-
ers all of stinking Galilee." Slumping onto Matthew's couch,
he helped himself to wine. "But let's stick to business, toll
collector. They're raising the rates."

"What!" exclaimed Matthew. "Half the people who use
the highway can hardly afford it as it is."

"Then they shouldn't be using the highway," said Bucco.
"Or," he added with a humorless laugh, "you don't have to
charge them the new rate. You can pay the difference yourself."

Matthew was startled to hear Bucco say exactly what he'd
been thinking. Bucco was joking, of course. Matthew looked
thoughtfully at the table on which the wine and cakes rested.
It was a fine piece of furniture, its top inlaid with a pattern of

lotus flowers and palm branches. He could sell that to raise some money. And he could sell the silver lamp stands, as well as several other costly items he didn't really need. He could let half of his servants go.

Matthew knew what was wrong with this plan. Sooner or later, he'd run out of furniture to sell and servants to let go. Then what? He didn't know. But for now, Matthew was sure of what he wanted to do.

TWENTY

POSSESSED

As the tax collector and his son disappeared into the storm, Phomelei made me rail at Susannah: "Is that what you think I deserve, a filthy traitor who works for the Romans?" I followed her into the bedchamber, where the baby was whimpering and Kanarit was trying to soothe him. "Do you want me to become an outcast?"

"Hush!" said Susannah. "You're frightening the children." She picked up the baby from his cradle and pulled Kanarit close to her side. The little girl hid her face in Susannah's robe.

"You're frightening the children," chirped the sparrow through my mouth.

"Mari, you've already become an outcast." My cousin

looked horrified at her own words, but she took a deep breath and looked me squarely in the face. "What's the matter with you? Everyone asks me, 'Why does your cousin talk to herself on the street—sometimes in different voices? What really happened to Eleazar?' They ask me, 'Aren't you afraid to have her in the house with your children?'"

Phomelei raised my hand to slap her. Then I noticed Kanarit peering fearfully at me, and I let my arm fall. I walked out of the chamber and through the common room, where Silas stood looking dazed. I dashed down the stairs through the rain.

The voices beat on my mind like the drumming raindrops. *How dare your cousin and her husband treat you like this!* Phomelei hissed. Aiandictor said, *Don't they understand how powerful you are?* Zaphaunt brayed, *They deserve to be punished.* A hoarse and grating voice broke in, *Yes, punish them. Make the baby sick, and see how they like that.*

"No!" I exclaimed. "That's an evil thought. I command you, go back to the garden!" I sat down in my apartment, shaking. *Quiet, fool!* exclaimed Phomelei. *Who let you out? She isn't ready.* The voices trickled off to an inaudible mutter.

Toward suppertime, Susannah came to my door and said she was sorry. I said I was sorry, too. Neither of us took back what we'd said during the shouting, but we hugged in a gingerly way. I came to supper and helped Susannah serve while Kanarit followed me with big eyes and Silas avoided looking at me.

During the meal, Silas talked in his quiet, matter-of-fact way, relating some dull bits of news about the fishing catch in Capernaum and a dispute between two landowners near Bethsaida-Julias. Obviously, he must have learned these things as he'd made inquiries about a husband for me, but he didn't mention that.

"They say there's a new preacher in that area," Silas went on. "He's from Nazareth, but he's living in Capernaum now, in the house of one of his disciples."

This didn't strike me as any more fascinating than the fishing catch, but Susannah asked, "A new preacher? Is he any different from all the other preachers?"

"I don't know," said Silas. "This Yeshua bar Yosef is gathering a large following. They say he performs healings. He drives out unclean spirits, too. Maybe he'll come to Magdala."

Suddenly I had a hard time paying attention to Silas because a murmuring began in my head, growing louder and louder.

Watch out for that holy man! chirped the sparrow.

Oh, worse than a holy man, brayed Zaphaunt. *Curse his name!*

Do not say his name, warned Phomelei. *That's asking for trouble.*

Curse him, then. That was Aiandictor, although his usually smooth voice sounded strained.

"Maybe Herod Antipas will cut off his head," suggested the harsh voice. I was afraid he might be right; after all, Herod Antipas had done just that to another such preacher, John the Baptizer.

"The Lord forbid it!" exclaimed Silas. "And I, as head of this family, forbid you to say such things."

"For shame, Mari!" said Susannah.

Oh no—they'd heard what the voice said about Herod Antipas. I stammered some kind of apology to Silas and Susannah, but I was distracted by Phomelei giving me hurried advice: *Of course, it was Odjit speaking, not you, but best not to try to explain that.*

It seemed that my advisors and protectors, with all their powers, were badly frightened of this preacher Yeshua. It made me afraid, too.

On the Sabbath, it was still raining. I started to go to the synagogue as usual with Susannah and Silas. We hurried down the avenue to the meeting hall, holding our shawls over our heads. I was looking forward to hearing the Scripture read and praying with the congregation. I hoped it would soothe my spirit.

They won't let you in, you know, a voice brayed in my head. *You're disgusting, with those beetles crawling all over you.*

"What beetles?" I recognized that voice; it was Zaphaunt, the donkey head. I wasn't going to let him annoy me. But now I felt a tickle on my left ankle. Tiny feet—many, many feet—hundreds and hundreds—creeping up my right ankle, too, over my knees . . .

"Aagh!" Pulling up my robe, I slapped at the green beetles on my legs.

The beetles fell off and disappeared. Susannah and Silas were staring at me. So was everyone else on the street. I dropped the hem of my robe.

Other Jews on their way to synagogue walked around me in a wide circle. "Look away from that woman!" a mother told her children.

"Mari, are you ill?" asked Susannah.

"Yes," I gasped. "I have to go home. Please, go on without me." Pulling my scarf over my face and ducking my head, I turned and hurried back to my apartment.

That's right, you'd better hide yourself, the mean voice told me. *You're unclean.*

In my room, I sat on the bench and stared at the plastered wall. How could I not have realized that I was indeed unclean, infested—infested with beings much worse than green beetles?

The demon voices were quiet for the moment, but my own thoughts told me the truth: I am possessed. Possessed. *Possessed.*

At first, I was too frightened to step out of my apartment, and I didn't even think of visiting my private garden. I huddled in a corner, reciting all the prayers I could remember, as the rainwater gurgled down the drain in the courtyard. The words of Scripture seemed to keep the voices down to a background murmur.

After a day or so, the rain let up. I felt calmer, and the voices were finally silent. Maybe I'd frightened too easily; maybe I could control them after all, by saying prayers. Surely, I could venture out to the market? I needed flour and oil, and at the same time, I could look for a little present for Kanarit.

As I walked down the avenue, the sun came out of the clouds and shone on the rain-washed paving stones. Outside the marketplace, the usual cluster of beggars held out their hands. There was a new face among them, a girl with pathetically shriveled legs. Deciding to give her my extra coin, I stepped toward her.

"Oh, poor me!" sneered a coarse voice through my mouth. "I can't walk right—I keep falling into camel dung— take pity on me!"

I was horrified, but I couldn't stop a guffaw from bursting out of my throat. *"Hawr, hawr!"* The laughter went on and on, as uncontrollable as vomiting. The crippled girl pulled back her hand, and another beggar snatched the coin from me. Passersby stared at me as I hurried on into the market, gasping.

I was a fool! I shouldn't have come out. Shrieks filled my ears, as if a flock of crows were flying around my head. I turned and ran back through the market, waving my arms to fend them off.

Before I reached Susannah's house, I was gasping for breath again, and I leaned against the wall in an alley. There was only one voice now, the cultured, cool voice of Phomelei. *Lady Mariamne, a thousand apologies. The others can be crude at times. But you and I understand that.*

"Silence!" I whispered.

My lady, I'm so sorry for that unfortunate incident. I'll make up for it, I vow. I'll help you . . . aren't I helping you right now? I have them under control, and they'll think twice about disobeying

you again. But you need to learn how to handle them. I can assist
you with that. . . . I long to assist you, dear Lady Mariamne!

"How can you possibly assist me?" I asked coldly.

Why, I can help you get the new husband you deserve, my
lady. Oh yes, I know I said we didn't deal with such ordinary mat-
ters, but finding your new husband is a more serious matter than
I realized. Silas means well, but he's been going about it all
wrong.

"Never mind a husband," I snapped. "Those spirits must
not get out of hand again. Promise me that, and I might listen to you."

I promise, with all my heart, on the honor of my name,
Phomelei. Her voice rang with sincerity. *Your wish will be easy*
to fulfill because you possess such gifts, Lady Mariamne! When
you learn how to use your powers, you'll only have to lift your lit-
tle finger and the spirit world will grovel at your feet.

The sweet words ran over me like honey. Yes, it made
sense that I still had much to learn about tapping and controlling my special gifts. After all, when I began to learn embroidery stitches, as a little girl, my work was slow and
awkward. But by the time I was twelve, I could sew embroidery that a noblewoman would be proud to wear.

But about your husband! Phomelei went on. *The first step is*
for you to decide on the man you want. Then I'll advise you about

how to apply the correct love charm. The very next day, the man himself will approach Silas and beg for a speedy betrothal. She chuckled gently. *It's that easy.*

I walked slowly through the alley to my cousin's house and stepped into the courtyard. Susannah and the serving woman were at work on a pile of flax stalks, beating them to expose the fibers. The baby lay in his basket in the shade, fussing a little from his teeth coming in. Kanarit was getting in the women's way, dashing under their arms as she tried to help.

"Kanarit, come with me," I said to the little girl. "I want to show you a surprise." Susannah cast me an uneasy look, but she didn't object as I led her daughter up to the roof.

"Did you bring me something from the market, cousin Mari?" piped Kanarit. She spoke well for such a young child.

The market. It seemed like days ago that I'd set out for the market. I hadn't bought the treat I'd intended for Kanarit, I realized, or even flour and oil. "I have something even better for you," I promised. I had no idea what I meant, but I'd make up something. "I'm going to teach you . . ."

Kanarit gazed up at me with wide, shining eyes. Aiandictor urged me, *She deserves something really wonderful, not just an ordinary game.*

"I'm going to teach you how to fly!" This was the best idea I'd ever had! *I* might be an outcast, a woman fit only to marry a toll collector, but Kanarit was young enough that she could still achieve marvelous things. In great excitement, I pulled her to the low railing at the edge of the rooftop.

Kanarit looked down on the awning of the kitchen shed, and the courtyard below it, then back at me. Excitement and fear mixed in her face. "I can't," she said. "People can't fly."

"*Most* people can't fly," I corrected her. "But you're a girl with rare gifts! For you, it'll be easy." Lifting under her arms, I set Kanarit on the edge of the wall. "All you have to do is think about where you're going to land. Do you see the top of my apartment, across the courtyard?"

The little girl nodded uncertainly, but she flexed her knees for the jump.

Just then, Susannah paused in her work and glanced up. "What are you doing up there? Kanarit!" There was a sharp note of fear in her voice. "Get down this instant!"

At Susannah's voice, the spell was broken. Kanarit stiffened and twisted around, clutching at me. "Imma!" she screamed back to her mother. She managed to grab a strand of my hair. Yelping with pain, I pried at her hands.

And then somehow—it seemed to happen very slowly— Kanarit squirmed out of my grasp. For an instant, she clung to me by my hair, but her weight pulled the strands out by the roots. Tumbling backward off the wall, she crashed onto the kitchen awning, slid to the edge, grabbed a handful of thatch and hung from it for a moment, then thumped onto the pile of flax in the courtyard.

TWENTY-ONE

A GOOD BROTHER

I guess she can't fly after all, brayed an idiotic voice in my head. Other voices chuckled.

I pounded down the steps; Susannah was already kneeling by her daughter. "Little girl, my heart, Kanarit, speak," she pleaded. The child lay still, eyes closed, one hand still clutching the lock of my hair and the other hand a wisp of thatch.

As I dropped to my knees beside them, Susannah turned on me. "You killed my child!" she screamed. "Are you possessed?"

Then—Kanarit must have been only stunned—she blinked, drew in breath, and let out a howl. From the basket against the wall, the baby gave an answering wail. A neighbor shouted from the nearest rooftop, "What's the matter? We're coming!" The racket almost drowned out the voices in my head.

Susannah began to feel Kanarit's arms and legs for broken bones. I reached out, trying to soothe the child. "Kanarit, dear—"

My cousin hit me away with the back of her hand. "Go!" she snarled. "Leave!"

"Cousin, I don't blame you for being upset," said Phomelei through my mouth, "but she wasn't in danger until you screamed. You frightened her, making her lose—"

"Go!"

It's no use trying to talk to her until they all calm down, Phomelei told me in a concerned tone. *Leave for a while and let it blow over.*

I wasn't sure it would blow over, but I didn't know what else to do. Holding my sore scalp, I retreated to my apartment.

I wasn't alone there because the invisible beings swirled around, discussing me and arguing. The sparrow chirped primly, *Your advisors are very disappointed in you, and I can't say that I blame them.*

Voices darted in like stinging wasps:

She doesn't have the courage to follow through.

If you ask me, she's not gifted at all.

She fancies herself as Queen Mariamne!

Queen of the dung heap is more like it, sneered Odjit's raw, hideous voice. It spoke directly to me. *Here, you! Yes, you with the bald patch—I'm talking to you. Why don't you go into business as a prostitute? At least that way, you'd be performing a valuable service.*

Or, even better—a new voice, as cold and hard as stone—*walk into the lake tonight and don't come back.*

Walk into the lake? I thought bleakly. Yes, that might be the best idea.

I realized dimly that someone, a real person, was in the doorway. It was my cousin. I struggled to focus on her. "Susannah . . . my dear friend from childhood . . . Forgive me for frightening you so badly. I wasn't myself . . . I didn't mean . . ."

"Here," she said, holding out a handful of silver coins. "Here is the rent you paid us. You are no longer my cousin. Leave this house."

"But where could we go?" Aiandictor made me plead.

"Get out! Go! Get out!"

Silas appeared behind Susannah and, behind him, the neighbor who'd gone to fetch him. "Hush," Silas told his wife. "Kanarit is safe now. We'll take your cousin to the council. They'll know what to do."

Gripping my arms, the two men hustled me out the gate. The voices continued to speak through me. Phomelei protested, "This is simply outrageous." Aiandictor tried to explain: "Can't we be reasonable about this? It was an accident, it could have happened to anyone, but then Susannah became hysterical and blamed *us*." Dionesiona leaned against Silas and asked in a husky voice, "Did you know it was your wife who got me involved with magic?" She gave a low, seductive chuckle. "What a good joke—Susannah, the model Jewish wife, as a channel to the dark powers!"

The neighbor threw Silas a fearful glance. Silas nodded grimly. "That's them speaking. Don't listen." The men pulled me through the alley to the avenue.

They're going to chain you up in the hills like the wild boy! warned my advisors in a chorus. Zaphaunt bucked and brayed, but the men only gripped me tighter. As we struggled down the avenue, I was dimly aware of onlookers gathering, horrified but fascinated.

The cloud of spirits swarmed around us, almost choking me as they shrieked, snarled, and cajoled: "I must insist that you unhand me at once." "Good people, have pity on a poor woman unjustly accused!" "Stone these men! Beat them!"

At the synagogue, Elder Thomas came out on the porch accompanied by a scribe. Silas called up the steps, "Revered elder, my wife's cousin is demon-ridden."

"Demon-ridden!" brayed Zaphaunt. "Not that!"

"Stay there," the elder told Silas, looking alarmed. "You must not bring the unclean woman into the house of prayer."

It hurt my feelings that Elder Thomas called me unclean, and I thought I would burst into tears. Instead, with Odjit's monstrous strength I wrenched free of the men's grasp. Odjit's voice grated, "You're afraid of us, aren't you, revered elder? Better run inside! Quick, or we might *touch* you!" Stomping up the steps, Odjit reached out his claws. "We're coming to get you! *Hawr, hawr, hawr!*"

Silas and his neighbor lunged after me and dragged me back down the steps. Panting with the effort, Silas explained to Elder Thomas that I'd tried to make his little girl fly off the roof. "What should be done with my wife's cousin, Elder?" he asked. "Could she be kept in the hospitality rooms next to the synagogue?"

As the elder put up a horrified hand to fend off that idea, the scribe spoke to him. "Isn't this young woman Mariamne, daughter of Tobias, widow of Eleazar—and sister of your son-in-law, Alexandros?"

Elder Thomas squinted at me. Phomelei spoke up in her most imperious tone. "Yes, I am your cousin's widow and your son-in-law's sister. Surely you will not allow these ruffians to malign and manhandle me."

"Revered elder," said Silas, "I bring this woman to you

only because her brother and uncle have washed their hands of her."

Elder Thomas sighed heavily. "This is not right." He nodded to the scribe. "Send to the docks for Alexandros bar Tobias and his uncle Reuben."

A servant was sent, but it took some time for Alexandros to appear. Meanwhile, my advisors and I hit out and cursed and made lewd suggestions. "I'm Artemis of Ephesus, you know," Dionesiona told the men. "Let me show you my many breasts."

The men covered their ears. When Dionesiona began to tear off my clothes, Silas took off his belt and bound my hands. Just as he finished tying the knot, my brother hurried around the corner with the messenger. Uncle Reuben was close behind him.

Alexandros stared at me, aghast. "Mari?" Zaphaunt brayed, thinking it was a good joke that my appearance frightened Alexandros.

Uncle Reuben said, "Peace, Elder Thomas," and my brother added, "Peace, Father-in-law." But they looked the opposite of peaceful.

"This woman is your niece and your sister, is she not?" asked the elder. "I am deeply disappointed to be allied with a family so lacking in responsibility for its members." He went on at some length, sprinkling his lecture with quotations from the Law.

As Alexandros visibly struggled to gather his wits, Uncle Reuben was the first to speak: "With all due respect, Elder, isn't it harsh to say that my nephew has abandoned his responsibility? My niece has always been difficult—willful and selfish."

"She herself asked to live under Silas's roof, rather than mine," Alexandros finally put in. "I have my widowed mother, my wife, and now a child to take care of. Business is bad."

"No matter how many excuses you give," said Elder Thomas sharply, "you must now take charge of your sister. This is our way, as people of the Law. We are not beasts or Gentiles, to cast off our kin when they inconvenience us."

"But what can I *do* with her, Father-in-law?" pleaded Alexandros. "Surely you wouldn't want your daughter Sarah and your little grandson exposed to unclean spirits?"

"No one could expect us to keep her in *our* house," said Uncle Reuben.

"That house is not *yours,* uncle!" Zaphaunt mocked him.

Elder Thomas fingered his silver belt buckle and frowned. He opened his mouth as if to make a pronouncement, then shut it again. My brother's argument about Sarah and the baby must have hit home.

"Revered elder," the scribe spoke up, "if I might suggest . . . Perhaps your son-in-law could take the woman to an exorcist."

Elder Thomas's eyebrows lifted thoughtfully, and he nodded several times. "Yes, an excellent idea. Don't they say there's a new exorcist in Capernaum? Take her to Capernaum."

Alexandros began to protest that he was much too busy to leave his business for the day, and Uncle Reuben added that they couldn't afford to pay an exorcist. But I could barely hear them because my spirit advisors were also protesting, all trying to speak at once. They shouted threats: they would mutilate Alexandros's manly organs, send a pack of unclean dogs to swim in the *mikvah,* destroy the coming harvest with hail.

Undoing a pouch from his belt, Elder Thomas tossed it to Alexandros. "See, now you have the exorcist's fee. Depart without delay." Dismissing us with a wave, he disappeared into the synagogue.

Silas also seemed to think he'd done all anyone could expect of him. "It might be wise to tie her hands before I take back my belt," he suggested to Alexandros. So my brother was forced to untie his own belt and bind me with that. Silas then nodded to Alexandros, as if to wish him good luck, and hurried off with his neighbor, tying his belt back around his waist.

Uncle Reuben said grimly to Alexandros, "Elder Thomas may be a wise and important man, but he doesn't have to take a harridan into *his* house. Listen, nephew." He dropped his voice and continued in an urgent tone. "Here's what we're going to do: We're going to take one of our fishing boats and sail north toward Capernaum. If the madwoman throws herself out of the boat before we get there . . . no one could blame us for such an accident."

My attendants, all but one, screamed a chorus of curses and insults. But Panhasaziel and I approved of my uncle's plan. Panhasaziel showed me the water closing over my head, and I agreed that would be a great relief.

My brother hesitated, looking from me, to the clinking pouch in his hand, to our uncle, and back to me again. To my surprise, he said slowly, "No."

"What?" exclaimed Uncle Reuben. "Are you also possessed? To speak frankly, your father-in-law has misjudged the case. You bear no further responsibility to this woman. One might even say she is no longer your sister."

"No," Alexandros repeated with a heavy sigh. "I promised Abba I would take care of my sisters. I cannot break my promise."

Our uncle sputtered, "You stubborn, foolish . . ." Then he threw up his hands and said, "As you wish. I know *my* responsibility: to put in a day's work at the packinghouse."

Uncle Reuben left, and Alexandros stood uncertainly in front of the synagogue. A few onlookers, curious but keeping their distance from my demons, peered from alleyways. "Good people," whined Aiandictor, "see how this man mistreats me! Have pity on me—do not let him take me away!" They didn't answer. Some stared and pointed; some whispered to one another.

Rousing himself, Alexandros took a firmer grip on my arm and headed for the waterfront. At first, when he approached the boats, several fishermen were eager to earn the fare to Capernaum. "Just you and the lady, sir?" asked one man as he dropped the net he was mending.

Alexandros opened his mouth to reply, but Phomelei's queenly voice announced first, "Not at all. My entire court will attend me. Hear their names."

My brother tried to clap his hand over my mouth, but I squirmed away. My attendants spoke in voice after distinct voice: "Dionesiona." "Odjit." "Zaphaunt." "Aiandictor." "Phomelei." "Panhasaziel."

The fishermen made the sign against the evil eye, and some of them threw pebbles at me. The one who'd offered to take us backed away, shouting, "I wouldn't let her in my boat for all the gold in the Temple!"

Alexandros hastily pulled me away from the shore. "All right," he said, gritting his teeth. "The journey by boat would be only half as long, but we'll take the road instead. I'll hire donkeys."

Sometime later, we rode north out of Magdala. My hands were still tied, and Alexandros's unbelted robe hung loose. "Four times the going rate for donkeys I had to pay!" he muttered, trying to keep the hem of his robe from dragging in the dirt. "You'd think they didn't know whose son-in-law I am."

We chortled and cackled and guffawed, *"Hawr, hawr!"*

As soon as we were outside the walls, Odjit seized his chance. He kicked the donkey; he pounded on its neck; he roared in its ears and bit them. The donkey bucked, throwing me against Alexandros's donkey and knocking my brother off.

Alexandros managed to hold on to his donkey's rope, but the animal wrenched its head free and bolted after my donkey into the hills. Alexandros and I sprawled in the dusty road.

"Now you've done it!" My brother scrambled to his feet and started to dash after the donkeys, then realized they were gone. He looked down at me, and Phomelei looked up at him with a smug smile.

Alexandros glared at me, sighed deeply, and raised his arms to the sky. "Oh Lord, what sin have I committed, that you burdened me with such a sister?" Then, dropping the donkey's rope around my neck, he led me like a beast up the road toward Capernaum.

TWENTY-TWO

CLEAN

Alexandros and I struggled along the lakeshore road all day. "From Magdala to Capernaum should take only half a day, even on foot," moaned my brother. "Even though we left late in the morning, even if we paused at Gennesaret for a midday meal and rest. But not Alexandros bar Tobias and his demented sister, oh no! For us, it's two steps forward, one step back."

Indeed, to me it seemed that I traveled the same short stretch of road over and over, like a donkey plodding around an olive press. Moving as if through a mist, I hardly saw the blue lake on one side or the fresh green fields on the other. The demons jostled around me and through me, muttering and bickering among themselves.

"If only she had behaved like a lady of distinction and kept her head scarf on," hissed Phomelei, "we would be treated as befits our dignity."

"I've always maintained that discretion is the key," said Aiandictor. "Smile, speak softly, slip the dagger into the ribs." Zaphaunt chanted a stupid song over and over, guffawing after every chorus.

I looked for the sparrow, thinking to send him for help, but he was nowhere to be seen. It occurred to me that slavering Odjit might have eaten him. I couldn't see Panhasaziel, but I sensed he was behind me, breathing out dread at every step.

From time to time, other travelers appeared through the mist. I heard a man tell his companion, "Step aside until they pass! Look how her loose hair hangs over her face—look how his robe flaps open. See how they rant at the empty air."

Alexandros was offended. "I am not possessed, you fools!" he called out to them. "I'm going to great expense and trouble to take my sister to an exorcist, and if you think it's easy, you should try it yourselves." He gave a yank on my halter.

The travelers, pointing and shaking their heads, watched us pass from a distance. My brother trudged forward, grim-faced, and I staggered over the pavement behind him.

Dionesiona called over my shoulder to the travelers, "Come see me at my temple in Sepphoris!" and Zaphaunt laughed long and senselessly.

Time passed. I heard Aiandictor plotting something with Odjit, but the others were bickering too loudly for me to make it out. I didn't know what they intended until Aiandictor exclaimed, "Now!" We leaped on Alexandros's back and hooked my bound arms under his chin, choking him. Falling together, my brother and I rolled around on the dusty paving stones. Odjit managed to jab my knee into the small of Alexandros's back before he wrenched himself free.

The demons came through the struggle unscathed although I was badly bruised and scraped. My brother ordered me to walk in front of him. "You won't pull that trick again," he snarled.

"We'll try another trick, then," said Zaphaunt, laughing at his own wit.

And in fact, just as Alexandros remarked, "We've reached Gennesaret, at least," they caught him in an unguarded moment. Whirling on him, we kicked the end of the bridle from my brother's hand, then dashed off the road into the brush.

Alexandros followed, shouting curses at me and at his loose robes, which kept catching on thorns and branches. I ran awkwardly with my hands tied, but the deadly, cold voice of Panhasaziel drove me on past endurance until I fell, gasping for breath.

My brother dragged me back to the road, and we struggled on. Alexandros muttered as he walked, his voice fading in and out of the demons' babble. Sometimes he complained to my father, sometimes to the Lord. He said the same things over and over, always ending by reminding Abba (or the Lord) that once he got me to the exorcist, his obligations were over.

Time passed. "What's this?" my brother said suddenly. "There must be hundreds of people—yes, several hundred, on the grass over there." He pulled me onward. "Oh . . . they're listening to a preacher."

The demons stiffened to attention. The mist around me cleared a bit, and I saw that we were at the edge of a great crowd. They sat on a hillside that sloped down to the water. In front of them, at the water's edge, a man stood in a fishing boat.

"Not just a preacher, stranger," said a man at the edge of the crowd. "That's Yeshua of Nazareth."

"That's the exorcist?" exclaimed my brother. "Thank the Lord!"

Then Alexandros asked the man who'd spoken to him a question. But I couldn't make it out because the demons all began to scream. "There's the exorcist! Flee! Flee for your lives! If he gets hold of us, we're doomed!"

The fiends twisted my limbs this way and that, and I fell to the ground, hitting the back of my head. I must have been knocked senseless. The next thing I knew, I was rolled up in a fishing net and swinging from a long pole. Alexandros carried the front end. Pain pounded through my head, and spittle ran out of my mouth as the unclean spirits shrieked and howled.

The crowd on the shore parted to let us through. Between the cords pressed against my face, I caught their stares of horror and their hands making the sign against the evil eye. At the end of the corridor of people was the lake, with the boat a few lengths from shore. The sun, hanging low over Mount Arbel, shone on the man in the boat.

"Rabbi, my sister Mariamne is possessed," called Alexandros. Turning to a bystander, he asked doubtfully, "Is he truly an exorcist? He's dressed like an ordinary workman."

"Miryam," said the man in the boat. It was a voice that spoke to the ears of my soul, ears that could still hear after all. I was struck breathless by the tenderness in his voice. And the eyes of my soul were not quite blind, either. This plainly dressed man with a thin face was looking at me as if he saw his own dear sister in the net.

The demons seemed stunned for a moment, and I seized my chance. "Help me," I said.

The rabbi spoke to Alexandros. "Let her out."

My brother launched into an explanation of why that was impossible, and how much he was willing to pay for an exorcism but no more, and how he'd done even more than a brother could be expected to—

The rabbi interrupted, "Let her out." He didn't raise his voice, but there was authority in it like a king's. Alexandros and the other man hurried to obey. While they lowered me to the pebbly shore and untied the net, the rabbi stepped over the side of the boat and waded out of the water.

The demons made me fling myself back and forth and call on them by name. They snarled through my mouth, "We know you, Yeshua of Nazareth! Leave us alone—this woman is ours!" All the nastiness and ugliness in my spirit spewed out for this holy man to see, as disgusting as if I were relieving my bowels in front of him. I thought I would die of shame. At the same time, I was terrified that he might change his mind about helping me.

Rabbi Yeshua's dark eyes flashed with anger, but his voice was calm and sure. "I know *you*, Phomelei, Aiandictor, Dionesiona, Odjit, Zaphaunt, Panhasaziel. I command you, leave this woman."

They streamed out through my mouth, like a rush of foul air. And then the whole tribe of unclean spirits was gone—simply gone. Was it possible that they *were* gone? I lay on my back, gazing up at Rabbi Yeshua.

He gazed back at me, and his face broke into a grin of pure delight. He reached down and pulled me to my feet. "*Shalom,* peace, Miryam."

"*Shalom,* Rabbi," I said, brushing the tangled hair from my eyes. I smiled back at him although it hurt a cut on my lip. I held out my bound hands, and he untied them.

"Come with me," he said.

Then the crowd closed around Rabbi Yeshua, and Alexandros and I were squeezed off to the side. My knees wobbled; my mind was still. I sank down on a rock. I was clean; I was pure; I was at peace.

Peace. How many hundreds and hundreds of times had I heard the greeting "Peace" but never thought about what it meant? Now I *felt* what it meant: being still inside, so that I could see how precious the most ordinary things around me were. I ran my hand over the rock, marveling at how black and solid it was. I lifted my face to the sky, blue overhead but shading toward yellow above the hills.

I pondered what the rabbi had said: "Come with me." I couldn't imagine that he actually wanted me to follow him. Still, he had invited me, and that warmed my heart.

"Miryam, you must be thirsty." A well-dressed woman stooped beside me with a gourd of water.

I hadn't realized it before, but indeed I was parched. I drank, feeling the water soothe my hoarse throat. Tears of gratitude filled my eyes, and it occurred to me to wonder why this woman dressed in a noblewoman's robe was waiting on me. "Who are you?" I asked.

"I am Joanna of Tiberias," she said. "My husband is Herod Antipas's steward. I had a wasting illness, and Rabbi Yeshua healed me. And then I saw how I could help the rabbi's mission—with my money, for one thing. So I left Tiberias last year, and I've followed Yeshua ever since."

Joanna said this in a matter-of-fact way as she offered the gourd to Alexandros, sitting nearby. My brother drank deeply, too, and thanked her, but all the while he kept his eyes on me. "You've come to your senses?" he asked.

I was so intrigued by Joanna's story that it took me a moment to focus on my brother. Poor Alexandros! He looked as if he'd been attacked by bandits. "Brother, are you all right?" I dipped a somewhat clean corner of my robe in the water and dabbed at a scratch over his eye. "I'm sorry I hurt you! I'm truly sorry."

"You speak in your own voice," said Alexandros. Closing his eyes, he let out a ragged sigh of relief. "Thank the Lord!"

"Thank the Lord!" I echoed, as did Joanna.

"I had my doubts about this healer," Alexandros went on, opening his eyes. "I'd expected him to pronounce incantations and wave his arms, that kind of thing. And to be frank,

I wasn't sure anyone could help you." Then he added, "Well. The holy man did drive out your demons, so I must pay what I offered." He stood up, pulled his loose robes together, and began to work his way into the crowd again.

Joanna sat down beside me. I said wonderingly, "It must be a great change for you, following the rabbi, after living in the palace."

She smiled. "Yes, we live very simply with the rabbi. Our home is wherever Yeshua is. Our family is his band of followers. Tonight we'll sleep at Simon's house in Capernaum. Tomorrow, who knows? The rabbi has to keep traveling, to spread his message."

While Joanna was explaining how she'd arranged to receive the income from her inheritance, Alexandros returned. "Come, I've paid the healer, and I've found a boat to take us back to Magdala," he said to me. "We must be home by dark."

Joanna looked at me with a question in her eyes. "So you return to your family."

"Yes," I answered, puzzled.

Joanna pressed my hand in both of hers. "Perhaps we'll meet again," she said. "I hope so. There aren't many women among the disciples."

I was sorry to leave her, but I followed my brother to the boat.

TWENTY-THREE

COME WITH ME

The way back to Magdala was as easy as the journey to Capernaum had been toilsome. Our boat slid through pink light shed on the lake by swirls of glowing sunset clouds above Mount Arbel. I, too, was glowing, glowing with good will. Making amends with my family would be a pleasure, starting with my brother. "Alexandros," I told him as the boatman worked the sail, "you were a faithful brother to bring me to the rabbi for healing, even though I caused you so much grief. I'm more grateful than I can say."

Alexandros looked mildly pleased. "It was the right thing to do. I was bound to follow Elder Thomas's judgment." He yawned hugely.

It struck me that my brother was not glowing. "Brother,

when we met Rabbi Yeshua . . . did you feel true peace, as if for the first time?" As he regarded me with a baffled frown, I went on, "What *did* you feel?"

Alexandros shrugged. "Well, naturally, I was relieved that he was able to exorcise the evil spirits. And I was satisfied that I'd done my duty—more than my duty, many would say." He yawned again. "I need to rest."

I was disappointed, but I reminded myself what an ordeal I'd put him through that day. He did look weary. "You must be exhausted," I said.

My brother nodded, slumping onto a pile of nets. By the time the boat had rocked once or twice, he was asleep.

Strangely, I wasn't tired at all. As I watched the shore glide past, my thoughts turned back to Rabbi Yeshua. Who had ever looked at me so lovingly? Only my father, my grandmother, and (in a rare moment or two) my mother. The rabbi had seen me at my worst, and yet he'd regarded me with such compassion. I felt that my life would never be the same again.

Why, I wondered, hadn't Alexandros been affected the way I was by meeting Rabbi Yeshua? My brother was "relieved," he said; "satisfied." He'd spoken as if the rabbi were a carpenter who'd built an extra storeroom on his warehouse. The exorcist did his job; Alexandros paid him for his work. No reason to make a fuss about it.

This was so absurd that it made me smile. I looked over at Alexandros as he slept. His mouth was open, and the lines of strain in his face had relaxed; he seemed much younger.

Later I'd share my sense of blessing with Alexandros. I'd tell my whole family! Everyone should feel the way I did, clean and free.

But it was not the way I'd imagined, walking into the house where I had grown up. Of course, my grandmother was no longer there, and although I'd expected that, it made me sad. But I'd forgotten that Chloe would also be gone—she was living with her betrothed's family now.

Uncle Reuben *was* there, and I thought he looked disappointed to see me again. The rest of them embraced me, as well as Alexandros, and they seemed relieved that we'd returned safely. But no one wanted to hear how Rabbi Yeshua had healed me.

Imma gave me fresh clothes to put on and helped me wash my scrapes. "I'm glad you're cleansed, Mariamne," she said. "But it's not something we should dwell on. Let's see, where will you sleep? I'll have Yael put a cot next to mine."

Many things had changed, I realized, since the last time I'd lived at home. Some were big changes, such as Chloe's absence. Some were smaller but still made a difference—

Alexandros and his wife had the bedchamber now, and my mother slept in the common room.

At supper, my uncle said, "Thank the Lord that the exorcist didn't expect more money. There's an exorcist at Herod Antipas's court in Tiberias who charges several silver denarii, they say, to drive out demons. We couldn't have afforded that." At first, I was hurt, but then I felt sad for Uncle Reuben. My grandmother had been stingy with her love for him, giving it all to my father, and now my uncle was stingy with me.

Alexandros's wife, Sarah, smiled uneasily when she caught me looking at her. She kept well away from me with her baby. It struck me that she must have heard the dreadful story of how I let Kanarit fall off the roof. Oh, that made me flinch! I was healed, but the harm I'd done while I was possessed was not healed. I would go to Susannah first thing the following day.

The next morning, I noticed that the manservant, rather than Yael, carried the water jars from the well. I supposed Yael wasn't strong enough to heft the heavy jars anymore. I saw that her shoulders had become hunched, and the lines in her face dragged her mouth down at the corners.

I also heard Yael talking to herself—and to anyone within

earshot—as she swept the courtyard: "Woe! Oh, I see it coming. I see how they look at me, as if to say, 'The old donkey's wearing out. Better sell her for hide and tallow while we can.'"

I assumed this was just Yael's usual self-pity. Surely, my family wouldn't turn her out to join the crowd of beggars at the market.

When I told my mother I was going to see Susannah, she tried to discourage me. "I wouldn't bother your cousin just now if I were you," said Imma. "'Once bitten, twice shy,' as the proverb goes. Besides, Sarah and I could use some help with combing the flax."

My mother and her never-ending proverbs! "I must ask Susannah's forgiveness—I can't put it off," I said. "I won't be long."

Silas and Susannah's house in the cloth-dyers' quarter was on the other side of town. At first, I walked quickly, but as I came closer, I began to wish it were farther away. I told myself that surely Susannah would be able to see that I was myself again—better, in fact, than my old self?

But Susannah would not let me in the courtyard. She wouldn't even open the gate. "I don't know you," she said in a grim voice. "I had a cousin once, but she is dead to me."

"Please listen to what I have to say," I pleaded through a

crack in the wood, "if only for the sake of our grand-mother"—tears stung my eyes—"who loved both of us."

Desperate, I dropped down on the dirt lane in a beggar's crouch, with my forehead on the ground and my open hands outstretched. "Forgive me, forgive me," I asked over and over.

After a time, I heard the bar of the gate being lifted, and I jumped up. But it was only Susannah's serving woman, and she opened the gate just wide enough to push a bundle through. "Mistress says take your things and go." I recognized a rug I'd brought from home when I married.

As I leaned against the gate, forlornly clutching my bundle, I heard faint footsteps approaching. "Cousin Mari?" piped a voice very quietly. "Are you still there?"

"Kanarit?" I seized the small hand reaching through a crack in the gate. "My dear!"

"Imma said you were dead," Kanarit went on.

"No, I'm alive," I said. How lucky I am, I thought, to be alive and holding my little cousin's hand! "I'm sorry I let you fall off the roof. I'm sorry you were hurt. I wish I'd fallen instead. I hope . . ." I hesitated, because it seemed like too much to ask. "I hope you can forgive me."

"I forgive you," she said seriously. "Cousin Mari?"

"Yes, dear?"

"Why did you try to make me fly?" She added quickly, "I asked Imma, but she hushed me up. Why did you?"

When Kanarit asked that way, it was easy to give her a straightforward answer. "I did it because I wasn't in my right mind. I was possessed by demons. They tricked me into thinking it was a good idea."

"Oh," Kanarit said. "Are the demons gone now?"

Before I could answer, Susannah called from the house. Kanarit pulled her hand back. "Imma wants me. I have to go. Good-bye, cousin Mari!"

"Good-bye, dear!" Under my breath, I murmured, "Thanks be to the Lord."

As I made my way back through the tangle of lanes and alleys, I had a good idea. Maybe I'd never be allowed to see Susannah's daughter again, but I could still do something for her. I could ask Alexandros to manage a portion of my property for me. He could set aside a certain amount every year for Kanarit. Then when she was grown, she wouldn't have to marry for money.

At home, I found my mother on the roof under the awning, combing flax. Sarah had taken the baby downstairs for a nap. Sitting beside Imma, I picked up combs and a bunch of flax.

After we'd been working a little while, Imma remarked,

"Sarah's a good girl, but still young and impressionable. It would be best if you didn't talk to her." She added, "I don't think you realize how hard your . . . er . . . condition was on Alexandros. He felt responsible, you know, that he didn't bring you home after Eleazar died. He wondered if he could have saved you."

I doubted this, but I swallowed the angry answer that came to my lips. Instead, I said, "If Alexandros did feel guilty, he doesn't need to anymore. In the end, he brought me to Rabbi Yeshua, and the rabbi saved me." As I spoke, that moment came back to me. The rabbi *saw* me, just as I was, with such loving eyes, and I was healed! "Imma . . ." I turned eagerly to my mother, to share the moment with her.

Before I could put what I felt into words, my mother said, "Yes, saved—that's well and good, but now what's to be done with you?" She talked on, more to herself than to me. "I'm not sure Alexandros has thought this through. As the first step, Elder Thomas should interview her and certify that she's free of . . . mm, er . . . now."

"The first step?" I wondered what she was talking about.

"Of course," Imma continued, "some might say that he was only doing so to help his son-in-law. But no—the elder is known as a just man. His opinion would carry a great deal of weight." She nodded several times.

I felt my glow fade as I realized what she was getting at. The day before, I'd been full of new, clean life, and my spirit was free. Now it seemed that we were all back where we'd started: I was in my family's house, and Alexandros and my uncle and Imma were searching for a husband for me. It felt like trying to cram my foot into Kanarit's sandal.

Still, I thought soberly, I owed my family a great debt, for the shame I'd brought on them. The next day, when Alexandros spoke to me in private, I made an effort to listen respectfully.

He'd found a possible husband for me already, he said. The new marriage prospect was actually the same as the last one: Matthew bar Alphaeus.

"I know he rejected you before, when Silas . . . when you were . . . er, mm . . . But we have reason to think he'd reconsider now," Alexandros went on hastily. "It seems he failed at toll collecting, and the Romans sent him away. Now he's making only a small living as an accountant for Tabbai, the Syrian wool merchant. So your income would naturally look more attractive to him, and if he can believe that you're truly healed . . ."

"You're willing to marry me off to the tax collector's son, who isn't even rich anymore?" I protested. Then I fell silent. After all, why did I think I deserved better? Perhaps this was what I was supposed to do.

That evening, Alexandros had further news about Matthew bar Alphaeus. "I'd gotten the impression from Alphaeus that they'd reconsider the match, but today I talked to Matthew." My brother blew out his breath in exasperation. "I couldn't make sense of what he was telling me, and I'm not sure he could, either. He told me he didn't plan to marry. He said he was 'waiting for a sign.' It had something to do with a wandering preacher, the same Rabbi Yeshua who drove away your . . . you know."

My brother talked on, but I hardly heard him. Matthew the toll collector was connected with Rabbi Yeshua, the holy man? That seemed impossible.

But after all, Yeshua had connected himself with *me*—I who had wished the death of my husband, and almost caused the death of an innocent child, and raved lewdness and blasphemy! I remembered how Yeshua looked at me when we met—looked straight through the layers of grime to my soul.

How would Yeshua see Matthew? I thought of that time years ago when I'd seen the tax collector's son, as I was about to spit on his doorstep and glimpsed a tender heart. Yeshua must have seen *that* Matthew hidden inside the vile toll collector.

"It's just as well," my brother was saying. "Elder Thomas has graciously offered to interview you and vouch that you're healed, and then we won't have to stoop quite as low as

Matthew bar Alphaeus. Uncle Reuben thought perhaps one of his connections in Tiberias . . ."

I felt the bars of a cage closing in on me again, and it was hard to take a deep breath. Making a hasty excuse to my brother, I left the rooftop.

As I stumbled down the stairs, which were lit only by a small lamp, a concerned voice spoke in my head. *What good is it to be healed if you have to be married off to another Eleazar? If only you could get away, just for a short while. . . .*

Your family has so little appreciation for the ordeal you've been through! exclaimed another voice. *They never did realize how gifted you were, how special.*

They should suffer for it, added a hideous grating that was hardly a voice.

My heart pounded. The demons had returned. What was to keep them from infesting me again?

Desperately I sought something to hold on to, as if I were sliding off a cliff. Words from a psalm came to mind, and I gasped them out: "For your name's sake lead and guide me, take me out of the net which is hidden for me. . . ."

Then I blinked as sunlight flooded the courtyard. Only it wasn't the courtyard but a lakeshore. Before I could even take in the scene, a sense of well-being washed over my spirit. In front of me stood a tall man with a thin face. "Miryam," said Yeshua. "Come with me."

While I watched, he turned and began walking up a path that led away from the lake. The path was steep and rocky, climbing quickly into the hills. At a turning where the path disappeared behind boulders, Yeshua paused, looked over his shoulder, and beckoned to me.

The scene faded, leaving me in the dark. My legs shook all over so that I had to sit down on the stairs. But I was filled with gratitude for the vision. At last, I recognized the path that the prophet Miryam had told me of. Indeed, it was not the path of my mother, my grandmother, my sister, my cousin, and every other woman I knew. It was the way of the rabbi and his disciples.

A short while later, as I was falling asleep on my cot next to my mother, a practical question came to me. I must join Yeshua; I would join him. There was no question in my mind about that. But how would I travel back to Capernaum? I couldn't go by myself.

In the morning, I woke up still puzzled. I went down to the kitchen and began helping Yael with the morning bread. While I patted the rounds of dough flat for baking, my thoughts took shape also: I must speak to Matthew. As soon as Matthew received the sign he was waiting for, he would go to follow Yeshua, I was sure of that. The son of the tax collector didn't want to marry me, but maybe he would let me travel with him.

What if he'd received his sign the previous night, at the same time I'd received mine? He might have left Magdala already. Or maybe right this minute, as I slapped bread onto the baking stone, he was leading his donkey out the north gate.

Praying that he would still be at the wool merchant's, I made myself wait until the rest of the family had left the courtyard or started their day's work. Then I wound a scarf around my head and slipped out the gate.

TWENTY-FOUR

SEEKING YESHUA

I got some strange looks walking through the Gentile quarter, but I found the warehouse of Tabbai the wool trader without too much trouble. There were more strange looks from the doorkeeper when I asked for Matthew bar Alphaeus. I told him I was Matthew's sister, my excuse for approaching a man in a public place, but he probably didn't believe that. However, he pointed out the office, where a man with thick, earnest eyebrows sat cross-legged, sliding the counters across a bronze abacus.

Matthew's finely woven striped coat may have been the same one he'd worn the night he came to Susannah's house, only now the edges of the coat looked shabby. The rings and gold chains were gone from his hands and neck. As he glanced up from his work, I was troubled by doubt. Maybe he wasn't going to join Rabbi Yeshua after all. Even if he was, would he want to be bothered taking a strange woman along?

"Shalom," I said uncertainly. "I am Mariamne . . ." My voice trailed off at Matthew's look of dismay.

"Mariamne, widow of Eleazar." (I winced at that, but of course it was my name.) He stood up. "Why are you here? I told your brother . . . he said you were healed . . . surely your brother told you . . ."

I felt my face redden as I understood: he was afraid that I was still possessed after all. He thought I'd come to berate him, or perhaps to demand that he marry me anyway. "Don't worry," I said. "This doesn't have anything to do with what Alexandros talked to you about, except that he told me you were waiting for a sign."

Matthew nodded, looking puzzled.

"I thought the sign might have come to you, because *I* had a vision last night." As I spoke, the vision came back to me, and I forgot to be embarrassed. "I saw Yeshua looking at me with eyes of love. He said, 'Come.' So now I must go find Rabbi Yeshua again."

Matthew seemed to be struck speechless. Maybe he was horrified at being confronted, once again, by such a bold woman. I went on, more hesitantly, "I hoped I might travel with you."

As I spoke, Matthew's expression softened into wonder. Again the memory of the boy on the doorstep flashed in my mind, and I could imagine Yeshua seeing through Matthew to his tender soul.

"Why are you hesitating, Matthew bar Alphaeus?" I exclaimed. "You don't belong here, either. Go join Rabbi Yeshua. Don't wait to receive a sign!"

Taking a deep breath, Matthew finally spoke in a dazed voice. "I think I've just received it."

Matthew and I agreed to meet inside the south gate of the city shortly after midday. Returning to my family's house, I thought at first that I'd leave without telling anyone. What if they tried to stop me?

But when I went upstairs to find a traveling cloak, I saw my mother at the other end of the room pushing her shuttle through the threads of the loom. Poor Imma, striving day in and day out for a well-run household and a family to be proud of. She would never be proud of me now.

At least, I wouldn't make her worry about what had become of me. Kneeling beside the loom, I said, "Imma, I'm leaving. I'm going to follow Rabbi Yeshua."

I expected my mother to be shocked, but she hardly looked surprised. Sighing, she said, "Maybe it's for the best. If the tax collector's son won't have you, I don't know who would. I suppose it's better to follow a penniless wandering preacher than to lurk in the hills with demons coming out of your ears." Then something occurred to her, and she frowned. "But who will escort you to the rabbi? Alexandros can't be expected to leave the packinghouse again."

When I explained that I was traveling with Matthew, Imma dropped her shuttle and stared at me. "No wonder he won't marry you. He doesn't have to. *Ai,* all my years of work for nothing!" Then her face cleared, and she exclaimed, "I have it! Yael must go with you as a chaperone."

"Yael? She's not strong enough for a journey," I protested.

"Yes, that would solve more than one problem," my mother continued. She nodded several times. "Yael can't carry the water jars from the well anymore. The manservant had to add that to his other chores, and he's been grumbling."

"No." I spoke with such authority that my mother stared, and I was surprised at myself. "Yael isn't able to travel," I went on. "But you must not think of turning her out, now that she's getting feeble. Respect all the years of work she's done for you, and respect my father's memory. He would at least let her have her bread, and a corner of the courtyard."

Imma looked stunned. She started to say something, then

stopped. She plied her shuttle for a few moments. Then she said in a matter-of-fact voice, as if she'd never mentioned Yael, "Bread. You'll need bread for the journey, and cheese, and you may as well take a string of dried figs, too." Rising from the loom, she went down to the kitchen shed with me to pack some provisions.

As I approached the gate where I was to meet Matthew, I had to admit that my mother's words about traveling without a chaperone bothered me. It had been highly improper of me to visit Matthew at his place of work, but to go on a journey with him . . . ! Only a prostitute would travel alone with men not of her family. According to Matthew, Rabbi Yeshua was up in the hill country of Galilee now, so it might be a few days before we found him.

To my relief, when I joined Matthew at the south gate, he'd already found a group to travel with. They were a family of peasants, conscripted to bring firewood to the lighthouse in the Magdala harbor. They were in a hurry to get back to the hills, where their crops needed tending.

As the peasants—a man, his wife, and their half-grown sons—walked ahead of us, Matthew fell into step with me. "I feel for them," he said quietly, nodding toward our fellow travelers. "They have so little as it is, and they can't really afford to take time away from the fields. My brother, James, used to talk about how unfair it was, that the Romans made them supply firewood."

"Your brother *used to?*" I asked, wondering if his brother had died of the Tishri fever, like many others.

"My brother is lost to me," he answered. There was such pain in his voice that I let it go.

Our route was the same as the one I'd traveled with my father three years before, climbing through pomegranate orchards, then terraced olive groves. After we'd been walking for a time, Matthew mentioned that Rabbi Yeshua was supposed to be somewhere near Arbel at the moment.

"I have an aunt in Arbel," I said. "Maybe we can stay with her." Ordinarily, I wouldn't doubt that, but after all that had happened, even my aunt Deborah might not welcome me with delight. She must have heard that her brother's elder daughter had been possessed, but maybe not that I'd been healed.

I *had* been healed, and I knew I was on the right way, but still I didn't feel quite out of danger. I was eager to reach Yeshua. In his presence, surely, the unclean spirits would not dare to approach me again.

When the road became steeper, Matthew stopped and cut a walking stick for each of us. As we walked on, I asked him how he'd first met Rabbi Yeshua. Matthew seemed glad that I wanted to hear his story. Gazing over the rocky goat-pastures, he described the time that Yeshua had walked up to the tollgate. He told how the encounter had drawn him into a different way of seeing, a different way of acting.

"Then one day, when I was standing at the back of the crowd, listening to Yeshua preach, he noticed me again." Matthew grinned as if remembering a good joke. "He said, 'Matthew bar Alphaeus, I'm coming to your house for dinner tonight.'"

I smiled, too. The holy man, inviting himself to break bread with the outcast toll collector! I could imagine how shocked everyone, including Yeshua's disciples and Matthew himself, must have been.

But Matthew recovered himself enough, he said, to call out to the whole crowd, "Everyone is welcome!"

Matthew's eyes sparkled as he described for me that dinner party at his villa above Capernaum. The roasted ox! The dining room decked with garlands, and wreaths of flowers for all the guests! The fine wines! The musicians!

"At first, I was afraid I'd overdone it," Matthew admitted. "I don't think the rabbi's fishermen disciples had ever seen a dining couch before, let alone reclined on one. But they followed Rabbi Yeshua's example, and he seemed perfectly at home." Matthew shook his head in wonderment. "That man would be at home anywhere—in the emperor's throne room, or sharing a crust with beggars."

Yeshua's joyous mood spread to everyone else, Matthew said, and soon they were all eating and drinking and talking with gusto. Matthew found himself thinking, This is what money is for: a celebration like this. Looking around the hall, he felt great affection for each of the people at his tables. But then a sobering thought came to him. Some of these guests at his banquet were also the travelers he'd overcharged, or turned back from the gate.

After the main course, Matthew stood up, motioning a musician to beat the drum for attention. "Friends, I have something to say." He looked around the room at the faces turned to him. There was the blind man, although he didn't seem to be blind anymore; there was the dried-fruit vendor; there was the man with the five children and the sick father.

Their expressions showed wonderment—except for Rabbi Yeshua's; he watched Matthew like a proud father. Matthew went on, "I'm going to repay everyone I cheated. In fact, I'm going to pay them back double what I owe."

There was a stunned silence, and then the dining hall rang with applause: shouts, whistles, stamping feet. Yeshua hugged Matthew in beaming silence.

"It was the happiest moment of my life," Matthew ended his story. "I was sure I knew, in that moment, what Yeshua meant by 'the kingdom of heaven.'"

"That's it," I said passionately. "That's the way I felt after he drove out the demons." I told Matthew my story, beginning with my miserable marriage. When I came to the moment when Yeshua looked into my eyes like a loving brother, Matthew interrupted.

"Yes! That's the way he looked at me, like a brother." He choked on the last words. I thought of what he'd said earlier, about a brother who had been "lost."

I started to go on with my story, describing how the rabbi commanded the unclean spirits to leave me. But Matthew broke in again: "Rabbi Yeshua!"

He explained that he'd just remembered a story he'd heard some time ago. It was about an exorcist named Rabbi Yeshua who'd tricked demons into possessing a herd of pigs. "Granted, Yeshua is a common name," said Matthew, "but I'm sure it must have been the same man. I can picture it all happening."

"So can I," I said. And I could, as if I'd been hiding behind a rock in that Gentile cemetery, watching the rabbi drive out the demons.

After a moment, Matthew returned to his thoughts about

his banquet. "So I was granted a glimpse of the kingdom of heaven. But then what?" He gave a baffled sigh. "The very next day, my Roman overseer came by and dismissed me for gross incompetence. It turned out that my most trustworthy guard had sent him word about what I was doing, and he replaced me with that man."

"So I came back to Magdala, not knowing what else to do. My father was . . . is . . . disgusted with me. The only work I could get was what you saw: as an accountant for a Gentile merchant."

"Rabbi Yeshua will make everything clear for us, don't you think?" I asked.

"I hope so," said Matthew.

Below the top of Mount Arbel, the road split, and one branch continued on around the back of the mountain. The peasant family was waiting for us at the fork, resting under a scrubby lone olive tree. "The road isn't so steep from here on," called the father encouragingly. "Over the next rise, it's downhill all the way to Arbel."

Matthew produced a skin full of watered wine, and we each had a sip. Then we followed the road down into the small valley behind Mount Arbel. The fields and pastures were green from the winter rains. Before we reached Arbel, the peasant family said good-bye, pointing out their field and house and the cart track that led to them. I'd never thought much about how peasants lived. Now the sight of these people's stone hut, and their little field, hardly big enough to feed a goat, gave me a pang.

Matthew must have felt the same way, because he gave the young son the extra tunic in his sack. I gave the wife my string of dried figs. Thanking them for their company, we walked on into the village.

In Arbel, a few of the village men were standing under the synagogue shed, talking. Matthew stopped to ask them about Yeshua. He found out that the rabbi had come that way, but he and his followers had left the day before.

"None too soon," said the village elder. "They'd eat us into poverty. That teacher charms the women into bringing out the hidden stores so that everyone can eat their fill, whether they have a right to or not."

My aunt Deborah, who owned the largest house in the village, was delighted to see me. "I'd heard you were . . ." She made the sign against the evil eye. She wanted to hear about Alexandros and Sarah's baby, and she asked after my uncle's and my mother's health. Aunt Deborah looked troubled when she realized I was traveling with Matthew, but she welcomed him and showed him the shelter on the roof where he could sleep.

It was almost evening by then, and I helped my aunt carry water jars to the village well. She was amazed, but not disbelieving, when I told her that Rabbi Yeshua had driven out my demons. "I *knew* Elder Jonas was mistaken. He thought the holy man was fooling us with magic tricks, and getting on the right side of the women by paying attention to their children. He ordered Rabbi Yeshua and his disciples to leave."

Other women were gathered at the well, and we waited as they filled their jars first. When my aunt introduced me as seeking Rabbi Yeshua, each of them had something good to say about him. One woman said, "The rabbi cured my neighbor's boy of his stutter." Another said, "And he healed a lame nanny goat, the leader of our herd." A third woman added, "Who knows what he might have done for the grape harvest, if the elder hadn't sent him away?"

"It was wrong of Elder Jonas," agreed my aunt. "But he's the elder, like his father before him."

"I wanted to listen to the rabbi some more," said a shy young woman with a baby tucked into her shawl. "I hoped he'd explain . . ." She waved a hand at the hillside above the village, bright yellow even in the fading light. "He said the kingdom of heaven is like a *mustard seed.*"

A mustard seed! I stared straight ahead, seeing not the well but a brown dot like a grain of sand. As I watched, it sprouted, branched, and bloomed, and my heart expanded with the healthy plant. I felt a mighty power in the seed, stronger than armies. But if the seedling were yanked from the soil . . .

The thought hurt me, as if my own roots were being torn up, and I cried out.

"Mariamne?" Aunt Deborah's voice brought me out of my vision. I clutched the edge of the well, waiting for my head to stop whirling. The circle of women watched with mixed expressions: puzzlement, hope, worry.

"It *is* like the kingdom of heaven," I gasped.

"Do you understand that?" asked the young woman. "What did the rabbi mean?"

I told her what I'd seen, the whole plant unfolding miraculously. "A mustard seed is so tiny; it's so common. Yet it's a miracle waiting to happen. And the same thing's true of us."

I looked around the circle, remembering the way Yeshua had looked over a crowd of listeners and spoken to each person's heart. "We can remain dry little seeds . . . or we can sprout and grow into the kingdom of heaven."

"The kingdom of heaven?" asked another woman, glancing toward the field of mustard. "Right here in Arbel? In us?" She gave an unhappy laugh.

I started to say yes, but before I could get the word out, the woman with the baby breathed, "Yes." Her face shone.

Later, as I lay down to sleep, the young mother's face

came back to me. I thought, My vision helped her see! I was grateful for that, and I said a prayer of thanks.

The next morning, we thanked my aunt for her hospitality. We took a road through the hills on the far side of the Arbel valley, the same road by which Yeshua had left two days before.

At first, we walked in silence. It was strange, I thought, to walk alone side by side with a man who was not my father, my brother, my cousin, or even my husband. (Not that Eleazar had ever walked beside me in a companionable way!) And yet, it felt natural.

After a time, I told Matthew about the women at the well and the mustard seed. He listened intently, then said, "You . . . *see* things, don't you? Not only because you were possessed."

My heart tripped. It was one thing to think about my visions by myself, and another to speak freely to someone else about them. "I—I always have, even as a child," I stammered. Matthew nodded encouragingly, and I went on, "But when I tried to tell other people, they usually thought I was just being odd. Now I wonder . . . could it be a gift to share? When we find the rabbi, I want to ask him."

Glancing up at Matthew, I was struck by his eager

expression, and I ventured a guess. "Maybe you, too, have something to ask the rabbi?"

Matthew admitted, "I have an idea. There must be others like me, not only tax collectors, but landowners, merchants, judges—many people who grow rich by cheating the poor and helpless. Meanwhile, their souls wither. Maybe I could seek them out, the way Yeshua sought me out. . . ." Matthew's voice trailed off, and he glanced at me. "It's foolish of me to think I could help the rabbi in that way. *He* can inspire people to repent because he's a great prophet—maybe as great as Elijah."

"Still, you should ask him," I said. "Maybe Yeshua does need our help."

As we followed the road downhill, I puzzled over my own words. It hadn't occurred to me that Yeshua might need *us* in order to accomplish his mission.

The kingdom of heaven is like a mustard seed, Rabbi Yeshua had said. I quickened my steps, and so did Matthew. He must have felt the same sense of urgency. Suddenly it seemed to me that in spite of Yeshua's power, his mission could be crushed as easily as a young seedling.

TWENTY-FIVE

YESHUA'S FAMILY

Following a trail that wound through the folds of the hills, we caught up with Yeshua in Rumah. It was midday as we neared the village, and we could tell from a distance that there was a celebration going on. The music of wooden flutes and drums, as well as the smell of roasting meat, wafted in the breeze up the gorge. The village's threshing floor was full of circling dancers, with merrymakers around them clapping and singing.

"Simon?" said Matthew to a burly man on the edge of the group. "*Shalom.* I am Matthew bar Alphaeus. I used to work at a . . . er, a post near Capernaum."

"I remember you, toll collector," said Simon. He grinned. "That was some dinner party at your house! Well, here we are at another party. The rabbi loves celebrations."

He went on to explain that this was a feast for a childless couple who'd been blessed by Yeshua the previous year. Now they were celebrating a *brit milah,* the circumcision and naming of their baby boy.

While the two men talked, I caught sight of Yeshua bobbing among the dancers, hands raised. It was a moment before I was sure it was him, because he looked so carefree, laughing and calling out like any party guest. The last time I'd seen Yeshua, I'd felt he was taking on the needs and longings of every person in the crowd—including mine.

"James!" At the urgent note in Matthew's shout, I turned to stare at him, and so did several of the partygoers.

One of them broke from the rest and pushed his way toward Matthew. "Brother!" he shouted back. Even if he hadn't said that, I would have known they were brothers. James was slighter than Matthew, but he had the same thick, mild-looking eyebrows.

"I thought you were lost to the Dead Sea sect," muttered Matthew as they embraced, his fine but threadbare robe pressing against James's rough homespun coat.

"I thought *you* were lost to the Romans," said James pointedly. Even as tears ran down their faces, they burst out laughing, punching each other's shoulders like boys.

Now Yeshua, too, separated himself from the dancers and came to greet us. "Matthew, Miryam!" he exclaimed, looking from one to the other. "Have you come to join our family?" With a delighted smile, he answered for us: "Yes!" Matthew and James grinned helplessly, and I felt the same foolish smile on my face.

There was a touch on my arm, and then a woman hugged me. "Welcome, Miryam!" It was Joanna, the disciple who'd offered me water after my healing.

As the celebration wound down, the rabbi's disciples followed him out of the village to a shady grove of oaks. We sat on the grass around Yeshua. I felt uneasy with all these strange men, and I seated myself near Joanna and the few other women.

"Friends," said Yeshua, "you already know Matthew, son of Alphaeus. He's one of us now. So is Miryam from Magdala." The rabbi went on around the circle, naming each disciple for us. "Simon, otherwise known as the Rock. " Yeshua said this with a teasing smile, knocking on Simon's head with his knuckles. Simon grinned sheepishly.

There was Simon's brother, Andrew, and then there were the two sons of the fisherman Zebedee. Yeshua called them Sons of Thunder. (As I learned later, they tended to talk in loud, self-important voices.) Several others also had affectionate nicknames, and I wished I did, too.

After naming all the disciples, Yeshua looked up through the leaves of the oaks and said quite naturally, "Lord, Abba, I thank you for drawing Matthew and Miryam to us." Then he turned to the two of us with an eager light in his eyes. "Tell me what you bring for our mission."

This was our chance to explain our ideas, but I was taken aback, and Matthew looked dismayed. "I—I'm afraid I don't have much to offer," he stammered.

Simon spoke up, in a tone of good-natured teasing: "Matthew can keep our money for us! He's had a lot of experience handling coins."

Some of the others laughed, but Judas said stiffly, "Keeping the money is my job."

Yeshua didn't laugh either; he waited quietly for Matthew's answer. Speaking haltingly, Matthew explained what he'd told me earlier. After he finished, Yeshua nodded. "I want to think more about this. It's already come to me that soon some of you should go out on your own missions. There's so much to do. I won't have time. . . . Thank you, Matthew."

Now was the moment I'd been dreading. My heart seemed to beat in my throat. Yeshua turned to me. "What about you, Miryam? What do you bring us?"

It seemed like an unfair question. I had gone through so much, dared so much, just to get here. I was only a woman. Why couldn't I just quietly join the group?

Joanna was nodding encouragingly at me, and finally she

spoke up. "Rabbi, Miryam has some land and a share in her family's business. She can help support us."

"*No,*" I said quickly. At their puzzled stares, I added, "I mean, of course I'll share my income, but what I really want to bring . . ." I thought of the young woman at the well in Arbel, and how she drank in my description of the mustard seed. "I want to share my visions."

The disciples didn't laugh at me as they had at Matthew. "You claim to have visions from heaven?" asked Andrew. "Like a prophet?"

"I think she does have them," protested Matthew, but the others ignored him. They looked appalled.

Joanna whispered to me, "You didn't mean it, did you?"

I didn't dare to look at the rabbi, for fear he'd be as shocked as the others. I saw now how close to blasphemy it was, for me to talk as if I could be a prophet. Had a demon spoken through my mouth again, even in Yeshua's presence? "I do want to share my bride-gift," I said, trembling. "Please let me stay."

The rabbi looked intently into my eyes, as if he was turning over new ideas. Finally, he said in a reassuring tone, "There's no need to understand everything all at once. I do understand one thing: everyone the Lord sends us brings gifts." But I hardly heard him, I was so shaken.

Again Yeshua thanked the Lord for us two new disciples.

Then he told the group, "Friends, it's time to move on. There's so much to do. We'll start out for the next village tomorrow morning."

Various villagers invited Yeshua's followers into their homes for the night. Joanna and another woman, Arsinoe, took me with them to the potter's house. Before we lay down on our pallets, Joanna whispered to me, "Don't worry, Miryam. The rabbi won't be angry with you."

Although I was weary, I lay awake for a while after the others had gone to sleep. My mood shifted, and I felt I had been slighted. *I* was the one who was angry. *We could teach that Andrew a thing or two,* whispered a voice.

"Be gone!" I exclaimed aloud, causing the other two women to moan in their sleep.

The voice did not speak again, but I felt sad and confused. Were my visions, which had inspired Matthew and the woman in Arbel, only demon's tricks? Where was the freedom and joy I'd expected to find in Yeshua's presence? The rabbi's family appeared to be just as difficult as my own. Or . . . maybe I was the one who was difficult.

The next morning at dawn, we thanked our hosts and set off with the rising sun on our backs. We were on the road that led to the city of Sepphoris, Joanna said, although Yeshua would avoid that city. It was a stronghold of Herod Antipas. Joanna thought Yeshua wanted to visit his mother, who still lived in Nazareth. He'd have to be careful there, too, since he'd been thrown out of that village on his last visit.

For the most part, the men walked ahead of the women, as one would expect. Matthew and James walked together, each with a hand on the other's shoulder, talking and gesturing without pause to catch up on their years apart. Yeshua moved freely up and down the road, first conferring with Zebedee's sons and Simon, then laughing with Joanna and Arsinoe, then talking quietly with Matthew and James.

In the fresh morning, traveling as one of Yeshua's twenty or so disciples, I felt more cheerful. They might think *I* was peculiar, but they were an odd mix themselves! Here was Joanna, apparently a noblewoman, but she didn't ride in a litter or even on a donkey. She walked the dusty road along with the farmers and fisherfolk. No one called her *Lady* Joanna, not even the former beggars in our band, who had been lower than stray dogs.

Then there was Matthew, the despicable, Roman-loving, neighbor-gouging toll collector. Not only did Yeshua and all his followers not spit at Matthew, they *ate meals* with him. So a strange young woman who was seized with visions now and then should fit right into this group. A smile tugged at my lips.

As I looked up and down the road at the little band, I felt something I hadn't felt for years. I felt like my young self back in the days when I took it for granted that I was safe and cared for. I felt like a chick, one in a nestful. I felt at home.

Tears stung my eyes. Joanna must have noticed, because she put an arm around my shoulders as we walked. "Don't grieve, Miryam. The sadness is behind you now. Yeshua tells us to rejoice in being together, as if we were at a wedding."

I wiped my eyes with a corner of my scarf and smiled at her. "I am rejoicing. But I'm not used to it, so it makes me cry."

TWENTY-SIX

MIRYAM, MY SISTER

When the sun was overhead, we paused by a creek. These streams dried up in the summer's heat, but now they were still running, watering the oaks and bay trees in the folds of the hills. Yeshua blessed the bread and broke it, we ate, and then most of the group lay down in the shade for a rest.

I wasn't tired, and I noticed Yeshua going off by himself. He climbed the grassy hillside for a distance and sat down under a tree. On an impulse, I stood up and followed him. I almost turned back, thinking that he might want to be alone for a while. But he could see me climbing toward him. I thought that if he didn't want my company, he had only to frown or make a gesture.

Instead, Yeshua watched me with friendly interest. As I

came closer, he motioned to the grass nearby, and I sat down. "What is on your heart, Miryam?" he asked.

I wanted to tell him, but at the same time, I was afraid I would give the wrong answer. Speaking hesitantly, watching the rabbi for any sign of disgust or anger, I told him about my worry that the demons could reinfest me. "When you first healed me, I thought they were gone for good. *You'd* driven them out, so how could they return? But now I'm worried that they're only awaiting their chance. . . ." Frightened by my own words, I stopped talking.

Yeshua nodded. "I think you're right. That's the way of demons."

I stared at him, horror-struck. I'd expected him to reassure me that the demons were banished forever.

Yeshua himself looked sober but not worried. He gazed into the distance as if remembering. Then he said, "Miryam . . . tell me about your visions."

My throat constricted, and I was afraid to speak. What if the rabbi decided that I might infect the whole group with unclean spirits and ordered me not to follow him? At the same time, I wanted very badly to tell him about the mission that had beckoned to me since I was a child. So I began, haltingly at first, and then more easily as his face showed wonder and delight.

I told Yeshua about my vision of the mustard seed, and about the mustard seedling that Chava tore up. Encouraged by his attention, I went on to tell him about the time I stood on Mount Arbel with my father and saw the world with the eyes of my soul. And I told him how the prophet Miryam had appeared to me in a dream, and cleansed me in her well in the *mikvah.*

Yeshua's eyes shone as he listened. He was silent for a moment, and then he said hoarsely, "Miryam, my sister. I've been so lonely. I've prayed for a companion who would understand. . . ." He looked into my eyes, and then suddenly he laughed. "To tell the truth, I prayed for a *brother* to be my soul mate. The Lord loves a joke, doesn't he?"

Light with relief, I laughed, too. All I cared about was that Yeshua was glad for my company.

He nodded in the direction of the creek, where the others were rousing themselves, splashing water on their faces, shaking out their cloaks. "Good, then!" said Yeshua. "It's time to go on."

"Wait—" I jumped to my feet, remembering his first comment on my visions. "You said I was right that *they*"—I didn't want to name the demons—"were only waiting for their chance. You'll protect me, won't you?"

He gazed at me with his deep eyes. "Your own visions will protect you, if you honor them. I'm sure of that."

I didn't really understand what he meant, but for now, I was happy. I climbed down the slope after him.

Over the next few days, Yeshua led us from village to village in the Galilee hills. Almost every day, either walking or resting, Yeshua took time to talk with me. He explained further what he'd meant about my visions protecting me. "If you try not to use the gift, your soul will be like an empty house, and the demons will move back in. But if you choose to nurture the gift and use it for other people, you'll be filled with *sophia,* the spirit of holy wisdom. Your soul will be like a house full of fierce angels, and the demons will flee from you."

Yeshua was so free in his own way of thinking that he freed me to say aloud my most startling ideas. The day before we reached Nazareth, I told him that the prophet Miryam had appeared to me once again, in a dream. "I'm meant to be the sister of your soul, as she was Moses's sister," I said. "She says you are the new Moses that everyone has been waiting for. I am to watch over you, the way Miryam of old watched over her brother Moses in the Nile River." A further thought struck me, and I smiled. "And I actually did find you in the reeds at the water's edge!"

"You'll watch over me?" Yeshua gave me a teasing look. "*You* found *me*? I seem to remember finding *you* in the reeds, rolled up in a net like a poisonous fish." Immediately his face softened into a tender expression. "The Lord did send you to me. I know that."

Toward evening, we reached Nazareth, a large village of stone houses clustered around a stone synagogue. Yeshua stopped outside the village. On his last visit, the elders had told him in no uncertain terms never to come back. Since Joanna and I had not been with the group at that time, we were sent to find his mother, Miryam, the widow of Yosef.

As the two of us came through the village, a boy directed us to a small house on the other side of Nazareth where Yosef's widow lived with her older stepson. The rest of the family must have been out in the fields, because the house was empty. Yeshua's mother knelt by a cook fire in the tiny courtyard, grinding spices for a stew.

When Joanna told her that Yeshua had come to see her, Yeshua's mother clapped her hands like a child. "I knew he'd come back for me!" She took a cloak and a sack, already packed, from a peg, and I realized that she meant to join us for good. Yeshua's mother had a fresh, sweet look, I thought; she reminded me a bit of my grandmother.

Yeshua's face lit up as we approached the pile of boulders where he and the rest waited. Watching him and his mother embrace, I thought what a great joy it must be to have a son. And at the same time, what a dreadful blow it must be, to lose a son. Such a sorrow had untethered my grandmother's mind.

We traveled on, circling back through the hills toward the lake and Capernaum. Yeshua walked beside his mother from time to time. They didn't talk much, but she touched his arm, and he smiled at her.

Each village we passed through looked much the same: rough stone houses scattered over a hillside among terraces of grapevines and olive trees. In each, the stray dogs would rush out to bark at us as we neared the village. If the day was almost gone, there would be women at the well with their water jars.

But the character of each village was distinct, the way families will be different from one another. In one village, the elder would come out to greet Yeshua and offer hospitality. In another, the elder would send a surly nephew to warn us away. In still another, the villagers would slowly gather, neither welcoming nor rejecting but waiting to see what we would do. Almost always there was a desperate mother or father with a sick child. In that case, Yeshua stopped to pray for healing, even if the village men were threatening him with rocks.

If the people welcomed us, whether immediately or cautiously, Yeshua gave a blessing to each person. Then he had them sit down on a hillside, and he stood in front of them to talk.

Yeshua began by gazing over the audience, whether it was twenty people or hundreds. He looked at each one of them with such fondness, as if he knew them well and was glad to be with them at last. And I saw the men and women gaze back at him like children with their father.

Although they hung on every word of Yeshua's, I don't think anyone understood half the things he said. It wasn't that he spoke in Hebrew quotations, as scholars in the synagogue often did. His words were plain—but mysterious: "The kingdom of heaven is in the midst of you."

Listening to Yeshua reminded me of when I was a child and tried looking at things upside down. His sayings turned my mind upside down: "Blessed are the poor." "The last shall be first." But then, when I thought about it, Yeshua's behavior was as surprising as his words. He was courteous to the village elder, but he was just as courteous to the village idiot.

Even more startling to the villagers, I think, was the way the women in our group were treated. When we were on the road, I'd almost get used to it. Yeshua listened to women, he talked to women; he expected us to have opinions and feelings and even valuable insight. Some of his male disciples accepted this more readily than others, but most of them followed his example.

Then we'd enter another village, and I'd see again the puzzled faces as they watched me and the other female disciples. I could almost hear their thoughts: Who are these women, that they look men straight in the eye? Who allows them to speak freely in front of men? Surely the rabbi will rebuke them for their boldness? And I'd remember how unusual, almost unheard of, it was for men to treat women as Yeshua did. The most unusual thing about it was, Yeshua seemed unaware that he was doing anything out of the ordinary.

One afternoon, as we walked another hilly stretch of road, Yeshua sought out my company. "Miryam," he said, "I've been thinking about your gift for communing with the unseen world. You will be a bridge for the other disciples. They'll need you for this."

"You are the bridge, Rabbi!" I protested.

"Not forever," he sighed. I opened my mouth to ask what he meant, but he went on quickly. "Let me tell you about the visions I had in the desert, before I came back to Galilee."

A few years earlier, Yeshua said, he had been unsure

about how he should lead his life. He'd gone on a long, solitary fast in the desert, seeking an answer. For many days, he prayed for guidance and waited.

Out in the wilderness, wandering among barren outcroppings of rock, Yeshua had had visions of the power he could seize. "Miryam, I saw that I could be as mighty as Herod Antipas." His voice turned grim. "I could gather an army tomorrow, march into Tiberias, and push the tyrant off his throne."

His words called up my view of the world, years ago, from the top of Mount Arbel. I had seen the earth cut up into sections ruled by unjust governors and kings and emperors, grabbing from each other like selfish children with toys.

My heart hammered, almost choking me with excitement. "Yes!" I cried out. "You aren't the new Moses—you are the Anointed One!" Why hadn't I seen it before? Of course: our beloved Yeshua was *the Messiah*! Yeshua was shaking his head but I rushed on, "Not only Galilee but the whole world—you can conquer it! You can rule in peace and righteousness!"

Yeshua looked at me sorrowfully, waiting until I calmed down and closed my mouth. "Yes, Miryam, that's what our people want. I wanted it, too, when I saw that vision. I burned to rush out, raise my army, and smash the tyrants. But if I did sit on Antipas's throne, what would that accomplish? What if I even overthrew the Romans and reigned as emperor?"

His tone of voice was low and soft, but it made shivers of horror run down my spine. I remembered a time I'd tried to forget, when the demons had crowned me Queen Mariamne. I remembered my drunken glee at my own power.

"In the end," Yeshua went on, "it would only accomplish a great evil. It would turn *me* into Herod Antipas, or into Caesar. And Satan would have another worshipper." He gazed into my eyes. "Do you see, Miryam?"

Shuddering, I nodded.

After a pause, Yeshua spoke again. "No, I'm not working for a kingdom that will rise and then fall, like Herod's or Caesar's. My kingdom is the kingdom of heaven on earth. For those who dwell in it, it lasts forever. Do you understand?"

I remembered the moment when I was healed, and how a world of wonders had opened to me. I nodded again.

"You do see, Miryam! You do understand! Thanks be to the Lord." Taking me by the shoulders, Yeshua kissed me on one side of my face, then the other.

"Thanks be to the Lord!" I echoed.

Yeshua always talked with me in view of the other

disciples, and I could tell from their looks that the men wondered why he spent so much time with me. "Rabbi," I overheard Simon saying that evening, "why do you speak privately with Miryam? What could you have to say to a woman that you couldn't say in front of me?"

A plaintive note in his voice made me think of my uncle Reuben, watching my grandmother gaze lovingly at my father. It made me sad. Why was there never enough love to go around?

"Simon the Rock!" sighed Yeshua. "How well your nickname suits you!" (By this time, the rabbi had given me a nickname, too. Finding out about my family's smelly business, he began calling me Sardine Mari.)

As if Yeshua hadn't just indicated that Simon had said something dense, Andrew went on in the same vein. "It's bad enough, Rabbi, that people see you traveling with women. They're saying it doesn't look right, for a holy man. It gives people the wrong idea about your Way."

"So you think women have no place in the kingdom of heaven?" asked Yeshua gently.

"No, of course, women can contribute money for the mission," said Andrew. "But they ought to stay at home."

"Andrew, Andrew!" Yeshua sighed again. "Where should I begin? Let me tell you two a story. . . ."

I waited for a day to let Yeshua's words to Simon sink in. Then I found a chance to speak with him out of earshot of the others. "I only want to say, I would never try to take your place with the rabbi. I can see how precious you are to him. He depends on you."

Simon looked at me half-suspiciously, but he said, "Do you think so?"

"Everyone knows it," I said earnestly. "You're the most solid, dependable one of all the disciples. That's what he means, even when he teases you and calls you the Rock."

I was only speaking the truth to Simon. But there was a larger truth behind it: every one of us was precious to Yeshua. He spent time with *each* of us, somehow giving each one his full attention. I remarked on this to Joanna, and she nodded. "He's so eager to find the jewel in each person," she said, "so sure the jewel is there."

"Is that how you felt—when he healed you?" I asked. I knew that Joanna had first come to Yeshua with a wasting illness.

"Yes," she said quietly. "The rabbi made me see what my life could be if I understood that the Lord loves me—loves each one of us—so dearly."

"It's a shock to feel so cherished," I said, thinking of the moment when I stared at Yeshua through the fishing net.

"And another shock to realize how much he expects of you," said Joanna wryly.

Indeed. I thought of what Yeshua had told me, that I would be a bridge to the unseen world for the others. The very idea made me gasp. And yet, I saw that I'd already begun to serve in this way: for Matthew as he waited for a sign to follow Yeshua, and for the young mother who asked about the mustard seed. Maybe I'd even helped Simon to feel more confident of his worth.

Each one of the disciples seemed to be growing their gifts, as fast as barley sprouts when the rains come. Late one afternoon, as we stopped to camp between villages, Matthew joined me in gathering firewood. He told me that his brother, James, had set about memorizing all of Rabbi Yeshua's sayings and deeds. He was talking to the other disciples, gathering whatever each one remembered.

"Your brother can remember as much as twenty others put together?" I was impressed.

Matthew explained that before James joined Yeshua's family, he'd studied with a scholarly sect near the Dead Sea. "They taught him how to store many scrolls' worth of words in his mind. For instance," Matthew said with a note of pride, "James can recite the Torah from beginning to end. So I told him the deeds I knew about: how Yeshua cast out your demons, and also how Yeshua healed the possessed man on the other side of the lake."

"Does James know the rabbi's saying about the kingdom of heaven being like a mustard seed?" I asked.

"Yes, I reminded him of that one," Matthew assured me. "Also 'Blessed are the merciful, for they—'" He had to stop, overcome with emotion.

I finished the saying for him: "'For they shall receive mercy.'"

After I'd been with Yeshua's family for a few months, I ran across someone I'd never expected to see again: Ramla. I'd assumed that she'd gone back to Tiberias after the elders of Magdala banished her, but she turned up in Bethsaida-Julias.

Yeshua generally avoided cities, which were expensive and inhospitable to strangers. But at this time, he was more concerned with avoiding Herod Antipas's soldiers. Friends had brought word that Antipas wanted to question the wandering preacher who drew such large crowds. So we left Capernaum and headed for the east side of the lake, outside Antipas's territory. Just over the border, we came to the city of Bethsaida-Julias.

And there, in a curtained stall in the market, was a woman in shimmering robes and a crescent-moon headdress.

She scowled when she caught sight of me, but I went up to her anyway. *"Shalom—"*

She cut me off. "Spare me your poisoned honey. You saved your own skin, didn't you, and let the council drive me out of town? I suppose you wouldn't have lifted a finger if they'd flogged me, too."

I flinched at "poisoned honey." I knew how it felt, to be betrayed by someone I trusted. "I did you wrong," I admitted. "I hope you'll come to forgive me." I started to explain how I'd become controlled by the demonic spirits I met in my private garden, and how, under possession, I'd done harm to everyone around me.

But the more I explained, the angrier Ramla looked. "Demons!" She gave a caustic laugh. "What a good excuse! Stars above, now *I* feel a possession coming on, and it's forcing me to . . ." Deliberately she leaned forward and spit in my face. "I hope you'll come to forgive me," she added in a mincing tone.

I wiped my face. "I do hope so, even if you don't believe me. For your own sake, won't you at least come into the Jewish market and listen to Rabbi Yeshua?"

"Yeshua of Nazareth, that one?" Ramla made the sign to ward off the evil eye. "I've heard of him. If he had his way, all the magicians of Galilee and Judea would be out of business."

"Don't you remember what you said, that afternoon at Susannah's house?" I pleaded. "You told us it was a time of new beginnings. You were right! Rabbi Yeshua's message could be a new beginning for you, too. Please come and listen."

Ramla wasn't paying attention; her eyes were on someone behind me. I turned to see a man with two young boys in tow. "How much for a good fortune for each of my sons?" he asked.

"Only a silver denarius apiece, sir," said Ramla, beckoning them into the curtained booth. As I left, I heard Ramla say in her best Egyptian accent, "Of course, I cannot guarantee the outcome of the reading, sir. Ramla only discerns the truth as it is revealed in the stars."

What is it that makes one person listen to Rabbi Yeshua and another close her ears? As we left the city, I asked Yeshua that question. "Nothing *makes* them listen, or not listen," he said. "They choose."

TWENTY-SEVEN

MIRYAM FROM MAGDALA

Now I am living a new life, my life as Miryam from Magdala, disciple and dear friend of Rabbi Yeshua. This life is so different from the life of Mariamne, daughter of Tobias, or wife and widow of Eleazar, or sister of Alexandros, that it's hard to believe I'm the same person. And yet, I know this is what I was born for.

I would gladly spend the rest of my life this way, with the rabbi and his odd mix of followers. But I sense that a change is coming. We're planning a trip to Jerusalem for the Passover next spring, and then . . . I don't know.

Sometimes Simon's mother-in-law chides Yeshua, "Rabbi, you're tired; you should rest. You're so thin . . . sit and eat!"

He looks at her fondly and answers, "Time is short." The simple words fill me with dread.

And what of the sparrow? I began my story with a sparrow, so I'll end the same way. Here's another of Rabbi Yeshua's upside-down pronouncements: "Your heavenly Father cares about every sparrow that falls to the ground."

When I heard Yeshua declare that last sentence, I blurted out, "He does?" I seemed to be a young child again, grieving over the sparrow felled by my brother's slingshot. Then, I'd been sure that no one but me cared about the small, common bird.

Now I see, with the eyes of my soul, that every sparrow is a messenger from heaven.

AUTHOR'S NOTE

For centuries, people have imagined Mary of Magdala as a re-
formed prostitute. We've seen her portrayed this way in nu-
merous paintings and sculptures, books and movies. So it's
hard for us to accept the fact that there is *no* evidence that she
was ever a prostitute of any kind. The text of the Gospels
(and other texts written close to these dates) gives no such in-
dication.

Depending on which Gospel you read, they do say that
she was a follower of Jesus, one from whom he drove out seven
demons. ("Seven" used in this sense means "completely," "to
the nth degree.") The Gospels also say that she stood by him
while he was crucified, that she discovered the empty tomb,
and that she was the first to see the resurrected Jesus.

During the centuries following Jesus's lifetime, information about the role Mary played in his movement was gradually lost. In the sixth century, Pope Gregory I (probably with
good intentions) preached sermons identifying Mary Magdalene with the "sinning" woman who washed Jesus's feet with
her tears (Luke 7:37–39) and with the "woman taken in adul-
tery" (John 8:3–11), although there was no reason to think
either of these women was Mary Magdalene. The legend of
the Magdalene, the repentant whore, was officially launched.

In medieval times, many legends grew up around Mary Magdalene, including one that she traveled from Galilee to southern France, where she lived for the rest of her life and performed many miracles. Recently the bestselling novel *The Da Vinci Code* has promoted this legend, as well as a more controversial one, that Mary was Jesus's wife and the mother of his child. But I haven't found any convincing evidence that Mary of Magdala ever traveled outside Galilee and Judea, or that she was married to anyone, much less Jesus, at the time she was following him.

What does seem reasonable to assume about Mary is that:

she was from Magdala, a town on the shore of the Sea of Galilee (Lake Gennesaret);

she was tormented by what she believed to be a horde of demons;

she was healed by Jesus and joined his movement;

she became one of his closest disciples.

Working from these points, I began to write my story.

All my quotations from the Bible follow the Revised Standard Version, 1977, published by Oxford University Press.